PENGUIN MODERN CLASSICS

A SAHIBS' WAR AND OTHER STORIES

Rudyard Kipling, son of John Lockwood Kipling, the author of *Beast and Man in India*, was born in Bombay in 1865. He was educated at the United Services College, Westward Ho!, and was engaged in journalistic work in India from 1882 to 1889. His fame rests principally on his short stories, dealing with India, the sea, the jungle and its beasts, the army, the navy, and a multitude of other subjects. His verse, as varied in subject as his prose, also enjoyed great popularity. Among his more famous publications are *Plain Tales from the Hills* (1888), *Life's Handicap* (1891), *Barrack-Room Ballads* (1892), *The Jungle Book* (1894), *The Day's Work* (1898), *Kim* (1901), *Just So Stories* (1902), *Puck of Pook's Hill* (1906), and *Rewards and Fairies* (1910). Kipling, who was awarded a Nobel Prize in 1907, died in 1936.

RUDYARD KIPLING

Short Stories: 1

A SAHIBS' WAR
AND OTHER STORIES

Selected by
Andrew Rutherford

PENGUIN BOOKS

PENGUIN BOOKS

Published by the Penguin Group
Penguin Books Ltd, 27 Wrights Lane, London W8 5TZ, England
Penguin Books USA Inc., 375 Hudson Street, New York, New York 10014, USA
Penguin Books Australia Ltd, Ringwood, Victoria, Australia
Penguin Books Canada Ltd, 10 Alcorn Avenue, Toronto, Ontario, Canada M4V 3B2
Penguin Books (NZ) Ltd, 182–190 Wairau Road, Auckland 10, New Zealand

Penguin Books Ltd, Registered Offices: Harmondsworth, Middlesex, England

First published in Great Britain by Macmillan & Co. Ltd
Published in Penguin Books 1971
Published in Penguin Books in the United States of America
by arrangement with Doubleday & Company, Inc.
Reprinted 1976, 1977, 1979, 1981, 1982, 1984, 1986, 1988
1 3 5 7 9 10 8 6 4 2

Printed in England by Clays Ltd, St Ives plc
Set in Linotype Georgian

Volume 1

Preface

THESE two volumes of short stories* are selected from the following five collections, which have been made available to Penguin Books by Macmillan and Co. Ltd: *Traffics and Discoveries* (1904), *Actions and Reactions* (1909), *A Diversity of Creatures* (1917), *Debits and Credits* (1926) and *Limits and Renewals* (1932). These comprise the best of Kipling's prose fiction after 1900, apart from *Kim* (1901) and the short stories collected in *Puck of Pook's Hill* (1906) and *Rewards and Fairies* (1910).

Kipling's fiction is characteristically a rich blend of invention with experience, his own or others'; and his autobiography, *Something of Myself* (1937), suggests origins for many of these tales. 'A Sahibs' War' and 'The Captive' both derive from his first-hand knowledge of British and Boer practice in South Africa; 'Little Foxes' was based on an anecdote told him by an officer who had been Master of the original 'Gihon Hunt'; 'Regulus' draws on recollections of his own schooldays at Westward Ho!; a barmaid seen in Auckland, and a petty officer's remarks overheard in a train near Cape Town, were the starting points for 'Mrs Bathurst'; his interest in Freemasonry ('In the Interests of the Brethren') dates from his induction to the multi-racial, multi-religious Lodge at Lahore in 1885; in a house at Torquay, formerly inhabited by three old maids, he and his wife had felt in 1896 'a growing depression which enveloped us both – a gathering blackness of mind and sorrow of the heart', which he attributed to the Spirit of the house itself, and recreated in the symptoms which afflict his characters in 'The House Surgeon'; while his experiences at Bateman's, their eventual home in Sussex, provided the technicalities of 'Below the

* ***A Sahibs' War and Other Stories*** **and** ***Friendly Brook and Other Stories.***

Mill Dam' and the insights into rural life and character which he drew on in stories like 'Friendly Brook', 'My Son's Wife', and 'An Habitation Enforced'.

Deeper emotional levels are suggested by Charles Carrington's official but less reticent biography, *Rudyard Kipling: His Life and Work* (1955). Behind the delicate pathos of 'They', for example, lies Kipling's grief at the death of his little daughter Josephine in 1899; and although 'Mary Postgate' was written before his only son was killed at Loos in 1915, our knowledge of his loss gives added poignancy to a story like 'The Gardener'. Such information, however, is not necessary for our understanding and enjoyment of the tales themselves; and further speculation would run counter to Kipling's own request (in 'The Appeal') that his art be judged impersonally, and his privacy respected posthumously as he made sure it was in his own lifetime:

> If I have given you delight
> By aught that I have done,
> Let me lie quiet in that night
> Which shall be yours anon:
>
> And for the little, little, span
> The dead are borne in mind,
> Seek not to question other than
> The books I leave behind.

This selection from five of the books he left behind presents the twentieth-century Kipling who developed from the more familiar prodigy of the eighties and nineties; and it illustrates the range, variety, and technical originality of his fiction of this period.* There are fewer tales of Empire than the popular stereotype of Kipling might lead readers to expect: as 'Little Foxes' demonstrates, he still held firmly the

*The poems which accompany the stories in these collections have not been included (though they are always thematically relevant), except in the case of 'MacDonough's Song', which is quoted and referred to in 'As Easy as A.B.C.', and must be regarded as an essential element of the story itself.

ideals and prejudices which had inspired much of his work in the previous two decades, but the general incompetence revealed by the Boer War diminished his confidence in Britain's ability to sustain her imperial role, while her very will to do so, or even to prepare to defend herself against hostile European powers, was being sapped, it seemed to him, by decadence and political irresponsibility. Increasingly, therefore, he was preoccupied by the condition of England herself, as he rebuked her blindness, folly and complacency, and sought reassurance in groups, types, or individuals who might still redeem her backslidings. Simultaneously, he found himself involved in a fascinating process of discovery, for the countryside, its people and traditions, came as a revelation to him once he settled in Sussex: 'England,' he wrote to a friend in 1902, 'is the most wonderful foreign land I have ever been in.' Yet even while making it peculiarly his own, he was aware (as 'Below the Mill Dam' shows) of the baneful influence of inert tradition, and the need for technological advance. For socially parasitic intellectuals, especially those of 'the Immoderate Left', he felt the savage contempt expressed in 'My Son's Wife'; but his fable of decadence in 'The Mother Hive' goes beyond this sectional antagonism to diagnose moral-political sickness in a whole community, while the suspicion of democracy which he shared with so many major authors of the century is projected into an ambiguously Utopian future in 'As Easy as A.B.C'. Such public themes bulk large in Volume 1, as his preoccupation with the Great War does in Volume 2; but these coexist with more personal, more psychological, and more spiritual interests, especially in his later years. Individual human beings, their characters, their actions, their behaviour under stress, remain his main concern; and using a remarkable variety of settings and of *dramatis personae,* he offers stories on a characteristic range of themes – stories of revenge, seen sometimes as wild justice, sometimes as an almost pathological obsession; stories of forgiveness, human and divine; stories of the supernatural, to be taken now literally, now symbolically, but never trivially as mere spine-chilling entertainment; stories of hatred and cruelty, but stories also of compassion and of love; stories of work, of craftsmanship, of artistry; of comradeship and isolation; and stories of healing, sometimes physical, but more often moral, spiritual or psychological.

Technically, his fiction shows a comparable variety, but for modern readers the most interesting development is probably his evolution of that complex, closely organized, elliptical and symbolic mode of writing which ranks him as an unexpected contributor to 'modernism' and a major innovator in the art of the short story. This mode, with its obliquities and ironies, its multiple levels of meaning, and what have been described by Miss J. M. S. Tompkins as its 'complexities of substance and ... of method', was first attempted in 'Mrs Bathurst' and 'They', but is to be found fully developed in his later stories, especially those dated from 1924 onwards in Volume 2 of this selection. Detailed discussion of this and other aspects of his artistry may be found in such studies as J. M. S. Tompkins, *The Art of Rudyard Kipling* (1959); C. A. Bodelsen, *Aspects of Kipling's Art* (1964); *Kipling's Mind and Art,* ed. Andrew Rutherford (1964); and Bonamy Dobrée, *Rudyard Kipling: Realist and Fabulist* (1967).

ANDREW RUTHERFORD

A Sahibs' War

(1901)

PASS? Pass? Pass? I have one pass already, allowing me to go by the *rêl* from Kroonstadt to Eshtellenbosch, where the horses are, where I am to be paid off, and whence I return to India. I am a – trooper of the Gurgaon Rissala (cavalry regiment), the One Hundred and Forty-first Punjab Cavalry. Do not herd me with these black Kaffirs. I am a Sikh – a trooper of the State. The Lieutenant-Sahib does not understand my talk? Is there *any* Sahib on this train who will interpret for a trooper of the Gurgaon Rissala going about his business in this devil's devising of a country, where there is no flour, no oil, no spice, no red pepper, and no respect paid to a Sikh? Is there no help? . . . God be thanked, here is such a Sahib! Protector of the Poor! Heaven-born! Tell the young Lieutenant-Sahib that my name is Umr Singh; I am – I was – servant to Kurban Sahib, now dead; and I have a pass to go to Eshtellenbosch, where the horses are. Do not let him herd me with these black Kaffirs! . . . Yes, I will sit by this truck till the Heaven-born has explained the matter to the young Lieutenant-Sahib who does not understand our tongue.

What orders? The young Lieutenant-Sahib will not detain me? Good! I go down to Eshtellenbosch by the next *terain*? Good! I go with the Heaven-born? Good! Then for this day I am the Heaven-born's servant. Will the Heaven-born bring the honour of his presence to a seat? Here is an empty truck; I will spread my blanket over one corner thus – for the sun is hot, though not so hot as our Punjab in May. I will prop it up thus, and I will arrange this hay thus, so the Presence can sit at ease till God sends us a *terain* for Eshtellenbosch . . .

The Presence knows the Punjab? Lahore? Amritzar? Attaree, belike? My village is north over the fields three miles from Attaree, near the big white house which was copied from a certain place of the Great Queen's by – by – I have forgotten the name. Can the Presence recall it? Sirdar Dyal Singh Attareewalla! Yes, that is the very man; but how does the Presence know? Born and bred in Hind, was he? O-o-oh! This is quite a different matter. The Sahib's nurse was a Surtee woman from the Bombay side? That was a pity. She should have been an up-country wench; for those make stout nurses. There is no land like the Punjab. There are no people like the Sikhs. Umr Singh is my name, yes. An old man? Yes. A trooper only after all these years? Ye-es. Look at my uniform, if the Sahib doubts. Nay – nay; the Sahib looks too closely. All marks of rank were picked off it long ago, but – but it is true – mine is not a common cloth such as troopers use for their coats, and – the Sahib has sharp eyes – that black mark is such a mark as a silver chain leaves when long worn on the breast. The Sahib says that troopers do not wear silver chains? No-o. Troopers do not wear the Arder of Beritish India? No. The Sahib should have been in the Police of the Punjab. I am not a trooper, but I have been a Sahib's servant for nearly a year – bearer, butler, sweeper, any and all three. The Sahib says that Sikhs do not take menial service? True; but it was for Kurban Sahib – my Kurban Sahib – dead these three months!

Young – of a reddish face – with blue eyes, and he lilted a little on his feet when he was pleased, and cracked his finger-joints. So did his father before him, who was Deputy-Commissioner of Jullundur in my father's time when I rode with the Gurgaon Rissala. *My* father? Jwala Singh. A Sikh of Sikhs – he fought against the English at Sobraon and carried the mark to his death. So we were knit as it were by a blood-tie, I and my Kurban Sahib. Yes, I was a trooper first – nay, I had risen to a Lance-Duffadar, I remember – and my father gave me a dun stallion of his own breeding on that day; and *he* was a little baba, sitting upon a wall by the parade-ground with his ayah – all in white, Sahib – laughing at the end of our drill. And his father and mine talked together, and mine beckoned to me, and I dismounted, and the baba put his hand into mine – eighteen – twenty-five – twenty-seven years gone now – Kurban Sahib – my Kurban Sahib! Oh, we were great friends after that! He cut his teeth on my sword-hilt, as the saying is. He called me Big Umr Singh – Buwwa Umwa Singh, for he could not speak plain. He stood only this high, Sahib, from the bottom of this truck, but he knew all our troopers by name – every one. . . . And he went to England, and he became a young man, and back he came, lilting a little in his walk, and cracking his finger-joints – back to his own regiment and to me. He had not forgotten either our speech or our customs. He was a Sikh at heart, Sahib. He was rich, open-handed, just, a friend of poor troopers, keen-eyed, jestful, and careless. *I* could tell tales about him in his first years. There was very little he hid from *me*. I was his Umr Singh, and when we were alone he called me Father, and I called him Son. Yes, that was how we spoke. We spoke freely together on everything – about war, and women, and money, and advancement, and such all.

We spoke about this war, too, long before it came. There were many box-wallahs, pedlars, with Pathans a few, in this country, notably at the city of Yunasbagh (Johannesburg), and they sent news in every week how the Sahibs lay without weapons under the heel of the Boer-log; and how big guns were hauled up and down the streets to keep Sahibs in order; and how a Sahib called Eger Sahib (Edgar?) was killed for a jest by the Boer-log. The Sahib knows how we of Hind hear all that passes over the earth? There was not a gun cocked in Yunasbagh that the echo did not come into Hind in a month. The Sahibs are very clever, but they forget their own cleverness has created the *dak* (the post), and that for an anna or two all things become known. We of Hind listened and heard and wondered; and when it was a sure thing, as reported by the pedlars and the vegetable-sellers, that the Sahibs of Yunasbagh lay in bondage to the Boer-log, certain among us asked questions and waited for signs. Others of us mistook the meaning of those signs. *Wherefore, Sahib, came the long war in the Tirah!* This Kurban Sahib knew, and we talked together. He said, 'There is no haste. Presently we shall fight, and we shall fight for all Hind in that country round Yunasbagh.' Here he spoke truth. Does the Sahib not agree? Quite so. It is for Hind that the Sahibs are fighting this war. Ye cannot in one place rule and in another bear service. Either ye must everywhere rule or everywhere obey. God does not make the nations ringstraked. True – true – true!

So did matters ripen – a step at a time. It was nothing to me, except I think – and the Sahib sees this, too? – that it is foolish to make an army and break their hearts in idleness. Why have they not sent for the men of the Tochi – the men of the Tirah – the men of Buner? Folly, a thousand times. *We* could have done it all so gently – so gently.

Then, upon a day, Kurban Sahib sent for me and said, 'Ho, Dada, I am sick, and the doctor gives me a certificate for many months.' And he winked, and I said, 'I will get leave and nurse thee, Child. Shall I bring my uniform?' He said, 'Yes, and a sword for a sick man to lean on. We go to Bombay, and thence by sea to the country of the Hubshis (niggers).' Mark his cleverness! He was first of all our men among the native regiments to get leave for sickness and to come here. Now they will not let our officers go away, sick or well, except they sign a bond not to take part in this war-game upon the road. But *he* was clever. There was no whisper of war when he took his sick-leave. I came also? Assuredly. I went to my Colonel, and sitting in the chair (I am – I was – of that rank for which a chair is placed when we speak with the Colonel) I said, 'My child goes sick. Give me leave, for I am old and sick also.'

And the Colonel, making the word double between English and our tongue, said, 'Yes, thou art truly *Sikh*', and he called me an old devil – jestingly, as one soldier may jest with another; and he said my Kurban Sahib was a liar as to his health (that was true, too), and at long last he stood up and shook my hand, and bade me go and bring my Sahib safe again. My Sahib back again – aie me!

So I went to Bombay with Kurban Sahib, but there, at sight of the Black Water, Wajib Ali, his bearer, checked, and said that his mother was dead. Then I said to Kurban Sahib, 'What is one Mussulman pig more or less? Give me the keys of the trunks, and I will lay out the white shirts for dinner.' Then I beat Wajib Ali at the back of Watson's Hotel, and that night I prepared Kurban Sahib's razors. I say, Sahib, that I, a Sikh of the Khalsa, an unshorn man, prepared the razors. But I did not put on my uniform while I did it. On the other hand, Kurban Sahib took for me, upon the steamer, a room in all respects like to his own, and would have given me a servant. We spoke of many things on the way to this country; and Kurban Sahib told me what he perceived would be the conduct of the war. He said, 'They have taken men afoot to fight men ahorse, and they will foolishly show mercy to these Boer-log because it is believed that they are white.' He said, 'There is but one fault in this war, and that is that the Government have not employed *us*, but have made it altogether a Sahibs' war. Very many men will thus be killed, and no vengeance will be taken.' True talk – true talk! It fell as Kurban Sahib foretold.

And we came to this country, even to Cape Town over yonder, and Kurban Sahib said, 'Bear the baggage to the big dak-bungalow, and I will look for employment fit for a sick man.' I put on the uniform of my rank and went to the big dak-bungalow, called Maun Nihâl Seyn,* and I caused the heavy baggage to be bestowed in that dark lower place – is it known to the Sahib? – which was already full of the swords and baggage of officers. It is fuller now – dead men's kit all! I was careful to secure a receipt for all three pieces. I have it in my belt. They must go back to the Punjab.

Anon came Kurban Sahib, lilting a little in his step, which sign I knew, and he said, 'We are born in a fortunate hour. We go to Eshtellenbosch to oversee the dispatch of horses.' Remember, Kurban Sahib was squadron-leader of the Gurgaon Rissala, and *I* was Umr Singh. So I said, speaking as we

*Mount Nelson?

do – we did – when none was near, 'Thou art a groom and I am a grass-cutter, but is this any promotion, Child?' At this he laughed, saying, 'It is the way to better things. Have patience, Father.' (Aye, he called me father when none were by.) 'This war ends not tomorrow nor the next day. I have seen the new Sahibs,' he said, 'and they are fathers of owls – all – all – all!'

So we went to Eshtellenbosch, where the horses are; Kurban Sahib doing the service of servants in that business. And the whole business was managed without forethought by new Sahibs from God knows where, who had never seen a tent pitched or a peg driven. They were full of zeal, but empty of all knowledge. Then came, little by little from Hind, those Pathans – they are just like those vultures up there, Sahib – they always follow slaughter. And there came to Eshtellenbosch some Sikhs – Muzbees, though – and some Madras monkey-men. They came with horses. Puttiala sent horses. Jhind and Nabha sent horses. All the nations of the Khalsa sent horses. All the ends of the earth sent horses. God knows what the army did with them, unless they ate them raw. They used horses as a courtesan uses oil: with both hands. These horses needed many men. Kurban Sahib appointed me to the command (what a command for me!) of certain woolly ones – *Hubshis* – whose touch and shadow are pollution. They were enormous eaters; sleeping on their bellies; laughing without cause; wholly like animals. Some were called Fingoes, and some, I think, Red Kaffirs, but they were all Kaffirs – filth unspeakable. I taught them to water and feed, and sweep and rub down. Yes, I oversaw the work of sweepers – a *jemadar* of *mehtars* (headman of a refuse-gang) was I, and Kurban Sahib little better, for five months. Evil months! The war went as Kurban Sahib had said. Our new men were slain and no vengeance was taken. It was a war of fools armed with the weapons of magicians. Guns that slew at half a day's march, and men who, being new, walked blind into high grass and were driven off like cattle by the Boer-log! As to the city of Eshtellenbosch, I am not a Sahib – only a Sikh. I would have quartered one troop only of the Gurgaon Rissala in that city – one little troop – and I would have schooled that city till its men learned to kiss the shadow of a Government horse upon the ground. There are many *mullahs* (priests) in Eshtellenbosch. They preached the Jehad against us. This is true – all the camp knew it. And most of the houses were thatched! A war of fools indeed!

At the end of five months my Kurban Sahib, who had grown lean, said, 'The reward has come. We go up towards the front with horses tomorrow, and, once away, I shall be too sick to return. Make ready the baggage.' Thus we got away, with some Kaffirs in charge of new horses for a certain new regiment that had come in a ship. The second day by *terain,* when we were watering at a desolate place without any sort of a bazaar to it, slipped out from the horse-boxes one Sikandar Khan, that had been a *jemadar* of *saises* (head-groom) at Eshtellenbosch, and was by service a trooper in a Border regiment. Kurban Sahib gave him big abuse for his desertion; but the Pathan put up his hands as excusing himself, and Kurban Sahib relented and added him to our service. So there were three of us – Kurban Sahib, I, and Sikandar Khan – Sahib, Sikh, and *Sag* (dog). But the man said truly, 'We be far from our homes and both servants of the Raj. Make truce till we see the Indus again.' I have eaten from the same dish as Sikandar Khan – beef, too, for aught I know! He said, on the night he stole some swine's flesh in a tin from a mess-tent, that in his Book, the Koran, it is written that whoso engages in a holy war is freed from ceremonial obligations. Wah! He had no more religion than the sword-point picks up of sugar and water at baptism. He stole himself a horse at a place where there lay a new and very raw regiment. I also procured myself a grey gelding there. They let their horses stray too much, those new regiments.

Some shameless regiments would indeed have made away with *our* horses on the road! They exhibited indents and requisitions for horses, and once or twice would have uncoupled the trucks; but Kurban Sahib was wise, and I am not altogether a fool. There is not much honesty at the front. Notably, there was one congregation of hard-bitten horse-thieves; tall, light Sahibs, who spoke through their noses for the most part, and upon all occasions they said, 'Oah Hell!' which, in our tongue, signifies *Jehannum ko jao*. They bore each man a vine-leaf upon their uniforms, and they rode like Rajputs. Nay, they rode like Sikhs. They rode like the Ustrelyahs! The Ustrelyahs, whom we met later, also spoke through their noses not little, and they were tall, dark men, with grey, clear eyes, heavily eyelashed like camel's eyes – very proper men – a new brand of Sahib to me. They said on all occasions, 'No fee-ah,' which in our tongue means *Durro mut* ('Do not be afraid'), so we called them the *Durro Muts*. Dark, tall men, most excellent horsemen, hot and angry, waging war *as* war, and drinking tea as a sandhill drinks water. Thieves? A little, Sahib. Sikandar Khan swore to me – and he comes of a horse-stealing clan for ten generations – he swore a Pathan was a babe beside a *Durro Mut* in regard to horse-lifting. The *Durro Muts* cannot walk on their feet at all. They are like hens on the high road. Therefore they must have horses. Very proper men, with a just lust for the war. Aah – 'No fee-ah,' say the *Durro Muts. They* saw the worth of Kurban Sahib. *They* did not ask him to sweep stables. They would by no means let him go. He did substitute for one of their troop-leaders who had a fever, one long day in a country full of little hills – like the mouth of the Khaibar; and when they returned in the evening, the *Durro Muts* said, 'Wallah! This is a man. Steal him!' So they stole my Kurban Sahib as they would have stolen anything else that they needed, and they sent a sick officer back to Eshtellenbosch in his place. Thus Kurban Sahib came to his own again, and I was his bearer, and Sikandar Khan was his cook. The law was strict that this was a Sahibs' war, but there was no order that a bearer and a cook should not ride with their Sahib – and we had naught to wear but our uniforms. We rode up and down this accursed country, where there is no bazaar, no pulse, no flour, no oil, no spice, no red pepper, no firewood; nothing but raw corn and a little cattle. There were no great battles as I saw it, but a plenty of gun-firing. When we were many, the Boer-log came out with coffee to greet us, and to show us *purwanas* (permits) from foolish English Generals who had gone that way before, certifying they were peaceful and well disposed. When we were few, they hid behind stones and shot us. Now the order was that they were Sahibs, and this was a Sahibs' war. Good! But, as I understand it, when a Sahib goes to war, he puts on the cloth of war, and only those who wear that cloth may take part in the war. Good! That also I understand. But these people were as they were in Burma, or as the Afridis are. They shot at their pleasure, and when pressed hid the gun and exhibited *purwanas,* or lay in a house and said they were farmers. Even such farmers as cut up the Madras troops at Hlinedatalone in Burma! Even such farmers as slew Cavagnari Sahib and the Guides at Kabul! We schooled *those* men, to be sure – fifteen, aye, twenty of a morning pushed off the verandah in front of the Bala Hissar. I looked that the Jung-i-lat Sahib (the Commander-in-Chief) would have remembered the old days; but – no. All the people shot at us everywhere, and he issued proclamations saying that he did not fight the people, but a certain army, which army, in truth, was all the Boer-log, who, between them, did not wear enough of uniform to make a loin-cloth. A fools' war from first to last; for it is manifest that he who fights should be hung if he fights with a gun in one hand and a *purwana* in the other, as did all these people. Yet we, when they had had their bellyfull for the time, received them with honour, and gave them permits, and refreshed them and fed their wives and their babes, and severely punished our soldiers who took their fowls. So the work was to be done not once with a few dead, but thrice and four times over. I talked much with Kurban Sahib on this, and he said, 'It is a Sahibs' war. That is the order'; and one night, when Sikandar Khan would have lain out beyond the pickets with his knife and shown them how it is worked on the Border, he hit Sikandar Khan between the eyes and came near to breaking in his head. Then Sikandar Khan, a bandage over his eyes, so that he looked like a sick camel, talked to him half one march, and he was more bewildered than I, and vowed he would return to Eshtellenbosch. But privately to me Kurban Sahib said we should have loosed the Sikhs and the Gurkhas on these people till they came in with their foreheads in the dust. For the war was not of that sort which they comprehended.

They shot us? Assuredly they shot us from houses adorned with a white flag; but when they came to know our custom, their widows sent word by Kaffir runners, and presently there was not quite so much firing. *No fee-ah!* All the Boer-log with whom we dealt had *purwanas* signed by mad Generals attesting that they were well disposed to the State. They had also rifles not a few, and cartridges, which they hid in the roof. The women wept very greatly when we burned such houses, but they did not approach too near after the flames had taken good hold of the thatch, for fear of the bursting cartridges. The women of the Boer-log are very clever. They are more clever than the men. The Boer-log are clever? Never, never, no! It is the Sahibs who are fools. For their own honour's sake the Sahibs must say that the Boer-log are clever; but it is the Sahibs' wonderful folly that has made the Boer-log. The Sahibs should have sent *us* into the game.

But the *Durro Muts* did well. They dealt faithfully with all that country thereabouts – not in any way as we of Hind should have dealt, but they were not altogether fools. One night when we lay on the top of a ridge in the cold, I saw far away a light in a house that appeared for the sixth part of an hour and was obscured. Anon it appeared again thrice for the twelfth part of an hour. I showed this to Kurban Sahib, for it was a house that had been spared – the people having many permits and swearing fidelity at our stirrup-leathers. I said to Kurban Sahib, 'Send half a troop, Child, and finish that house. They signal to their brethren.' And he laughed where he lay and said, 'If I listened to my bearer Umr Singh, there would not be left ten houses in all this land.' I said,

'What need to leave one? This is as it was in Burma. They are farmers today and fighters tomorrow. Let us deal justly with them.' He laughed and curled himself up in his blanket, and I watched the far light in the house till day. I have been on the Border in eight wars, not counting Burma. The first Afghan War; the second Afghan War; two Mahsud Waziri wars (that is four); two Black Mountain wars, if I remember right; the Malakand and Tirah. I do not count Burma, or some small things. *I* know when house signals to house!

I pushed Sikandar Khan with my foot, and he saw it too. He said, 'One of the Boer-log who brought pumpkins for the mess, which I fried last night, lives in yonder house.' I said, 'How dost thou know?' He said, 'Because he rode out of the camp another way, but I marked how his horse fought with him at the turn of the road; and before the light fell I stole out of the camp for evening prayer with Kurban Sahib's glasses, and from a little hill I saw the pied horse of that pumpkin-seller hurrying to that house.' I said naught, but took Kurban Sahib's glasses from his greasy hands and cleaned them with a silk handkerchief and returned them to their case. Sikandar Khan told me that he had been the first man in the Zenab valley to use glasses – whereby he finished two blood-feuds cleanly in the course of three months' leave. But he was otherwise a liar.

That day Kurban Sahib, with some ten troopers, was sent on to spy the land for our camp. The *Durro Muts* moved slowly at that time. They were weighted with grain and forage and carts, and they greatly wished to leave these all in some town and go on light to other business which pressed. So Kurban Sahib sought a short cut for them, a little off the line of march. We were twelve miles before the main body, and we came to a house under a high bushed hill, with a nullah, which they call a donga, behind it, and an old sangar of piled stones, which they call a kraal, before it. Two thorn bushes grew on either side of the door, like babul bushes, covered with a golden-coloured bloom, and the roof was all of thatch. Before the house was a valley of stones that rose to another bush-covered hill. There was an old man in the verandah – an old man with a white beard and a wart upon the left side of his neck; and a fat woman with the eyes of a swine and the jowl of a swine; and a tall young man deprived of understanding. His head was hairless, no larger than an orange, and the pits of his nostrils were eaten away by a disease. He laughed and slavered and he sported sportively before Kurban Sahib. The man brought coffee and the woman showed us *purwanas* from three General-Sahibs, certifying that they were people of peace and goodwill. Here are the *purwanas,* Sahib. Does the Sahib know the Generals who signed them?

They swore the land was empty of Boer-log. They held up their hands and swore it. That was about the time of the evening meal. I stood near the verandah with Sikandar Khan, who was nosing like a jackal on a lost scent. At last he took my arm and said, 'See yonder! There is the sun on the window of the house that signalled last night. This house can see that house from here,' and he looked at the hill behind him all hairy with bushes, and sucked in his breath. Then the idiot with the shrivelled head danced by me and threw back that head, and regarded the roof and laughed like a hyena, and the fat woman talked loudly, as it were, to cover some noise. After this I passed to the back of the house on pretence to get water for tea, and I saw fresh horse-dung on the ground, and that the ground was cut with the new marks of hoofs; and there had dropped in the dirt one cartridge. Then Kurban Sahib called to me in our tongue, saying, 'Is this a good place to make tea?' and I replied, knowing what he meant, 'There are over many cooks in the cook-house. Mount and go, Child.' Then I returned, and he said, smiling to the woman, 'Prepare food, and when we have loosened our girths we will come in and eat'; but to his men he said in a whisper, 'Ride away!' No. He did not cover the old man or the fat woman with his rifle. That was not his custom. Some fool of the *Durro Muts,* being hungry, raised his voice to dispute the order to flee, and before we were in our saddles many shots came from the roof – from rifles thrust through the thatch. Upon this we rode across the valley of stones, and men fired at us from the nullah behind the house, and from the hill behind the nullah, as well as from the roof of the house – so many shots that it sounded like a drumming in the hills. Then Sikandar Khan, riding low, said, 'This play is not for us alone, but for the rest of the *Durro Muts*'; and I said, 'Be quiet. Keep place!' for his place was behind me, and I rode behind Kurban Sahib. But these new bullets will pass through five men a-row! We were not hit – not one of us – and we reached the hill of rocks and scattered among the stones, and Kurban Sahib turned in his saddle and said, 'Look at the old man!' He stood in the verandah firing swiftly with a gun, the woman beside him and the idiot also – both with guns. Kurban Sahib laughed, and I caught him by the wrist, but – his fate was written at that hour. The bullet passed under my arm-pit and struck him in the liver, and I pulled him backward between two great rocks a-tilt – Kurban Sahib, my Kurban Sahib! From the nullah behind the house and from the hills came our Boer-log in number more than a hundred, and Sikandar Khan said, '*Now* we see the meaning of last night's signal. Give me the rifle.' He took Kurban Sahib's rifle – in this war of fools only the doctors carry swords – and lay belly-flat to the work, but Kurban Sahib turned where he lay and said, 'Be still. It is a Sahibs' war,' and Kurban Sahib put up his hand – thus; and then his eyes rolled on me, and I gave him water that he might pass the more quickly. And at the drinking his Spirit received permission ...

Thus went our fight, Sahib. We *Durro Muts* were on a ridge working from the north to the south, where lay our main body, and the Boer-log lay in a valley working from east to west. There were more than a hundred, and our men were ten, but they held the Boer-log in the valley while they swiftly passed along the ridge to the south. I saw three Boers drop in the open. Then they all hid again and fired heavily at the rocks that hid our men; but our men were clever and did not show, but moved away and away, always south; and the noise of the battle withdrew itself southward, where we could hear the sound of big guns. So it fell stark dark, and Sikandar Khan found a deep old jackal's earth amid rocks, into which we slid the body of Kurban Sahib upright. Sikandar Khan took his glasses, and I took his handkerchief and some letters and a certain thing which I knew hung round his neck, and Sikandar Khan is witness that I wrapped them all in the handkerchief. Then we took an oath together, and lay still and mourned for Kurban Sahib. Sikandar Khan wept till daybreak – even he, a Pathan, a Mohammedan! All that night we heard firing to the southward, and when the dawn broke the valley was full of Boer-log in carts and on horses. They gathered by the house, as we could see through Kurban Sahib's glasses, and the old man, who, I take it, was a priest, blessed them, and preached the holy war, waving his arm; and the fat woman brought coffee and the idiot capered among them and kissed their horses. Presently they went away in haste; they went over the hills and were not; and a black slave came out and washed the door-sills with bright water. Sikandar Khan saw through the glasses that the stain was blood, and he laughed, saying, 'Wounded men lie there. We shall yet get vengeance.'

About noon we saw a thin, high smoke to the southward, such a smoke as a burning house will make in sunshine, and Sikandar Kahn, who knows how to take a bearing across a hill, said, 'At last we have burned the house of the pumpkin-seller whence they signalled.' And I said, 'What need now that they have slain my child? Let me mourn.' It was a high smoke, and the old man, as I saw, came out into the verandah to behold it, and shook his clenched hands at it. So we lay till the twilight, foodless and without water, for we had vowed a vow neither to eat nor to drink till we had accomplished the matter. I had a little opium left, of which I gave Sikandar Khan the half, because he loved Kurban Sahib. When it was full dark we sharpened our sabres upon a certain softish rock, which, mixed with water, sharpens steel well, and we took off our boots and we went down to the house and looked through the windows very softly. The old man sat reading in a book, and the woman sat by the hearth; and the idiot lay on the floor with his head against her knee, and he counted his fingers and laughed, and she laughed again. So I knew they were mother and son, and I laughed, too, for I had suspected this when I claimed her life and her body from Sikandar Khan, in our discussion of the spoil. Then we entered with bare swords. ... Indeed, these Boer-log do not understand the steel, for the old man ran towards a rifle in the corner; but Sikandar Khan prevented him with a blow of the flat across the hands, and he sat down and held up his hands, and I put my fingers on my lips to signify they should be silent. But the woman cried, and one stirred in an inner room, and a door opened, and a man, bound about the head with rags, stood stupidly fumbling with a gun. His whole head fell inside the door, and none followed him. It was a very pretty stroke – for a Pathan. Then they were silent, staring at the head upon the floor, and I said to Sikandar Khan, 'Fetch ropes! Not even for Kurban Sahib's sake will I defile my sword.' So he went to seek and returned with three long leather ones, and said, 'Four wounded lie within, and doubtless each has a permit from a General,' and he stretched the ropes and laughed. Then I bound the old man's hands behind his back, and unwillingly – for he laughed in my face, and would have fingered my beard – the idiot's. At this the woman with the swine's eyes and the jowl of a swine ran forward, and Sikandar Khan said, 'Shall I strike or bind? She was thy property on the division.' And I said, 'Refrain! I have made a chain to hold her. Open the door.' I pushed out the two across the verandah into the darker shade of the thorn-trees, and she followed upon her knees and lay along the ground, and pawed at my boots and howled. Then Sikandar Khan bore out the lamp, saying that he was a butler and would light the table, and I looked for a branch that would bear fruit. But the woman hindered me not a little with her screechings and plungings, and spoke fast in her tongue, and

I replied in my tongue, 'I am childless tonight because of thy perfidy, and *my* child was praised among men and loved among women. He would have begotten men – not animals. Thou hast more years to live than I, but my grief is the greater.'

I stooped to make sure the noose upon the idiot's neck, and flung the end over the branch, and Sikandar Khan held up the lamp that she might well see. Then appeared suddenly, a little beyond the light of the lamp, the spirit of Kurban Sahib. One hand he held to his side, even where the bullet had struck him, and the other he put forward thus, and said, 'No. It is a Sahibs' war.' And I said, 'Wait a while, Child, and thou shalt sleep.' But he came nearer, riding, as it were, upon my eyes, and said, 'No. It is a Sahibs' war.' And Sikandar Khan said, 'Is it too heavy?' and set down the lamp and came to me; and as he turned to tally on the rope, the spirit of Kurban Sahib stood up within arm's reach of us, and his face was very angry, and a third time he said, 'No. It is a Sahibs' war.' And a little wind blew out the lamp, and I heard Sikandar Khan's teeth chatter in his head.

So we stayed side by side, the ropes in our hand, a very long while, for we could not shape any words. Then I heard Sikandar Khan open his water-bottle and drink; and when his mouth was slaked he passed to me and said, 'We are absolved from our vow.' So I drank, and together we waited for the dawn in that place where we stood – the ropes in our hand. A little after third cockcrow we heard the feet of horses and gun-wheels very far off, and so soon as the light came a shell burst on the threshold of the house, and the roof of the verandah that was thatched fell in and blazed before the windows. And I said, 'What of the wounded Boer-log within?' And Sikandar Khan said, 'We have heard the order. It is a Sahibs' war. Stand still.' Then came a second shell – good line, but short – and scattered dust upon us where we stood; and then came ten of the little quick shells from the gun that speaks like a stammerer – yes, pompom the Sahibs call it – and the face of the house folded down like the nose and the chin of an old man mumbling, and the forefront of the house lay down. Then Sikandar Khan said, 'If it be the fate of the wounded to die in the fire, *I* shall not prevent it.' And he passed to the back of the house and presently came back, and four wounded Boer-log came after him, of whom two could not walk upright. And I said, 'What hast thou done?' And he said, 'I have neither spoken to them nor laid hand on them. They follow in hope of mercy.' And I said, 'It is a Sahibs' war. Let them wait the Sahibs' mercy.' So they lay still, the four men and the idiot, and the fat woman under the thorn-tree, and the house burned furiously. Then began the known sound of cartouches in the roof – one or two at first; then a trill, and last of all one loud noise and the thatch blew here and there, and the captives would have crawled aside on account of the heat that was withering the thorn-trees, and on account of wood and bricks flying at random. But I said, 'Abide! Abide! Ye be Sahibs, and this is a Sahibs' war, O Sahibs. There is no order that ye should depart from this war.' They did not understand my words. Yet they abode and they lived.

Presently rode down five troopers of Kurban Sahib's command, and one I knew spoke my tongue, having sailed to Calcutta often with horses. So I told him all my tale, using bazaar-talk, such as his kidney of Sahib would understand; and at the end I said, 'An order has reached us here from the dead that this is a Sahibs' war. I take the soul of my Kurban Sahib to witness that I give over to the justice of the Sahibs these Sahibs who have made me childless.' Then I gave him the ropes and fell down senseless, my heart being very full, but my belly was empty, except for the little opium.

They put me into a cart with one of their wounded, and after a while I understood that they had fought against the Boer-log for two days and two nights. It was all one big trap, Sahib, of which we, with Kurban Sahib, saw no more than the outer edge. They were very angry, the *Durro Muts* – very angry indeed. I have never seen Sahibs so angry. They buried my Kurban Sahib with the rites of his faith upon the top of the ridge overlooking the house, and I said the proper prayers of the faith, and Sikandar Khan prayed in his fashion and stole five signalling-candles, which have each three wicks, and lighted the grave as if it had been the grave of a saint on a Friday. He wept very bitterly all that night, and I wept with him, and he took hold of my feet and besought me to give him a remembrance from Kurban Sahib. So I divided equally with him one of Kurban Sahib's handkerchiefs – not the silk ones, for those were given him by a certain woman; and I also gave him a button from a coat, and a little steel ring of no value that Kurban Sahib used for his keys, and he kissed them and put them into his bosom. The rest I have here in that little bundle, and I must get the baggage from the hotel in Cape Town – some four shirts we sent to be washed, for which we could not wait when we went up-country – and I must give them all to my Colonel-Sahib at Sialkote in the Punjab. For my child is dead – my baba is dead! . . .

I would have come away before; there was no need to stay, the child being dead; but we were far from the rail, and the *Durro Muts* were as brothers to me, and I had come to look upon Sikandar Khan as in some sort a friend, and he got me a horse and I rode up and down with them; but the life had departed. God knows what they called me – orderly, *chaprassi* (messenger), cook, sweeper, I did not know nor care. But once I had pleasure. We came back in a month after wide circles to that very valley. I knew it every stone, and I went up to the grave, and a clever Sahib of the *Durro Muts* (we left a troop there for a week to school those people with *purwanas*) had cut an inscription upon a great rock; and they interpreted it to me, and it was a jest such as Kurban Sahib himself would have loved. Oh! I have the inscription well copied here. Read it aloud, Sahib, and I will explain the jests. There are two very good ones. Begin, Sahib:

In Memory of
WALTER DECIES CORBYN
Late Captain 141st Punjab Cavalry

The Gurgaon Rissala, that is. Go on, Sahib.

Treacherously shot near this place by
The connivance of the late
HENDRIK DIRK UYS
A Minister of God
Who thrice took the oath of neutrality
And Piet his son,
This little work

Aha! This is the first jest. The Sahib should see this little work!

Was accomplished in partial
And inadequate recognition of their loss
By some men who loved him

Si monumentum requiris circumspice

That is the second jest. It signifies that those who would desire to behold a proper memorial to Kurban Sahib must look out at the house. And, Sahib, the house is not there, nor the well, nor the big tank which they call dams, nor the little fruit-trees, nor the cattle. There is nothing at all, Sahib, except the two trees withered by the fire. The rest is like the desert here – or my hand – or my heart. Empty, Sahib – all empty!

The Captive

(1902)

'He that believeth shall not make haste.' – *Isaiah.*

THE guard-boat lay across the mouth of the bathing-pool, her crew idly spanking the water with the flat of their oars. A red-coated militiaman, rifle in hand, sat at the bows, and a petty officer at the stern. Between the snow-white cutter and the flat-topped, honey-coloured rocks on the beach the green water was troubled with shrimp-pink prisoners-of-war bathing. Behind their orderly tin camp and the electric-light poles rose those stone-dotted spurs that throw heat on Simonstown. Beneath them the little *Barracouta* nodded to the big *Gibraltar,* and the old *Penelope,* that in ten years has been bachelors' club, natural history museum, kindergarten, and prison, rooted and dug at her fixed moorings. Far out, a three-funnelled Atlantic transport with turtle bow and stern waddled in from the deep sea.

Said the sentry, assured of the visitor's good faith, 'Talk to 'em? You can, to any that speak English. You'll find a lot that do.'

Here and there earnest groups gathered round ministers of the Dutch Reformed Church, who doubtless preached conciliation, but the majority preferred their bath. The God who Looks after Small Things had caused the visitor that day to received two weeks' delayed mails in one from a casual postman, and the whole heavy bundle of newspapers, tied with a strap, he dangled as bait. At the edge of the beach, cross-legged, undressed to his sky-blue army shirt, sat a lean, ginger-haired man, on guard over a dozen heaps of clothing. His eyes followed the incoming Atlantic boat.

'Excuse me, Mister,' he said, without turning (and the speech betrayed his nationality), 'would you mind keeping away from these garments? I've been elected janitor – on the Dutch vote.'

The visitor moved over against the barbed-wire fence and sat down to his mail. At the rustle of the newspaper-wrappers the ginger-coloured man turned quickly, the hunger of a press-ridden people in his close-set iron-grey eyes.

'Have you any use for papers?' said the visitor.

'Have I any use?' A quick, curved forefinger was already snicking off the outer covers. 'Why, that's the New York postmark! Give me the ads. at the back of *Harper's* and *M'Clure's* and I'm in touch with God's Country again! Did you know how I was aching for papers?'

The visitor told the tale of the casual postman.

'Providential!' said the ginger-coloured man, keen as a terrier on his task; 'both in time and matter. Yes! ... The *Scientific American* yet once more! Oh, it's good! it's good!' His voice broke as he pressed his hawk-like nose against the heavily-inked patent-specifications at the end. 'Can I keep it? I thank you – I thank you! Why – why – well – well! The *American Tyler* of all things created! Do you subscribe to that?'

'I'm on the free list,' said the visitor, nodding.

He extended his blue-tanned hand with that air of Oriental spaciousness which distinguishes the native-born American, and met the visitor's grasp expertly. 'I can only say that you have treated me like a Brother (yes, I'll take every last one you can spare), and if ever – ' He plucked at the bosom of his shirt. 'Psha! I forgot I'd no card on me; but my name's Zigler – Laughton O. Zigler. An American? If Ohio's still in the Union, I am, Sir. But I'm no extreme States'-rights man. I've used all of my native country and a few others as I have found occasion, and now I am the captive of your bow and spear. I'm not kicking at that. I am not a coerced alien, nor a naturalized Texas mule-tender, nor an adventurer on the instalment plan. *I* don't tag after our Consul when he comes around, expecting the American Eagle to lift me out o' this by the slack of my pants. No, Sir!

If a Britisher went into Indian Territory and shot up his surroundings with a Colt automatic (not that *she's* any sort of weapon, but I take her for an illustration), he'd be strung up quicker'n a snowflake 'ud melt in hell. No ambassador of yours 'ud save him. I'm my neck ahead on this game, anyway. That's how I regard the proposition.

'Have I gone gunning against the British? To a certain extent. I presume you never heard tell of the Laughton-Zigler automatic two-inch field-gun, with self-feeding hopper, single oil-cylinder recoil, and ball-bearing gear throughout? Or Laughtite, the new explosive? Absolutely uniform in effect, and one-ninth the bulk of any present effete charge – flake, cannonite, cordite, troisdorf, cellulose, cocoa, cord, or prism – I don't care what it is. Laughtite's immense; so's the Zigler automatic. It's me. It's fifteen years of me. You are not a gun-sharp? I am sorry. I could have surprised you. Apart from my gun, my tale don't amount to much of anything. I thank you, but I don't use any tobacco you'd be likely to carry. . . . Bull Durham? *Bull Durham!* I take it all back – every last word. Bull Durham – here! If ever you strike Akron, Ohio, when this fool-war's over, remember you've Laughton O. Zigler in your vest pocket. Including the city of Akron. We've a little club there. . . . Hell! What's the sense of talking Akron with no pants?

'My gun? . . . For two cents I'd have shipped her to our Filipeens. 'Came mighty near it too; but from what I'd read in the papers, you can't trust Aguinaldo's crowd on scientific matters. Why don't I offer it to our army? Well, you've an effete aristocracy running yours, and we've a crowd of politicians. The results are practically identical. I am not taking any U.S. Army in mine.

'I went to Amsterdam with her – to this Dutch junta that supposes it's bossing the war. I wasn't brought up to love the British for one thing, and for another I knew that if she got in her fine work (my gun) I'd stand more chance of receiving an unbiassed report from a crowd o' dam-fool British officers than from a hatful of politicians' nephews doing duty as commissaries and ordnance sharps. As I said, I put the brown man out of the question. That's the way *I* regarded the proposition.

'The Dutch in Holland don't amount to a row of pins. Maybe I misjudge 'em. Maybe they've been swindled too often by self-seeking adventurers to know a enthusiast when they see him. Anyway, they're slower than the Wrath o' God. But on delusions – as to their winning out next Thursday week at 9 a.m. – they are – if I may say so – quite British.

'I'll tell tell you a curious thing, too. I fought 'em for ten days before I could get the financial side of my game fixed to my liking. I knew they didn't believe in the Zigler, but they'd no call to be crazy-mean. I fixed it – free passage and freight for me and the gun to Delagoa Bay, and beyond by steam and rail. Then I went aboard to see her crated, and there I struck my fellow-passengers – all deadheads, same as me. Well, Sir, I turned in my tracks where I stood and besieged the ticket-office, and I said, "Look at here, Van Dunk. I'm paying for my passage and her room in the hold – every square and cubic foot." Guess he knocked down the fare to himself; but I paid. I paid. I wasn't going to deadhead along o' *that* crowd of Pentecostal sweepings. 'Twould have hoodooed my gun for all time. That was the way I regarded the proposition. No, Sir, they were not pretty company.

'When we struck Pretoria I had a hell-and-a-half of a time trying to interest the Dutch vote in my gun an' her potentialities. The bottom was out of things rather much just about that time. Kruger was praying some and stealing some, and the Hollander lot was singing, "If you haven't any money you needn't come round." Nobody was spending his dough on anything except tickets to Europe. We were both grossly neglected. When I think how I used to give performances in the public streets with dummy cartridges, filling the hopper and turning the handle till the sweat dropped off me, I blush, Sir. I've made her do her stunts before Kaffirs – naked sons of Ham – in Commissioner Street, trying to get a holt somewhere.

'Did I talk? I despise exaggeration – 'tain't American or scientific – but as true as I'm sitting here like a blue-ended baboon in a kloof, Teddy Roosevelt's Western tour was a maiden's sigh compared to my advertising work.

''Long in the spring I was rescued by a commandant called Van Zyl – a big, fleshy man with a lame leg. Take away his hair and his gun and he'd make a first-class Schenectady bar-keep. He found me and the Zigler on the veldt (Pretoria wasn't wholesome at that time), and he annexed me in a somnambulistic sort o' way. He was dead against the war from the start, but, being a Dutchman, he fought a sight better than the rest of that "God and the Mauser" outfit. Adrian Van Zyl. Slept a heap in the daytime – and didn't love niggers. I liked him. I was the only foreigner in his commando. The rest was Georgia Crackers and Pennsylvania Dutch – with a dash o' Philadelphia lawyer. I could tell you things about them would surprise you. Religion for one thing; women for another; but I don't know as their notions o' geography weren't the craziest. Guess that must be some sort of automatic compensation. There wasn't one blamed ant-hill in their district they didn't know *and* use; but the world was flat, they said, and England was a day's trek from Cape Town.

'They could fight in their own way, and don't you forget it. But I guess you will not. They fought to kill, and, by what I could make out, the British fought to be killed. So both parties were accommodated.

'I am the captive of your bow and spear, Sir. The position has its obligations – on both sides. You could not be offensive or partisan to me. I cannot, for the same reason, be offensive to you. Therefore I will not give you my opinions on the conduct of your war.

'Anyway, I didn't take the field as an offensive partisan, but as an inventor. It was a condition and not a theory that confronted me. (Yes, Sir, I'm a Democrat by conviction, and that was one of the best things Grover Cleveland ever got off.)

'After three months' trek, old man Van Zyl had his commando in good shape and refitted off the British, and he reckoned he'd wait on a British General of his acquaintance that did business on a circuit between Stompiesneuk, Jackhalputs, Vrelegan, and Odendaalstroom, year in and year out. He was a fixture in that section.

'"He's a dam good man," says Van Zyl. "He's a friend of mine. He sent in a fine doctor when I was wounded and our Hollander doc. wanted to cut my leg off. Ya, I'll guess we'll stay with him." Up to date, me and my Zigler had lived in innocuous desuetude owing to little odds and ends riding out of gear. How in thunder was I to know there wasn't the ghost of any road in the country? But raw hide's cheap and lastin'. I guess I'll make my next gun a thousand pounds heavier, though.

'Well, Sir, we struck the General on his beat – Vrelegen it was – and our crowd opened with the usual compliments at two thousand yards. Van Zyl shook himself into his greasy old saddle and says, "Now we shall be quite happy, Mr Zigler. No more trekking. Joost twelve miles a day till the apricots are ripe."

'Then we hitched on to his outposts, and vedettes, and cossack-picquets, or whatever they was called, and we wandered around the veldt arm in arm like brothers.

'The way we worked lodge was this way. The General, he had his breakfast at 8.45 a.m. to the tick. He might have been a Long Island commuter. At 8.42 a.m. I'd go down to the Thirty-fourth Street ferry to meet him – I mean I'd see the Zigler into position at two thousand (I began at three thousand, but that was cold and distant) – and blow him off to two full hoppers – eighteen rounds – just as they were bringing in his coffee. If his crowd was busy celebrating the anniversary of Waterloo or the last royal kid's birthday, they'd open on me with two guns (I'll tell you about them later on), but if they were disengaged they'd all stand to their horses and pile on the ironmongery, and washers, and typewriters, and five weeks' grub, and in half an hour they'd sail out after me and the rest of Van Zyl's boys; lying down and firing till 11.45 a.m. or maybe high noon. Then we'd go from labour to refreshment, resooming at 2 p.m. and battling till tea-time. Tuesday and Friday was the General's moving days. He'd trek ahead ten or twelve miles, and we'd loaf around his flankers and exercise the ponies a piece. Sometimes he'd get hung up in a drift – stalled crossin' a crick – and we'd make playful snatches at his wagons. First time that happened I turned the Zigler loose with high hopes, Sir; but the old man was well posted on rearguards with a gun to 'em, and I had to haul her out with three mules instead o' six. I was pretty mad. I wasn't looking for any experts back of the Royal British Artillery. Otherwise, the game was mostly even. He'd lay out three or four of our commando, and we'd gather in four or five of his once a week or thereon. One time, I remember, 'long towards dusk we saw 'em burying five of their boys. They stood pretty thick around the graves. We wasn't more than fifteen hundred yards off, but old Van Zyl wouldn't fire. He just took off his hat at the proper time. He said if you stretched a man at his prayers you'd have to hump his bad luck before the Throne as well as your own. I am inclined to agree with him. So we browsed along week in and week out. A war-sharp might have judged it sort of docile, but for an inventor needing practice one day and peace the next for checking his theories, it suited Laughton O. Zigler.

'And friendly? Friendly was no word for it. We was brothers in arms.

'Why, I knew those two guns of the Royal British Artillery as well as I used to know the old Fifth Avenoo stages. *They* might have been brothers too.

'They'd jolt into action, and wiggle around and skid and and cough and prise 'emselves back again during our hours of bloody battle till I could have wept, Sir, at the spectacle of modern white men chained up to these old hand-power, back-number, flint-and-steel reaping machines. One of 'em – I called her Baldy – she'd a long white scar all along her barrel – I'd made sure of twenty times. I knew her crew by sight, but she'd come switching and teetering out of the dust of my shells like – like a hen from under a buggy – and she'd dip into a gully, and next thing I'd know 'ud be her old nose peeking over the ridge sniffin' for us. Her runnin' mate had two grey mules in the lead, and a natural wood wheel re-painted, and a whole raft of rope-ends trailin' around. 'J'ever see Tom Reed with his vest off, steerin' Congress through a heat-wave? I've been to Washington often – too often – filin' my patents. I called her Tom Reed. We three 'ud play pussy-wants-a-corner all round the outposts on off-days – cross-lots through the sage and along the mezas till we was short-circuited by cañons. Oh, it was great for me and Baldy and Tom Reed! I don't know as we didn't neglect the legitimate interests of our respective commandoes sometimes for this ball-play. I know *I* did.

' 'Long towards the fall the Royal British Artillery grew shy – hung back in their breeching sort of – and their shooting was way – way off. I observed they wasn't taking any chances, not though I acted kitten almost underneath 'em.

'I mentioned it to Van Zyl, because it struck me I had knocked their Royal British morale endways.

' "No," says he, rocking as usual on his pony. "My Captain Mankeltow he is sick. That is all."

' "So's your Captain Mankeltow's guns," I said. "But I'm going to make 'em a heap sicker before he gets well."

' "No," says Van Zyl. "He has had the enteric a little. Now he is better, and he was let out from hospital at Jackhalputs. Ah, that Mankeltow! He always makes me laugh so. I told him – long back – at Colesberg, I had a little home for him at Nooitgedacht. But he would not come – no! He has been sick, and I am sorry."

' "How d'you know that?" I says.

' "Why, only today he sends back his love by Johanna Van der Merwe, that goes to their doctor for her sick baby's eyes. He sends his love, that Mankeltow, and he tells her tell me he has a little garden of roses all ready for me in the Dutch Indies – Umballa. He is very funny, my Captain Mankeltow."

'The Dutch and the English ought to fraternize, Sir. They've the same notions of humour, to my thinking.'

'"When he gets well," says Van Zyl, "you look out, Mr Americaan. He comes back to his guns next Tuesday. Then they shoot better."

'I wasn't so well acquainted with the Royal British Artillery as old man Van Zyl. I knew this Captain Mankeltow by sight, of course, and, considering what sort of a man with the hoe he was, I thought he'd done right well against my Zigler. But nothing epoch-making.

'Next morning at the usual hour I waited on the General, and old Van Zyl come along with some of the boys. Van Zyl didn't hang round the Zigler much as a rule, but this was his luck that day.

'He was peeking through his glasses at the camp, and I was helping pepper the General's sow-belly – just as usual – when he turns to me quick and says, "Almighty! How all these Englishmen are liars! You cannot trust one," he says. "Captain Mankeltow tells our Johanna he comes not back till Tuesday, and today is Friday, and there he is! Almighty! The English are all Chamberlains!"

'If the old man hadn't stopped to make political speeches he'd have had his supper in laager that night, I guess. I was busy attending to Tom Reed at two thousand when Baldy got in her fine work on me. I saw one sheet of white flame wrapped round the hopper, and in the middle of it there was one o' my mules straight on end. Nothing out of the way in a mule on end, but this mule hadn't any head. I remember it struck me as incongruous at the time, and when I'd ciphered it out I was doing the Santos-Dumont act without any balloon and my motor out of gear. Then I got to thinking about Santos-Dumont and how much better my new way was. Then I thought about Professor Langley and the Smithsonian, and wished I hadn't lied so extravagantly in some of my specifications at Washington. Then I quit thinking for quite a while, and when I resumed my train of thought I was nude, Sir, in a very stale stretcher, and my mouth was full of fine dirt all flavoured with Laughtite.

'I coughed up that dirt.

'"Hullo!" says a man walking beside me. "You've spoke almost in time. Have a drink?"

'I don't use rum as a rule, but I did then, because I needed it.

'"What hit us?" I said.

'"Me," he said. "I got you fair on the hopper as you pulled out of that donga; but I'm sorry to say every last round in the hopper's exploded and your gun's in a shocking state. I'm real sorry," he says. "I admire your gun, Sir."

'"Are you Captain Mankeltow?" I says.

'"Yes," he says. "I presoom you're Mister Zigler. Your commanding officer told me about you."

'"Have you gathered in old man Van Zyl?" I said.

'"Commandant Van Zyl," he says very stiff, "was most unfortunately wounded, but I am glad to say it's not serious. We hope he'll be able to dine with us tonight; and I feel sure," he says, "the General would be delighted to see you too, though he didn't expect," he says, "and no one else either, by Jove!" he says, and blushed like the British do when they're embarrassed.

'I saw him slide an Episcopalian Prayer-book up his sleeve, and when I looked over the edge of the stretcher there was half-a-dozen enlisted men – privates – had just quit digging and was standing to attention by their spades. I guess he was right on the General not expecting me to dinner; but it was all of a piece with their sloppy British way of doing business. Any God's quantity of fuss and flubdub to bury a man, and not an ounce of forehandedness in the whole outfit to find out whether he was rightly dead. And I am a Congregationalist anyway!

'Well, Sir, that was my introduction to the British Army. I'd write a book about it if anyone would believe me. This Captain Mankeltow, Royal British Artillery, turned the doctor on me (I could write another book about *him*) and fixed me up with a suit of his own clothes, and fed me canned beef and biscuits, and gave me a cigar – a Henry Clay and a whisky-and-sparklet. He was a white man.

'"Ye-es, by Jove," he said, dragging out his words like a twist of molasses, "we've all admired your gun and the way you've worked it. Some of us betted you was a British deserter. I won a sovereign on that from a yeoman. And, by the way," he says, "you've disappointed me groom pretty bad."

'"Where does your groom come in?" I said.

'"Oh, he was the yeoman. He's a dam poor groom," says my captain, "but he's a way-up barrister when he's at home. He's been running around the camp with his tongue out, waiting for the chance of defending you at the court-martial."

'"What court-martial?" I says.

'"On you as a deserter from the Artillery. You'd have had a good run for your money. Anyway, you'd never have been hung after the way you worked your gun. Deserter ten times over," he says, "I'd have stuck out for shooting you like a gentleman."

'Well, Sir, right there it struck me at the pit of my stomach – sort of sickish, sweetish feeling – that my position needed regularizing pretty bad. I ought to have been a naturalized burgher of a year's standing; but Ohio's my State, and I wouldn't have gone back on her for a desertful of Dutchmen. That and my enthoosiasm as an inventor had led me to the existing crisis; but I couldn't expect this Captain Mankeltow to regard the proposition that way. There I sat, the rankest breed of unreconstructed American citizen, caught red-handed squirting hell at the British Army for months on end. I tell *you,* Sir, I wished I was in Cincinnatah that summer evening. I'd have compromised on Brooklyn.

'"What d'you do about aliens?" I said, and the dirt I'd coughed up seemed all back of my tongue again.

'"Oh," says he, "we don't do much of anything. They're about all the society we get. I'm a bit of a pro-Boer myself," he says, "but between you and me the average Boer ain't over and above intellectual. You're the first American we've met up with, but of course you're a burgher."

'It was what I ought to have been if I'd had the sense of a

common tick, but the way he drawled it out made me mad.

' "Of course I am not," I says. "Would *you* be a naturalized Boer?"

' "I'm fighting against 'em," he says, lighting a cigarette, "but it's all a matter of opinion."

' "Well," I says, "you can hold any blame opinion you choose, but I'm a white man, and my present intention is to die in that colour."

'He laughed one of those big, thick-ended, British laughs that don't lead anywhere, and whacked up some sort of compliment about America that made me mad all through.

'I am the captive of your bow and spear, Sir, but I do not understand the alleged British joke. It is depressing.

'I was introdooced to five or six officers that evening, and every blame one of 'em grinned and asked me why I wasn't in the Filipeens suppressing our war! And that was British humour! They all had to get it off their chests before they'd talk sense. But they was sound on the Zigler. They had all admired her. I made out a fairy-story of me being wearied of the war, and having pushed the gun at them these last three months in the hope they'd capture it and let me go home. That tickled 'em to death. They made me say it three times over, and laughed like kids each time. But half the British *are* kids; specially the older men. My Captain Mankeltow was less of it than the others. He talked about the Zigler like a lover, Sir, and I drew him diagrams of the hopper-feed and recoil-cylinder in his note-book. He asked the one British question I was waiting for, "Hadn't I made my working-parts too light?" The British think weight's strength.

'At last – I'd been shy of opening the subject before – at last I said, "Gentlemen, you are the unprejudiced tribunal I've been hunting after. I guess you ain't interested in any other gun-factory, and politics don't weigh with you. How did it feel your end of the game? What's my gun done, anyway?"

' "I hate to disappoint you," says Captain Mankeltow, "because I know how you feel as an inventor." I wasn't feeling like an inventor just then. I felt friendly, but the British haven't more tact than you can pick up with a knife out of a plate of soup.

'"The honest truth," he says, "is that you've wounded about ten of us one way and another, killed two battery horses and four mules, and – oh, yes," he said, "you've bagged five Kaffirs. But, buck up," he says, "we've all had mighty close calls" – shaves, he called 'em, I remember. "Look at my pants."

'They was repaired right across the seat with Minneapolis flour-bagging. I could see the stencil.

'"I ain't bluffing," he says. "Get the hospital returns, Doc."

'The doctor gets 'em and reads 'em out under the proper dates. That doctor alone was worth the price of admission.

'I was pleased right through that I hadn't killed any of these cheerful kids; but none the less I couldn't help thinking that a few more Kaffirs would have served me just as well for advertising purposes as white men. No, Sir. Anywhichway you regard the proposition, twenty-one casualties after months of close friendship like ours was – paltry.

'They gave me taffy about the gun – the British use taffy where we use sugar. It's cheaper, and gets there just the same. They sat around and proved to me that my gun was too good, too uniform – shot as close as a Männlicher rifle.

'Says one kid chewing a bit of grass: "I counted eight of your shells, Sir, burst in a radius of ten feet. All of 'em would have gone through one waggon-tilt. It was beautiful," he says. "It was too good."

'I shouldn't wonder if the boys were right. My Laughtite is too mathematically uniform in propelling power. Yes; she was too good for this refractory fool of a country. The training-gear was broke, too, and we had to swivel her around by the trail. But I'll build my next Zigler fifteen hundred pounds heavier. Might work in a gasoline motor under the axles. I must think that up.

' "Well, gentlemen," I said, "I'd hate to have been the death of any of you; and if a prisoner can deed away his property, I'd love to present the Captain here with what he's seen fit to leave of my Zigler."

' "Thanks awf'ly," says my Captain. "I'd like her very much. She'd look fine in the mess at Woolwich. That is, if you don't mind, Mr Zigler."

' "Go right ahead," I says. "I've come out of all the mess I've any use for; but she'll do to spread the light among the Royal British Artillery."

'I tell you, Sir, there's not much of anything the matter with the Royal British Artillery. They're brainy men languishing under an effete system which, when you take good holt of it, is England – just all England. 'Times I'd feel I was talking with real live citizens, and times I'd feel I'd struck the Beef-eaters in the Tower.

'How? Well, this way. I was telling my Captain Mankeltow what Van Zyl had said about the British being all Chamberlains when the old man saw him back from hospital four days ahead of time.

' "Oh, dam it all!" he says, as serious as the Supreme Court. "It's too bad," he says. "Johanna must have misunderstood me, or else I've got the wrong Dutch word for these blarsted days of the week. I told Johanna I'd be out on Friday. The woman's a fool. Oah, da-am it all!" he says. "I wouldn't have sold old Van Zyl a pup like that," he says. "I'll hunt him up and apologize."

'He must have fixed it all right, for when we sailed over to the General's dinner my Captain had Van Zyl about half-full of sherry and bitters, as happy as a clam. The boys all called him Adrian, and treated him like their prodigal father. He'd been hit on the collar-bone by a wad of shrapnel, and his arm was tied up.

'But the General was the peach. I presume you're acquainted with the average run of British generals, but this was my first. I sat on his left hand, and he talked like – like the *Ladies Home Journal*. 'J'ever read that paper? It's refined, Sir – and innocuous, and full of nickel-plated sentiments guaranteed to improve the mind. He was it. He began by a Lydia Pinkham heart-to-heart talk about my health, and hoped the boys had done me well, and that I was enjoying my stay in their midst. Then he thanked me for the interesting and valuable lessons that I'd given his crowd – specially in the matter of placing artillery and rearguard attacks. He'd wipe his long thin moustache between drinks – lime-juice and water he used – and blat off into a long "a-aah," and ladle out more taffy for me or old man Van Zyl on his right. I told him how I'd had my first Pisgah-sight of the principles of the Zigler when I was a fourth-class postmaster on a star-route in Arkansas. I told him how I'd worked it up by instalments when I was machinist in Waterbury, where the dollar-watches come from. He had one on his wrist then. I told him how I'd met Zalinski (he'd never heard of Zalinski!) when I was an extra clerk in the Naval Construction Bureau at Washington. I told him how my uncle, who was a truck-farmer in Noo Jersey (he loaned money on mortgage too, for ten acres ain't enough now in Noo Jersey), how he'd willed me a quarter of a million dollars, because I was the only one of our kin that called him down when he used to come home with a hard-cider jag on him and heave ox-bows at his nieces. I told him how I'd turned in every red cent on the Zigler, and I told him the whole circus of my coming out with her, and so on, and so following; and every forty seconds he'd wipe his moustache and blat, "How interesting. Really, now? How interesting."

'It was like being in an old English book, Sir. Like *Bracebridge Hall*. But an American wrote *that*! I kept peeking around for the Boar's Head and the Rosemary and Magna Charta and the Cricket on the Hearth, and the rest of the outfit. Then Van Zyl whirled in. He was no ways jagged, but thawed – thawed, Sir, and among friends. They began discussing previous scraps all along the old man's beat – about sixty of 'em – as well as side-shows with other generals and columns. Van Zyl told 'im of a big beat he'd worked on a column a week or so before I'd joined him. He demonstrated his strategy with forks on the table.

'"There!" said the General, when he'd finished. "That proves my contention to the hilt. Maybe I'm a bit of a pro-Boer, but I stick to it," he says, "that under proper officers, with due regard to his race prejudices, the Boer'ud make the finest mounted infantry in the Empire. Adrian," he says, "you're simply squandered on a cattle-run. You ought to be at the Staff College with De Wet."

'"You catch De Wet and I come to your Staff College – eh," says Adrian, laughing. "But you are so slow, Generaal. Why are you so slow? For a month," he says, "you do so well and strong that we say we shall hands-up and come back to our farms. Then you send to England and make us a present of two – three – six hundred young men, with rifles and wagons and rum and tobacco, and such a great lot of cartridges, that our young men put up their tails and start all over again. If you hold an ox by the horn and hit him by the bottom he runs round and round. He never goes anywhere. So, too, this war goes round and round. You know that, Generaal!"

'"Quite right, Adrian," says the General; "but you must believe your Bible."

'"Hooh!" says Adrian, and reached for the whisky. I've never known a Dutchman a professing Atheist, but some few have been rather active Agnostics since the British sat down in Pretoria. Old man Van Zyl! – he told me – had soured on religion after Bloemfontein surrendered. He was a Free Stater for one thing.

'"He that believeth," says the General, "shall not make haste. That's in Isaiah. We believe we're going to win, and so we don't make haste. As far as I'm concerned I'd like this war to last another five years. We'd have an army then. It's just this way, Mr Zigler," he says, "our people are brim-full of patriotism, but they've been born and brought up between houses, and England ain't big enough to train 'em – not if you expect to preserve."

' "Preserve what?" I says. "England?"

' "No. The game," he says; "and that reminds me, gentlemen, we haven't drunk the King and Fox-hunting."

'So they drank the King and Fox-hunting. I drank the King because there's something about Edward that tickles me (he's so blame British); but I rather stood out on the Fox-hunting. I've ridden wolves in the cattle-country, and needed a drink pretty bad afterwards, but it never struck me as I ought to drink about it – he-red-it-arily.

' "No, as I was saying, Mr Zigler," he goes on, "we have to train our men in the field to shoot and ride. I allow six months for it; but many column-commanders – not that I ought to say a word against 'em, for they're the best fellows that ever stepped, and most of 'em are my dearest friends – seem to think that if they have men and horses and guns they can take tea with the Boers. It's generally the other way about, ain't it, Mr Zigler?"

' "To some extent, Sir," I said.

' "I'm *so* glad you agree with me," he says. "My command here I regard as a training depot, and you, if I may say so, have been one of my most efficient instructors. I mature my men slowly but thoroughly. First I put 'em in a town which is liable to be attacked by night, where they can attend riding-school in the day. Then I use 'em with a convoy, and last I put 'em into a column. It takes time," he says, "but I flatter myself that any men who have worked under me are at least grounded in the rudiments of their profession. Adrian," he says, "was there anything wrong with the men who upset Van Besters' apple-cart last month when he was trying to cross the line to join Piper with those horses he'd stole from Gabbitas?"

' "No, Generaal," says Van Zyl. "Your men got the horses back and eleven dead; and Van Besters, he ran to Delarey in his shirt. They was very good, those men. They shoot hard."

' "*So* pleased to hear you say so. I laid 'em down at the beginning of this century – a 1900 vintage. *You* remember 'em, Mankletow?" he says. "The Central Middlesex Broncho Busters – clerks and floor-walkers mostly," and he wiped his moustache. "It was just the same with the Liverpool Buck-jumpers, but they were stevedores. Let's see – they were a last-century draft, weren't they? They did well after nine months. *You* know 'em, Van Zyl? You didn't get much change out of 'em at Pootfontein?"

'"No," says Van Zyl. "At Pootfontein I lost my son Andries."

'"I beg your pardon, Commandant," says the General; and the rest of the crowd sort of cooed over Adrian.

'"Excoose," says Adrian. "It was all right. They were good men those, but it is just what I say. Some are so dam good we want to hands-up, and some are so dam bad, we say, 'Take the Vierkleur into Cape Town.' It is not upright of you, Generaal. It is not upright of you at all. I do not think you ever wish this war to finish."

'"It's a first-class dress-parade for Armageddon," says the General. "With luck, we ought to run half a million men through the mill. Why, we might even be able to give our Native Army a look in. Oh, not here, of course, Adrian, but down in the Colony – say a camp-of-exercise at Worcester. You mustn't be prejudiced, Adrian. I've commanded a district in India, and I give you my word the native troops are splendid men."

'"Oh, I should not mind them at Worcester," says Adrian. "I would sell you forage for them at Worcester – yes, and Paarl and Stellenbosch; but Almighty!" he says, "must I stay with Cronje till you have taught half a million of these stupid boys to ride? I shall be an old man."

'Well, Sir, then and there they began arguing whether St Helena would suit Adrian's health as well as some other places they knew about, and fixing up letters of introduction to Dukes and Lords of their acquaintance, so's Van Zyl should be well looked after. We own a fair-sized block of real estate – America does – but it made me sickish to hear this crowd fluttering round the Atlas (oh yes, they had an Atlas), and choosing stray continents for Adrian to drink his coffee in. The old man allowed he didn't want to roost with Cronje, because one of Cronje's kin had jumped one of his farms after Paardeberg. I forget the rights of the case, but it was interesting. They decided on a place called Umballa in India, because there was a first-class doctor there.

'So Adrian was fixed to drink the King and Fox-hunting, and study up the Native Army in India (I'd like to see 'em myself), till the British General had taught the male white citizens of Great Britain how to ride. Don't misunderstand me, Sir. I loved that General. After ten minutes I loved him, and I wanted to laugh at him; but at the same time, sitting there and hearing him talk about the centuries, I tell you, Sir, it scared me. It scared me cold! He admitted everything – he acknowledged the corn before you spoke – he was more pleased to hear that his men had been used to wipe the veldt with than I was when I knocked out Tom Reed's two lead-horses – and he sat back and blew smoke through his nose and matured his men like cigars and – he talked of the everlastin' centuries!

'I went to bed nearer nervous prostration than I'd come in a long time. Next morning me and Captain Mankeltow fixed up what his shrapnel had left of my Zigler for transport to the railroad. She went in on her own wheels, and I stencilled her "Royal Artillery Mess, Woolwich", on the muzzle, and he said he'd be grateful if I'd take charge of her to Cape Town, and hand her over to a man in the Ordnance there. "How are you fixed financially? You'll need some money on the way home," he says at last.

' "For one thing, Cap," I said, "I'm not a poor man, and for another I'm not going home. I am the captive of your bow and spear. I decline to resign office."

' "Skittles!" he says (that was a great word of his), "you'll take parole, and go back to America and invent another Zigler, a trifle heavier in the working-parts – I would. We've got more prisoners than we know what to do with as it is," he says. "You'll only be an additional expense to me as a taxpayer. Think of Schedule D," he says, "and take parole."

" 'I don't know anything about your tariffs," I said, "but when I get to Cape Town I write home for money, and I turn in every cent my board'll cost your country to any ten-century-old department that's been ordained to take it since William the Conqueror came along."

' "But, confound you for a thick-headed mule," he says, "this war ain't any more than just started! Do you mean to tell me you're going to play prisoner till it's over?"

' "That's about the size of it," I says, "if an Englishman and an American could ever understand each other."

' "But, in Heaven's Holy Name, why?" he says, sitting down of a heap on an ant-hill.

' "Well, Cap," I says, "I don't pretend to follow your ways of thought, and I can't see why you abuse your position to persecute a poor prisoner o' war on *his*!"

' "My dear fellow," he began, throwing up his hands and blushing, "I'll apologize."

' "But if you insist," I says, "there are just one and a half things in this world I can't do. The odd half don't matter here; but taking parole, and going home, and being interviewed by the boys, and giving lectures on my single-handed campaign against the hereditary enemies of my beloved country happens to be the one. We'll let it go at that, Cap."

' "But it'll bore you to death," he says. The British are a heap more afraid of what they call being bored than of dying, I've noticed.

' "I'll survive," I says, "I ain't British. I can think," I says.

' "By God," he says, coming up to me, and extending the right hand of fellowship, "you ought to be English, Zigler!"

'It's no good getting mad at a compliment like that. The English all do it. They're a crazy breed. When they don't know you they freeze up tighter'n the St Lawrence. When they *do*, they go out like an ice-jam in April. Up till we prisoners left – four days – my Captain Mankeltow told me pretty much all about himself there was; – his mother and sisters, and his bad brother that was a trooper in some Colonial corps, and how his father didn't get on with him, and – well, everything, as I've said. They're undomesticated, the British, compared with us. They talk about their own family affairs as if they belonged to someone else. 'Tain't as if they hadn't any shame, but it sounds like it. I guess they talk out loud what we think, and we talk out loud what they think.

'I liked my Captain Mankeltow. I liked him as well as any man I'd ever struck. He was white. He gave me his silver drinking-flask, and I gave him the formula of my Laughtite. That's a hundred and fifty thousand dollars in his vest-pocket, on the lowest count, if he has the knowledge to use it. No, I didn't tell him the money-value. He was English. He'd send his valet to find out.

'Well, me and Adrian and a crowd of dam Dutchmen was sent down the road to Cape Town in first-class carriages under escort. (What did I think of your enlisted men? They are largely different from ours, Sir: very largely.) As I was saying, we slid down south, with Adrian looking out of the car-window and crying. Dutchmen cry mighty easy for a breed that fights as they do; but I never understood how a Dutchman could curse till we crossed into the Orange Free State Colony, and he lifted up his hand and cursed Steyn for a solid ten minutes. Then we got into the Colony, and the rebs – ministers mostly and school-masters – came round the cars with fruit and sympathy and texts. Van Zyl talked to 'em in Dutch, and one man, a big red-bearded minister, at Beaufort West, I remember, he jest wilted on the platform.

' "Keep your prayers for yourself," says Van Zyl, throwing back a bunch of grapes. "You'll need 'em, and you'll need the fruit too, when the war comes down here. *You* done it," he says. "You and your picayune Church that's deader than Cronje's dead horses! What sort of a God have you been unloading on us, you black *aasvogels*? The British came, and we beat 'em," he says, "and you sat still and prayed. The British beat us, and you sat still," he says. "You told us to hang on, and we hung on, and our farms were burned, and you sat still

– you and your God. See here," he says, "I shot my Bible full of bullets after Bloemfontein went, and you and God didn't say anything. Take it and pray over it before we Federals help the British to knock hell out of you rebels."

'Then I hauled him back into the car. I judged he'd had a fit. But life's curious – and sudden – and mixed. I hadn't any more use for a reb than Van Zyl, and I knew something of the lies they'd fed us up with from the Colony for a year and more. I told the minister to pull his freight out of that, and went on with my lunch, when another man come along and shook hands with Van Zyl. He'd known him at close range in the Kimberley siege and before. Van Zyl was well seen by his neighbours, I judge. As soon as this other man opened his mouth I said, "You're Kentucky, ain't you?" "I am," he said; "and what may you be?" I told him right off, for I was pleased to hear good United States in any man's mouth; but he whipped his hands behind him and said, "I'm not knowing any man that fights for a Tammany Dutchman. But I presoom you've been well paid, you dam gun-runnin' Yank."

'Well, Sir, I wasn't looking for that, and it near knocked me over, while old man Van Zyl started in to explain.

' "Don't you waste your breath, Mister Van Zyl," the man says. "I know this breed. The South's full of 'em." Then he whirls round on me and says, "Look at here, you Yank. A little thing like a King's neither here nor there, but what *you've* done," he says, "is to go back on the White Man in six places at once – two hemispheres and four continents – America, England, Canada, Australia, New Zealand, and South Africa. Don't open your head," he says. "You know right well if you'd been caught at this game in our country you'd have been jiggling in the bight of a lariat before you could reach for your naturalization papers. Go on and prosper," he says, "and you'll fetch up by fighting for niggers, as the North did." And he threw me half-a-crown – English money.

'Sir, I do not regard the proposition in that light, but I

guess I must have been somewhat shook by the explosion. They told me at Cape Town one rib was driven in on to my lungs. I am not adducing this as an excuse, but the cold God's truth of the matter is – the money on the floor did it. ... I give up and cried. Put my head down and cried.

'I dream about this still sometimes. He didn't know the circumstances, but I dream about it. And it's Hell!

'How do you regard the proposition – as a Brother? If you'd invented your own gun, and spent fifty-seven thousand dollars on her – and had paid your own expenses from the word "go"? An American citizen has a right to choose his own side in an unpleasantness, and Van Zyl wasn't any Krugerite ... and I'd risked my hide at my own expense. I got that man's address from Van Zyl; he was a mining man at Kimberley, and I wrote him the facts. But he never answered. Guess he thought I lied. ... Damned Southern rebel!

'Oh, say. Did I tell you my Captain gave me a letter to an English Lord in Cape Town, and he fixed things so's I could lie up a piece in his house? I was pretty sick, and threw up some blood from where the rib had gouged into the lung – here. This Lord was a crank on guns, and he took charge of the Zigler. He had his knife into the British system as much as any American. He said he wanted revolution, and not reform, in your army. He said the British soldier had failed in every point except courage. He said England needed a Monroe Doctrine worse than America – a new doctrine, barring out all the Continent, and strictly devoting herself to developing her own Colonies. He said he'd abolish half the Foreign Office, and take all the old hereditary families clean out of it, because, he said, they was expressly trained to fool around with continental diplomats, and to despise the Colonies. His own family wasn't more than six hundred years old. He was a very brainy man, and a good citizen. We talked politics and inventions together when my lung let up on me.

'Did he know my General? Yes. He knew 'em all. Called

'em Teddie and Gussie and Willie. They was all of the very best, and all his dearest friends; but he told me confidentially they was none of 'em fit to command a column in the field. He said they were too fond of advertising. Generals don't seem very different from actors or doctors or – yes, Sir – inventors.

'He fixed things for me lovelily at Simonstown. Had the biggest sort of pull – even for a Lord. At first they treated me as a harmless lunatic; but after a while I got 'em to let me keep some of their books. If I was left alone in the world with the British system of book-keeping, I'd reconstruct the whole British Empire – beginning with the Army. Yes, I'm one of their most trusted accountants, and I'm paid for it. As much as a dollar a day. I keep that. I've earned it, and I deduct it from the cost of my board. When the war's over I'm going to pay up the balance to the British Government. Yes, Sir, that's how I regard the proposition.

'Adrian? Oh, he left for Umballa four months back. He told me he was going to apply to join the National Scouts if the war didn't end in a year. 'Tisn't in nature for one Dutchman to shoot another, but if Adrian ever meets up with Steyn there'll be an exception to the rule. Ye-es, when the war's over it'll take some of the British Army to protect Steyn from his fellow-patriots. But the war won't be over yet awhile. He that believeth don't hurry, as Isaiah says. The ministers and the school-teachers and the rebs 'll have a war all to themselves long after the north is quiet.

'I'm pleased with this country – it's big. Not so many folk on the ground as in America. There's a boom coming sure. I've talked it over with Adrian, and I guess I shall buy a farm somewhere near Bloemfontein and start in cattle-raising. It's big and peaceful – a ten-thousand-acre farm. I could go on inventing there, too. I'll sell my Zigler, I guess. I'll offer the patent rights to the British Government; and if they do the "reelly-now-how-interesting" act over her, I'll turn her over to Captain Mankeltow and his friend the Lord. They'll pretty quick find some Gussie, or Teddie, or Algie who can get her accepted in the proper quarters. I'm beginning to know my English.

'And now I'll go in swimming, and read the papers after lunch. I haven't had such a good time since Willie died.'

He pulled the blue shirt over his head as the bathers returned to their piles of clothing, and, speaking through the folds, added:

'But if you want to realize your assets, you should lease the whole proposition to America for ninety-nine years.'

Below the Mill Dam

(1902)

'BOOK – Book – Domesday Book!' They were letting in the water for the evening stint at Robert's Mill, and the wooden Wheel where lived the Spirit of the Mill settled to its nine-hundred-year-old song: 'Here Azor, a freeman, held one rod, but it never paid geld. *Nun-nun-nunquam geldavit.* Here Reinbert has one villein and four cottars with one plough – and wood for six hogs and two fisheries of sixpence and a mill of ten shillings – *unum molinum* – one mill. Reinbert's mill – Robert's Mill. Then and afterwards and now – *tunc et post et modo* – Robert's Mill. Book – Book – Domesday Book!'

'I confess,' said the Black Rat on the cross-beam, luxuriously trimming his whiskers – 'I confess I am not above appreciating my position and all it means.' He was a genuine old English black rat, a breed which, report says, is rapidly diminishing before the incursions of the brown variety.

'Appreciation is the surest sign of inadequacy,' said the Grey Cat, coiled up on a piece of sacking.

'But I know what you mean,' she added. 'To sit by right at the heart of things – eh?'

'Yes,' said the Black Rat, as the old mill shook and the heavy stones thuttered on the grist. 'To possess – er – all this environment as an integral part of one's daily life must insensibly of course.... You see?'

'I feel,' said the Grey Cat. 'Indeed, if *we* are not saturated with the spirit of the Mill, who should be?'

'Book – Book – Domesday Book!' The Wheel, set to his work, was running off the tenure of the whole rape, for he knew Domesday Book backwards and forwards: *'In Ferle tenuit Abbatia de Wiltuna unam hidam et unam virgam et dimidiam. Nunquam geldavit.* And Agemond, a freeman, has half a hide and one rod. I remember Agemond well. Charmin' fellow – friend of mine. He married a Norman girl in the days when we rather looked down on the Normans as upstarts. An' Agemond's dead? So he is. Eh, dearie me! dearie me! I remember the wolves howling outside his door in the big frost of Ten Fifty-Nine. . . . *Essewelde hundredum nunquam geldum reddidit.* Book! Book! Domesday Book!'

'After all,' the Grey Cat continued, 'atmosphere is life. It is the influences under which we live that count in the long run. Now, outside' – she cocked one ear towards the half-opened door – 'there is an absurd convention that rats and cats are, I won't go so far as to say natural enemies, but opposed forces. Some such ruling may be crudely effective – I don't for a minute presume to set up my standards as final – among the ditches; but from the larger point of view that one gains by living at the heart of things, it seems for a rule of life a little overstrained. Why, because some of your associates have, shall I say, liberal views on the ultimate destination of a sack of – er – middlings, don't they call them –'

'Something of that sort,' said the Black Rat, a most sharp and sweet-toothed judge of everything ground in the mill for the last three years.

'Thanks – middlings be it. *Why*, as I was saying, must I disarrange my fur and my digestion to chase you round the dusty arena whenever we happen to meet?'

'As little reason,' said the Black Rat, 'as there is for me, who, I trust, am a person of ordinarily decent instincts, to wait till you have gone on a round of calls, and then to assassinate your very charming children.'

'Exactly! It has its humorous side though.' The Grey Cat yawned. 'The miller seems afflicted by it. He shouted large and vague threats to my address, last night at tea, that he wasn't going to keep cats who "caught no mice". Those were his words. I remember the grammar sticking in my throat like a herring-bone.'

'And what did you do?'

'What does one do when a barbarian utters? One ceases to utter and removes. I removed – towards his pantry. It was a *riposte* he might appreciate.'

'Really those people grow absolutely insufferable,' said the

Black Rat. 'There is a local ruffian who answers to the name of Mangles – a builder – who has taken possession of the outhouses on the far side of the Wheel for the last fortnight. He has constructed cubical horrors in red brick where those deliciously picturesque pigstyes used to stand. Have you noticed?'

'There has been much misdirected activity of late among the humans. They jabber inordinately. I haven't yet been able to arrive at their reason for existence.' The Cat yawned.

'A couple of them came in here last week with wires, and fixed them all about the walls. Wires protected by some abominable composition, ending in iron brackets with glass bulbs. Utterly useless for any purpose and artistically absolutely hideous. What do they mean?'

'Aaah! I have known *four*-and-twenty leaders of revolt in Faenza,' said the Cat, who kept good company with the boarders spending a summer at the Mill Farm. 'It means nothing except that humans occasionally bring their dogs with them. I object to dogs in all forms.'

'Shouldn't object to dogs,' said the Wheel sleepily.... 'The Abbot of Wilton kept the best pack in the county. He enclosed all the Harryngton Woods to Sturt Common. Aluric, a freeman, was dispossessed of his holding. They tried the case at Lewes, but he got no change out of William de Warrenne on the bench. William de Warrenne fined Aluric eight and fourpence for treason, and the Abbot of Wilton excommunicated him for blasphemy. Aluric was no sportsman. Then the Abbot's brother married.... I've forgotten her name, but she was a charmin' little woman. The Lady Philippa was her daughter. That was after the barony was conferred. She rode devilish straight to hounds. They were a bit throatier than we breed now, but a good pack: one of the best. The Abbot kept 'em in splendid shape. Now, who was the woman the Abbot kept? Book – Book! I shall have to go right back to Domesday and work up the centuries: *Modo per omnia reddit burgum tunc – tunc – tunc!* Was it *burgum* or *hundredum*? I shall remember in a minute. There's no hurry.' He paused as he turned over, silvered with showering drops.

'This won't do,' said the Waters in the sluice. 'Keep moving.'

The Wheel swung forward; the Waters roared on the buckets and dropped down to the darkness below.

'Noisier than usual,' said the Black Rat. 'It must have been raining up the valley.'

'Floods maybe,' said the Wheel dreamily. 'It isn't the proper season, but they can come without warning. I shall never forget the big one – when the Miller went to sleep and forgot to open the hatches. More than two hundred years ago it was, but I recall it distinctly. Most unsettling.'

'We lifted that wheel off his bearings,' cried the Waters. 'We said, "Take away that bauble!" And in the morning he was five miles down the valley – hung up in a tree.'

'Vulgar!' said the Cat. 'But I am sure he never lost his dignity.'

'We don't know. He looked like the Ace of Diamonds when we had finished with him. ... Move on there! Keep on moving. Over! Get over!'

'And why on this day more than any other?' said the Wheel statelily. 'I am not aware that my department requires the stimulus of external pressure to keep it up to its duties. I trust I have the elementary instincts of a gentleman.'

'Maybe,' the Waters answered together, leaping down on the buckets. 'We only know that you are very stiff on your bearings. Over! Get over!'

The Wheel creaked and groaned. There was certainly greater pressure upon him than he had ever felt, and his revolutions had increased from six and three-quarters to eight and a third per minute. But the uproar between the narrow, weed-hung walls annoyed the Grey Cat.

'Isn't it almost time,' she said plaintively, 'that the person who is paid to understand these things shuts off those vehement drippings with that screw-thing on the top of that box-thing?'

'They'll be shut off at eight o'clock as usual,' said the Rat; 'then we can go to dinner.'

'But we shan't be shut off till ever so late,' said the Waters gaily. 'We shall keep it up all night.'

'The ineradicable offensiveness of youth is partially compensated for by its eternal hopefulness,' said the Cat. 'Our dam is not, I am glad to say, designed to furnish water for more than four hours at a time. Reserve is Life.'

'Thank goodness!' said the Black Rat. 'Then they can return to their native ditches.'

'Ditches!' cried the Waters; 'Raven's Gill Brook is no ditch. It is almost navigable, and *we* come from there away.' They slid over solid and compact till the Wheel thudded under their weight.

'Raven's Gill Brook,' said the Rat. '*I* never heard of Raven's Gill.'

'We are the waters of Harpenden Brook – down from under Callton Rise. Phew! how the race stinks compared with the heather country.' Another five foot of water flung itself against the Wheel, broke, roared, gurgled, and was gone.

'Indeed?' said the Grey Cat. 'I am sorry to tell you that Raven's Gill Brook is cut off from this valley by an absolutely impassable range of mountains, and Callton Rise is more than nine miles away. It belongs to another system entirely.'

'Ah, yes,' said the Rat, grinning, 'but we forget that, for the young, water always runs uphill.'

'Oh, hopeless! hopeless! hopeless!' cried the Waters, descending open-palmed upon the Wheel. 'There is nothing between here and Raven's Gill Brook that a hundred yards of channelling and a few square feet of concrete could not remove; and hasn't removed!'

'And Harpenden Brook is north of Raven's Gill and runs into Raven's Gill at the foot of Callton Rise, where the big ilex trees are, and *we* come from there!' These were the glassy, clear waters of the high chalk.

'And Batten's Ponds, that are fed by springs, have been led

through Trott's Wood, taking the spare water from the old Witches' Spring under Churt Haw, and we – we – *we* are their combined waters!' Those were the Waters from the upland bogs and moors – a porter-coloured, dusky, and foam-flecked flood.

'It's all very interesting,' purred the Cat to the sliding waters, 'and I have no doubt that Trott's Woods and Bott's Woods are tremendously important places; but if you could manage to do your work – whose value I don't in the least dispute – a little more soberly, I, for one, should be grateful.'

'Book – book – book – book – book – Domesday Book!' The urged Wheel was fairly clattering now: 'In Burgelstaltone a monk holds of Earl Godwin one hide and a half with eight villeins. There is a church – and a monk. . . . I remember that monk. Blessed if he could rattle his rosary off any quicker than I am doing now . . . and wood for seven hogs. I must be running twelve to the minute . . . almost as fast as Steam. Damnable invention, Steam! . . . Surely it's time we went to dinner or prayers – or something. Can't keep up this pressure, day in and day out, and not feel it. I don't mind for myself, of course. *Noblesse oblige*, you know. I'm only thinking of the Upper and the Nether Millstones. They came out of the common rock. They can't be expected to – '

'Don't worry on our account, please,' said the Millstones huskily. 'So long as you supply the power we'll supply the weight and the bite.'

'Isn't it a trifle blasphemous, though, to work you in this way?' grunted the Wheel. 'I seem to remember something about the Mills of God grinding "slowly". *Slowly* was the word!'

'But we are not the Mills of God. We're only the Upper and the Nether Millstones. We have received no instructions to be anything else. We are actuated by power transmitted through you.'

'Ah, but let us be merciful as we are strong. Think of all the beautiful little plants that grow on my woodwork. There are five varieties of rare moss within less than one square yard – and all these delicate jewels of nature are being grievously knocked about by this excessive rush of the water.'

'Umph!' growled the Millstones. 'What with your religious scruples and your taste for botany we'd hardly know you for the Wheel that put the carter's son under last autumn. You never worried about *him*!

'He ought to have known better.'

'So ought your jewels of nature. Tell 'em to grow where it's safe.'

'How a purely mercantile life debases and brutalizes!' said the Cat to the Rat.

'They were such beautiful little plants too,' said the Rat tenderly. 'Maiden's-tongue and hart's-hair fern trellising all over the wall just as they do on the sides of churches in the Downs. Think what a joy the sight of them must be to our sturdy peasants pulling hay!'

'Golly!' said the Millstones. 'There's nothing like coming to the heart of things for information'; and they returned to the song that all English water-mills have sung from time beyond telling:

There was a jovial miller once
Lived on the River Dee,
And this the burden of his song
For ever used to be.

Then, as fresh grist poured in and dulled the note:

I care for nobody – no, not I,
And nobody cares for me.

'Even these stones have absorbed something of our atmosphere,' said the Grey Cat. 'Nine-tenths of the trouble in this world comes from lack of detachment.'

'One of your people died from forgetting that, didn't she?' said the Rat.

'One only. The example has sufficed us for generations.'

'Ah! but what happened to Don't Care?' the Waters demanded.

'Brutal riding to death of the casual analogy is another mark of provincialism!' The Grey Cat raised her tufted chin. 'I am going to sleep. With my social obligations I must snatch rest when I can; but, as our old friend here says, *Noblesse oblige*. . . . Pity me! Three functions tonight in the village, and a barn-dance across the valley!'

'There's no chance, I suppose, of your looking in on the loft about two. Some of our young people are going to amuse themselves with a new sacque-dance – best white flour only,' said the Black Rat.

'I believe I am officially supposed not to countenance that sort of thing, but youth is youth. . . . By the way, the humans set my milk-bowl in the loft these days; I hope your youngsters respect it.'

'My dear lady,' said the Black Rat, bowing, 'you grieve me. You hurt me inexpressibly. After all these years, too!'

'A general crush is so mixed – highways and hedges – all that sort of thing – and no one can answer for one's best friends. *I* never try. So long as mine are amusin' and in full voice, and can hold their own at a tile-party, I'm as catholic as these mixed waters in the dam here!'

'We aren't mixed. We *have* mixed. We are one now,' said the Waters sulkily.

'Still uttering?' said the Cat. 'Never mind, here's the Miller coming to shut you off. Ye-es, I have known – *four* – or five, is it? – and twenty leaders of revolt in Faenza. . . . A little more babble in the dam, a little more noise in the sluice, a little extra splashing on the wheel, and then – '

'They will find that nothing has occurred,' said the Black Rat. 'The old things persist and survive and are recognized – our old friend here first of all. By the way,' he turned towards the Wheel, 'I believe we have to congratulate you on your latest honour.'

'Profoundly well deserved – even if he had never – as he has – laboured strenuously through a long life for the amelioration of millkind,' said the Cat, who belonged to many tile and oast-house committees. 'Doubly deserved, I may say, for the silent and dignified rebuke his existence offers to the clattering, fidgety-footed demands of – er – some people. What form did the honour take?'

'It was,' said the Wheel bashfully, 'a machine-moulded pinion.'

'Pinions! Oh, how heavenly!' the Black Rat sighed. 'I never see a bat without wishing for wings.'

'Not exactly that sort of pinion,' said the Wheel, 'but a really ornate circle of toothed iron wheels. Absurd, of course, but gratifying. Mr Mangles and an associate herald invested me with it personally – on my left rim – the side that you can't see from the mill. I hadn't meant to say anything about it – or the new steel straps round my axles – bright red, you know – to be worn on all occasions – but, without false modesty, I assure you that the recognition cheered me not a little.'

'How intensely gratifying!' said the Black Rat. 'I must really steal an hour between lights some day and see what they are doing on your left side.'

'By the way, have you any light on this recent activity of Mr Mangles?' the Grey Cat asked. 'He seems to be building small houses on the far side of the tail-race. Believe me, I don't ask from any vulgar curiosity.'

'It affects our Order,' said the Black Rat simply but firmly.

'Thank you,' said the Wheel. 'Let me see if I can tabulate it properly. Nothing like system in accounts of all kinds. Book! Book! Book! On the side of the Wheel towards the hundred of Burgelstaltone, where till now was a stye of three hogs, Mangles, a freeman, with four villeins and two carts of two thousand bricks, has a new small house of five yards and a half, and one roof of iron and a floor of cement. Then, now, and afterwards beer in large tankards. And Felden, a stranger, with three villeins and one very great cart, deposits on it one engine of iron and brass and a small iron mill of four feet, and a broad strap of leather. And Mangles, the builder, with two villeins, constructs the floor for the same, and a floor of new brick with wires for the small mill. There are there also chalices filled with iron and water, in number fifty-seven. The whole is valued at one hundred and seventy-four pounds. ... I'm sorry I can't make myself clearer, but you can see for yourself.'

'Amazingly lucid,' said the Cat. She was the more to be admired because the language of Domesday Book is not, perhaps, the clearest medium wherein to describe a small but complete electric-light installation, deriving its power from a water-wheel by means of cogs and gearing.

'See for yourself – by all means, see for yourself,' said the Waters, spluttering and choking with mirth.

'Upon my word,' said the Black Rat furiously, 'I may be at fault, but I wholly fail to perceive where these offensive eavesdroppers – er – come in. We were discussing a matter that solely affected our Order.'

Suddenly they heard, as they had heard many times before, the Miller shutting off the water. To the rattle and rumble of the labouring stones succeeded thick silence, punctuated with little drops from the stayed wheel. Then some water-bird in the dam fluttered her wings as she slid to her nest, and the plop of a water-rat sounded like the fall of a log in the water.

'It is all over – it always is all over at just this time. Listen, the Miller is going to bed – as usual. Nothing has occurred,' said the Cat.

Something creaked in the house where the pigstyes had stood, as metal engaged on metal with a clink and a burr.

'Shall I turn her on?' cried the Miller.

'Ay,' said the voice from the dynamo-house.

'A human in Mangles' new house!' the Rat squeaked.

'What of it?' said the Grey Cat. 'Even supposing Mr Mangles' cat's-meat-coloured hovel pullulated with humans, can't you see for yourself – that – ?'

There was a solid crash of released waters leaping upon the

Wheel more furiously than ever, a grinding of cogs, a hum like the hum of a hornet, and then the unvisited darkness of the old mill was scattered by intolerable white light. It threw up every cobweb, every burl and knot in the beams and the floor; till the shadows behind the flakes of rough plaster on the wall lay clear-cut as shadows of mountains on the photographed moon.

'See! See! See!' hissed the Waters in full flood. 'Yes, see for yourselves. Nothing has occurred. Can't you see?'

The Rat, amazed, had fallen from his foothold and lay half-stunned on the floor. The Cat, following her instinct, leaped nigh to the ceiling, and with flattened ears and bared teeth backed in a corner ready to fight whatever terror might be loosed on her. But nothing happened. Through the long aching minutes nothing whatever happened, and her wire-brush tail returned slowly to its proper shape.

'Whatever it is,' she said at last, 'it's overdone. They can never keep it up, you know.'

'Much you know,' said the Waters. 'Over you go, old man. You can take the full head of us now. Those new steel axle-straps of yours can stand anything. Come along, Raven's Gill, Harpenden, Callton Rise, Batten's Ponds, Witches' Spring, all together! Let's show these gentlemen how to work!'

'But – but – I thought it was a decoration. Why – why – why – it only means more work for *me*!'

'Exactly. You're to supply about sixty eight-candle lights when required. But they won't be all in use at once –'

'Ah! I thought as much,' said the Cat. 'The reaction is bound to come.'

'*And*,' said the Waters, 'you will do the ordinary work of the mill as well.'

'Impossible!' the old Wheel quivered as it drove. 'Aluric never did it – nor Azor, nor Reinbert. Not even William de Warrenne or the Papal Legate. There's no precedent for it. I tell you there's no precedent for working a wheel like this.'

'Wait a while! We're making one as fast as we can. Aluric and Co. are dead. So's the Papal Legate. You've no notion how dead they are, but we're here – the Waters of Five Separate Systems. We're just as interesting as Domesday Book. Would you like to hear about the land-tenure in Trott's Wood? It's squat-right, chiefly.' The mocking Waters leaped one over the other, chuckling and chattering profanely.

'In that hundred Jenkins, a tinker, with one dog – *unus canis* – holds, by the Grace of God and a habit he has of working hard, *unam hidam* – a large potato-patch. Charmin' fellow, Jenkins. Friend of ours. Now, who the dooce did Jenkins keep? ... In the hundred of Callton is one charcoal-burner *irreligiosissimus homo* – a bit of a rip – but a thorough sportsman. *Ibi est ecclesia. Non multum.* Not much of a church, *quia* because, *episcopus* the Vicar irritated the Nonconformists *tunc et post et modo* – then and afterwards and now – until they built a cut-stone Congregational chapel with red brick facings that did not return itself – *defendebat se* – at four thousand pounds.'

'Charcoal-burners, vicars, schismatics, and red brick facings,' groaned the Wheel. 'But this is sheer blasphemy. What waters have they let in upon me?'

'Floods from the gutters. Faugh, this light is positively sickening!' said the Cat, rearranging her fur.

'We come down from the clouds or up from the springs, exactly like all other waters everywhere. Is that what's surprising you?' sang the Waters.

'Of course not. I know my work if you don't. What I complain of is your lack of reverence and repose. You've no instinct of deference towards your betters – your heartless parody of the Sacred volume (the Wheel meant Domesday Book) proves it.'

'Our betters?' said the Waters most solemnly. 'What is there in all this damned race that hasn't come down from the clouds, or – '

'Spare me that talk, please,' the Wheel persisted. 'You'd *never* understand. It's the tone – your tone that we object to.'

'Yes. It's your tone,' said the Black Rat, picking himself up limb by limb.

'If you thought a trifle more about the work you're supposed to do, and a trifle less about your precious feelings, you'd render a little more duty in return for the power vested in you – we mean wasted on you,' the Waters replied.

'I have been some hundreds of years laboriously acquiring the knowledge which you see fit to challenge so lightheartedly,' the Wheel jarred.

'Challenge him! Challenge him!' clamoured the little waves riddling down through the tail-race. 'As well now as later. Take him up!'

The main mass of the Waters plunging on the Wheel shocked that well-bolted structure almost into box-lids by saying: 'Very good. Tell us what you suppose yourself to be doing at the present moment.'

'Waiving the offensive form of your question, I answer, purely as a matter of courtesy, that I am engaged in the trituration of farinaceous substances whose ultimate destination it would be a breach of the trust reposed in me to reveal.'

'Fiddle!' said the Waters. 'We knew it all along! The first direct question shows his ignorance of his own job. Listen, old thing. Thanks to us, you are now actuating a machine of whose construction you know nothing, that that machine may, over wires of whose ramifications you are, by your very position, profoundly ignorant, deliver a power which you can never realize, to localities beyond the extreme limits of your mental horizon, with the object of producing phenomena which in your wildest dreams (if you ever dream) you could never comprehend. Is that clear, or would you like it all in words of four syllables?'

'Your assumptions are deliciously sweeping, but may I point out that a decent and – the dear old Abbot of Wilton would have put it in his resonant monkish Latin much better than I can – a scholarly reserve does not necessarily connote blank vacuity of mind on all subjects?'

'Ah, the dear old Abbot of Wilton,' said the Rat sympathetically, as one nursed in that bosom. 'Charmin' fellow – thorough scholar and gentleman. Such a pity!'

'Oh, Sacred Fountains!' – the Waters were fairly boiling. 'He goes out of his way to expose his ignorance by triple bucketfuls. He creaks to high Heaven that he is hopelessly behind the common order of things! He invites the streams of Five Watersheds to witness his su-su-su-pernal incompetence, and then he talks as though there were untold reserves of knowledge behind him that he is too modest to bring forward. For a bland, circular, absolutely sincere impostor, you're a miracle, O Wheel!'

'I do not pretend to be anything more than an integral portion of an accepted and not altogether mushroom institution.'

'Quite so,' said the Waters. 'Then go round – hard – '

'To what end?' asked the Wheel.

'Till a big box of tanks in your house begins to fizz and fume – gassing is the proper word.'

'It would be,' said the Cat, sniffing.

'That will show that your accumulators are full. When the accumulators are exhausted, and the lights burn badly, you will find us whacking you round and round again.'

'The end of life as decreed by Mangles and his creatures is to go whacking round and round for ever,' said the Cat.

'In order,' the Rat said, 'that you may throw raw and unnecessary illumination upon all the unloveliness in the world. Unloveliness which we shall – er – have always with us. At the same time you will riotously neglect the so-called little but vital graces that make up Life.'

'Yes, Life,' said the Cat, 'with its dim delicious half-tones and veiled indeterminate distances. Its surprisals, escapes, encounters, and dizzying leaps – its full-throated choruses in honour of the morning star, and its melting reveries beneath the sun-warmed wall.'

'Oh, you can go on the tiles, Pussalina, just the same as

usual,' said the laughing Waters. '*We* shan't interfere with you.'

'On the tiles, forsooth!' hissed the Cat.

'Well, that's what it amounts to,' persisted the Waters. 'We see a good deal of the minor graces of life on our way down to our job.'

'And – but I fear I speak to deaf ears – do they never impress you?' said the Wheel.

'Enormously,' said the Waters. 'We have already learned six refined synonyms for loafing.'

'But (here again I feel as though preaching in the wilderness) it never occurs to you that there may exist some small difference between the wholly animal – ah – rumination of bovine minds and the discerning, well-apportioned leisure of the finer type of intellect?'

'Oh, yes. The bovine mind goes to sleep under a hedge and makes no bones about it when it's shouted at. We've seen *that* – in haying-time – all along the meadows. The finer type is wide awake enough to fudge up excuses for shirking, and mean enough to get stuffy when its excuses aren't accepted. Turn over!'

'But, my good people, no gentleman gets stuffy as you call it. A certain proper pride, to put it no higher, forbids –'

'Nothing that he wants to do if he really wants to do it. Get along! What are you giving us? D'you suppose we've scoured half heaven in the clouds and half earth in the mists, to be taken in at this time of the day by a bone-idle, old hand-quern of your type?'

'It is not for me to bandy personalities with you. I can only say that I simply decline to accept the situation.'

'Decline away. It doesn't make any odds. They'll probably put in a turbine if you decline too much.'

'What's a turbine?' said the Wheel quickly.

'A little thing you don't see, that performs surprising revolutions. But you won't decline. You'll hang on to your two nice red-strapped axles and your new machine-moulded pinions like – a – like a leech on a lily stem! There's centuries of work in your old bones if you'd only apply yourself to it; and, mechanically, an overshot wheel with this head of water is about as efficient as a turbine.'

'So in future I am to be considered mechanically? I have been painted by at least five Royal Academicians.'

'Oh, you can be painted by five hundred when you aren't at work, of course. But while you are at work you'll work. You won't half-stop and think and talk about rare plants and dicky-birds and farinaceous fiduciary interests. You'll continue to revolve, and this new head of water will see that you do so continue.'

'It is a matter on which it would be exceedingly ill-advised to form a hasty or a premature conclusion. I will give it my most careful consideration,' said the Wheel.

'Please do,' said the Waters gravely. 'Hullo! Here's the Miller again.'

The Cat coiled herself in a picturesque attitude on the softest corner of a sack, and the Rat, without haste, yet certainly without rest, slipped behind the sacking as though an appointment had just occurred to him.

In the doorway, with the young Engineer, stood the Miller grinning amazedly.

'Well – well – well! 'tis true-ly won'erful. An' what a power o' dirt! It come over me now looking at these lights, that I've never rightly seen my own mill before. She needs a lot bein' done to her.'

'Ah! I suppose one must make oneself moderately agreeable to the baser sort. They have their uses. This thing controls the dairy.' The Cat, mincing on her toes, came forward and rubbed her head against the Miller's knee.

'Ay, you pretty puss,' he said, stooping. 'You're as big a cheat as the rest of 'em that catch no mice about me. A won'erful smooth-skinned, rough-tongued cheat you be. I've more than half a mind –'

'She does her work well,' said the Engineer, pointing to where the Rat's beady eyes showed behind the sacking. 'Cats and Rats livin' together – see?'

'Too much they do – too long they've done. I'm sick and tired of it. Go and take a swim and larn to find your own vittles honest when you come out, Pussy.'

'My word!' said the Waters, as a sprawling Cat landed all unannounced in the centre of the tail-race. 'Is that you, Mewsalina? You seem to have been quarrelling with your best friend. Get over to the left. It's shallowest there. Up on that alder-root with all four paws. Good night!'

'You'll never get any they rats,' said the Miller, as the young Engineer struck wrathfully with his stick at the sacking. 'They're not the common sort. They're the old black English sort.'

'Are they, by Jove? I must catch one to stuff, some day.'

Six months later, in the chill of a January afternoon, they were letting in the Waters as usual.

'Come along! It's both gears this evening,' said the Wheel, kicking joyously in the first rush of the icy stream. 'There's a heavy load of grist just in from Lamber's Wood. Eleven miles it came in an hour and a half in our new motor-lorry, and the Miller's rigged five new five-candle lights in his cow-stables. I'm feeding 'em tonight. There's a cow due to calve. Oh, while I think of it, what's the news from Callton Rise?'

'The waters are finding their level as usual – but why do you ask?' said the deep outpouring Waters.

'Because Mangles and Felden and the Miller are talking of increasing the plant here and running a saw-mill by electricity. I was wondering whether we –'

'I beg your pardon,' said the Waters, chuckling. '*What* did you say?'

'Whether *we*, of course, had power enough for the job. It will be a biggish contract. There's all Harpenden Brook to be considered and Batten's Ponds as well, and Witches' Spring, and the Churt Haw system.'

'We've power enough for anything in the world,' said the Waters. 'The only question is whether you could stand the strain if we came down on you full head.'

'Of course I can,' said the Wheel. 'Mangles is going to turn me into a set of turbines – beauties.'

'Oh – er – I suppose it's the frost that has made us a little thick-headed, but to whom are we talking?' asked the amazed Waters.

'To me – the Spirit of the Mill, of course.'

'Not to the old Wheel, then?'

'I happen to be living in the old Wheel just at present. When the turbines are installed I shall go and live in them. What earthly difference does it make?'

'Absolutely none,' said the Waters, 'in the earth or in the waters under the earth. But we thought turbines didn't appeal to you.'

'Not like turbines? Me? My dear fellows, turbines are good for fifteen hundred revolutions a minute – and with our power we can drive 'em at full speed. Why, there's nothing we couldn't grind or saw or illuminate or heat with a set of turbines! That's to say if all the Five Watersheds are agreeable.'

'Oh, we've been agreeable for ever so long.'

'Then why didn't you tell me?'

'Don't know. Suppose it slipped our memory.' The Waters were holding themselves in for fear of bursting with mirth.

'How careless of you! You should keep abreast of the age, my dear fellows. We might have settled it long ago, if you'd only spoken. Yes, four good turbines and a neat brick penstock – eh? This old Wheel's absurdly out of date.'

'Well,' said the Cat, who after a little proud seclusion had returned to her place impenitent as ever. 'Praised be Pasht and the Old Gods, that whatever may have happened *I*, at least, have preserved the Spirit of the Mill!'

She looked round as expecting her faithful ally, the Black Rat; but that very week the Engineer had caught and stuffed him, and had put him in a glass case; he being a genuine old English black rat. That breed, the report says, is rapidly diminishing before the incursions of the brown variety.

Mrs Bathurst

(1904)

THE day that I chose to visit H.M.S. *Peridot* in Simon's Bay was the day that the Admiral had chosen to send her up the coast. She was just steaming out to sea as my train came in, and since the rest of the Fleet were either coaling or busy at the rifle-ranges a thousand feet up the hill, I found myself stranded, lunchless, on the sea-front with no hope of return to Cape Town before 5 p.m. At this crisis I had the luck to come across my friend Inspector Hooper, Cape Government Railways, in command of an engine and a brake-van chalked for repair.

'If you get something to eat,' he said, 'I'll run you down to Glengariff siding till the goods comes along. It's cooler there than here, you see.'

I got food and drink from the Greeks who sell all things at a price, and the engine trotted us a couple of miles up the line to a bay of drifted sand and a plank-platform half buried in sand not a hundred yards from the edge of the surf. Moulded dunes, whiter than any snow, rolled far inland up a brown and purple valley of splintered rocks and dry scrub. A crowd of Malays hauled at a net beside two blue and green boats on the beach; a picnic party danced and shouted barefoot where a tiny river trickled across the flat, and a circle of dry hills, whose feet were set in sands of silver, locked us in against a seven-coloured sea. At either horn of the bay the railway line, just above high-water mark, ran round a shoulder of piled rocks, and disappeared.

'You see, there's always a breeze here,' said Hooper, opening the door as the engine left us in the siding on the sand, and the strong south-easter buffeting under Elsie's Peak dusted sand into our tickey beer. Presently he sat down to a file full of spiked documents. He had returned from a long trip up-country, where he had been reporting on damaged rolling-stock, as far away as Rhodesia. The weight of the bland wind on my eyelids; the song of it under the car-roof, and high up among the rocks; the drift of fine grains chasing each other musically ashore; the tramp of the surf; the voices of the picnickers; the rustle of Hooper's file, and the presence of the assured sun, joined with the beer to cast me into magical slumber. The hills of False Bay were just dissolving into those of fairyland when I heard footsteps on the sand outside, and the clink of our couplings.

'Stop that!' snapped Hooper, without raising his head from his work. 'It's those dirty little Malay boys, you see: they're always playing with the trucks...'

'Don't be hard on 'em. The railway's a general refuge in Africa,' I replied.

' 'Tis – up-country at any rate. That reminds me,' he felt in his waistcoat-pocket, 'I've got a curiosity for you from Wankies – beyond Bulawayo. It's more of a souvenir perhaps than – '

'The old hotel's inhabited,' cried a voice. 'White men, from the language. Marines to the front! Come on, Pritch. Here's your Belmont. Wha – i – i!'

The last word dragged like a rope as Mr Pyecroft ran round to the open door, and stood looking up into my face. Behind him an enormous Sergeant of Marines trailed a stalk of dried seaweed, and dusted the sand nervously from his fingers.

'What are you doing here?' I asked. 'I thought the *Hierophant* was down the coast?'

'We came in last Tuesday – from Tristan d'Acunha – for overhaul, and we shall be in dockyard 'ands for two months, with boiler-seatings.'

'Come and sit down.' Hooper put away the file.

'This is Mr Hooper of the Railway,' I explained, as Pyecroft turned to haul up the black-moustached sergeant.

'This is Sergeant Pritchard, of the *Agaric*, an old shipmate,' said he. 'We were strollin' on the beach.' The monster blushed and nodded. He filled up one side of the van when he sat down.

'And this is my friend, Mr Pyecroft,' I added to Hooper, already busy with the extra beer which my prophetic soul had bought from the Greeks.

'*Moi aussi*,' quoth Pyecroft, and drew out beneath his coat a labelled quart bottle.

'Why, it's Bass!' cried Hooper.

'It was Pritchard,' said Pyecroft. 'They can't resist him.'

'That's not so,' said Pritchard mildly.

'Not *verbatim* per'aps, but the look in the eye came to the same thing.'

'Where was it?' I demanded.

'Just on beyond here – at Kalk Bay. She was slappin' a rug in a back verandah. Pritch 'adn't more than brought his batteries to bear, before she stepped indoors an' sent it flyin' over the wall.'

Pyecroft patted the warm bottle.

'It was all a mistake,' said Pritchard. 'I shouldn't wonder if she mistook me for Maclean. We're about of a size.'

I had heard householders of Muizenberg, St James, and Kalk Bay complain of the difficulty of keeping beer or good servants at the seaside, and I began to see the reason. None the less, it was excellent Bass, and I too drank to the health of that large-minded maid.

'It's the uniform that fetches 'em, an' they fetch it,' said Pyecroft. 'My simple navy blue is respectable, but not fascinatin'. Now Pritch in 'is Number One rig is always "purr Mary, on the terrace" – *ex officio* as you might say.'

'She took me for Maclean, I tell you,' Pritchard insisted. 'Why – why – to listen to him you wouldn't think that only yesterday – '

'Pritch,' said Pyecroft, 'be warned in time. If we begin tellin' what we know about each other we'll be turned out of the pub. Not to mention aggravated desertion on several occasions – '

'Never anything more than absence without leaf – I defy

you to prove it,' said the Sergeant hotly. 'An' if it comes to that, how about Vancouver in '87?'

'How about it? Who pulled bow in the gig going ashore? Who told Boy Niven . . . ?'

'Surely you were court-martialled for that?' I said. The story of Boy Niven who lured seven or eight able-bodied seamen and marines into the woods of British Columbia used to be a legend of the Fleet.

'Yes, we were court-martialled to rights,' said Pritchard, 'but we should have been tried for murder if Boy Niven 'adn't been unusually tough. He told us he had an uncle 'oo'd give us land to farm. 'E said he was born at the back o' Vancouver Island, and *all* the time the beggar was a balmy Barnado Orphan!'

'*But* we believed him,' said Pyecroft. 'I did – you did – Paterson did – an' 'oo was the Marine that married the cocoanut woman afterwards – him with the mouth?'

'Oh, Jones, Spit-Kid Jones. I 'aven't thought of 'im in years,' said Pritchard. 'Yes, Spit-Kid believed it, an' George Anstey and Moon. We were very young an' very curious.'

'*But* lovin' an' trustful to a degree,' said Pyecroft.

'Remember when 'e told us to walk in single file for fear o' bears? Remember, Pye, when 'e 'opped about in that bog full o' ferns an' sniffed an' said 'e could smell the smoke of 'is uncle's farm? An' *all* the time it was a dirty little outlyin' uninhabited island. We walked round it in a day, an' come back to our boat lyin' on the beach. A whole day Boy Niven kept us walkin' in circles lookin' for 'is uncle's farm! He said his uncle was compelled by the law of the land to give us a farm!'

'Don't get hot, Pritch. We believed,' said Pyecroft.

'He'd been readin' books. He only did it to get a run ashore an' have himself talked of. A day an' a night – eight of us – followin' Boy Niven round an uninhabited island in the Vancouver archipelago! Then the picket came for us an' a nice pack o' idiots we looked!'

'What did you get for it?' Hooper asked.

'Heavy thunder with continuous lightning for two hours.

Thereafter sleet-squalls, a confused sea, and cold, unfriendly weather till conclusion o' cruise,' said Pyecroft. 'It was only what we expected, but what we felt – an' I assure you, Mr Hooper, even a sailor-man has a heart to break – was bein' told that we able seamen an' promisin' marines 'ad misled Boy Niven. Yes, we poor back-to-the-landers was supposed to 'ave misled him! He rounded on us, o' course, an' got off easy.'

'Excep' for what we gave him in the steerin'-flat when we came out o' cells. 'Eard anything of 'im lately, Pye?'

'Signal Boatswain in the Channel Fleet, I believe – Mr L. L. Niven is.'

'An' Anstey died o' fever in Benin,' Pritchard mused. 'What come to Moon? Spit-Kid we know about.'

'Moon – Moon! Now where did I last ... ? Oh yes, when I was in the *Palladium*. I met Quigley at Buncrana Station. He told me Moon 'ad run when the *Astrild* sloop was cruising among the South Seas three years back. He always showed signs o' bein' a Mormonastic beggar. Yes, he slipped off quietly an' they 'adn't time to chase 'im round the islands even if the navigatin' officer 'ad been equal to the job.'

'Wasn't he?' said Hooper.

'Not so. Accordin' to Quigley the *Astrild* spent half her commission rompin' up the beach like a she-turtle, an' the other half hatching turtles' eggs on the top o' numerous reefs. When she was docked at Sydney her copper looked like Aunt Maria's washing on the line – an' her 'midship frames was sprung. The commander swore the dockyard 'ad done it haulin' the pore thing on to the slips. They *do* do strange things at sea, Mr Hooper.'

'Ah! I'm not a taxpayer,' said Hooper, and opened a fresh bottle. The Sergeant seemed to be one who had a difficulty in dropping subjects.

'How it all comes back, don't it?' he said. 'Why, Moon must 'ave 'ad sixteen years' service before he ran.'

'It takes 'em at all ages. Look at – you know,' said Pyecroft.

'Who?' I asked.

'A service man within eighteen months of his pension is the party you're thinkin' of,' said Pritchard. 'A warrant 'oo's name begins with a V., isn't it?'

'But, in a way o' puttin' it, we can't say that he actually did desert,' Pyecroft suggested.

'Oh no,' said Pritchard. 'It was only permanent absence up-country without leaf. That was all.'

'Up-country?' said Hooper. 'Did they circulate his description?'

'What for?' said Pritchard, most impolitely.

'Because deserters are like columns in the war. They don't move away from the line, you see. I've known a chap caught at Salisbury that way tryin' to get to Nyassa. They tell me, but o' course I don't know, that they don't ask questions on the Nyassa Lake Flotilla up there. I've heard of a P. and O. quartermaster in full command of an armed launch there.'

'Do you think Click 'ud ha' gone up that way?' Pritchard asked.

'There's no saying. He was sent up to Bloemfontein to take over some Navy ammunition left in the fort. We know he took it over and saw it into the trucks. Then there was no more Click – then or thereafter. Four months ago it transpired, and thus the *casus belli* stands at present,' said Pyecroft.

'What were his marks?' said Hooper again.

'Does the Railway get a reward for returnin' 'em, then?' said Pritchard.

'If I did d'you suppose I'd talk about it?' Hooper retorted angrily.

'You seemed so very interested,' said Pritchard with equal crispness.

'Why was he called Click?' I asked, to tide over an uneasy little break in the conversation. The two men were staring at each other very fixedly.

'Because of an ammunition hoist carryin' away,' said Pyecroft. 'And it carried away four of 'is teeth – on the lower port side, wasn't it, Pritch? The substitutes which he bought weren't screwed home, in a manner o' sayin'. When he talked fast they used to lift a little on the bedplate. 'Ence, "Click". They called 'im a superior man, which is what we'd call a long, black-'aired, genteelly-speakin', 'alf-bred beggar on the lower deck.'

'Four false teeth in the lower left jaw,' said Hooper, his hand in his waistcoat-pocket. 'What tattoo marks?'

'Look here,' began Pritchard, half rising. 'I'm sure we're very grateful to you as a gentleman for your 'orspitality, but per'aps we may 'ave made an error in –'

I looked at Pyecroft for aid – Hooper was crimsoning rapidly.

'If the fat marine now occupying the foc'-sle will kindly bring 'is *status quo* to an anchor yet once more, we may be able to talk like gentlemen – not to say friends,' said Pyecroft. 'He regards you, Mr Hooper, as a emissary of the Law.'

'I only wish to observe that when a gentleman exhibits such a peculiar, or I should rather say, such a *bloomin'* curiosity in identification marks as our friend here –'

'Mr Pritchard,' I interposed, 'I'll take all the responsibility for Mr Hooper.'

'An' *you'll* apologize all round,' said Pyecroft. 'You're a rude little man, Pritch.'

'But how was I –' he began, wavering.

'I don't know an' I don't care. Apologize!'

The giant looked round bewildered and took our little hands into his vast grip, one by one.

'I was wrong,' he said meekly as a sheep. 'My suspicions was unfounded. Mr Hooper, I apologize.'

'You did quite right to look out for your own end o' the line,' said Hooper. 'I'd ha' done the same with a gentleman I didn't know, you see. If you don't mind I'd like to hear a little more o' your Mr Vickery. It's safe with me, you see.'

'Why did Vickery run?' I began, but Pyecroft's smile made me turn my question to 'Who was she?'

'She kep' a little hotel at Hauraki – near Auckland,' said Pyecroft.

'By Gawd!' roared Pritchard, slapping his hand on his leg. 'Not Mrs Bathurst!'

Pyecroft nodded slowly, and the Sergeant called all the powers of darkness to witness his bewilderment.

'So far as I could get at it, Mrs B. was the lady in question.'

'But Click was married,' cried Pritchard.

'An' 'ad a fifteen-year-old daughter. 'E's shown me her photograph. Settin' that aside, so to say, 'ave you ever found these little things make – much difference? Because I haven't.'

'Good Lord Alive an' Watchin'! ... Mrs Bathurst ...' Then with another roar: 'You can say what you please, Pye, but you don't make me believe it was any of 'er fault. She wasn't *that!*'

'If I was going to say what I please, I'd begin by callin' you a silly ox an' work up to the higher pressures at leisure. I'm trying to say solely what transpired. M'rover, for once you're right. It wasn't her fault.'

'You couldn't 'aven't made me believe it if it 'ad been,' was the answer.

Such faith in a Sergeant of Marines interested me greatly. 'Never mind about that,' I cried. 'Tell me what she was like.'

'She was a widow,' said Pyecroft. 'Left so very young and never re-spliced. She kep' a little hotel for warrants and non-coms close to Auckland, an' she always wore black silk, and 'er neck – '

'You ask what she was like,' Pritchard broke in. 'Let me give you an instance. I was at Auckland first in '97, at the end o' the *Marroquin*'s commission, an' as I'd been promoted I went up with the others. She used to look after us all, an' she never lost by it – not a penny! "Pay me now," she'd say, "or settle later. I know you won't let me suffer. Send the money from home if you like." Why, gentlemen all, I tell you I've seen that lady take her own gold watch an' chain off her neck in the bar an' pass it to a bosun 'oo'd come ashore without 'is ticker an' 'ad to catch the last boat. "I don't know your name," she said, "but when you've done with it, you'll find plenty that know me on the front. Send it back by one o' them." And it was worth thirty pounds if it was worth 'arf-a-crown. The little gold watch, Pye, with the blue monogram at the back. But, as I was sayin', in those days she kep' a beer that agreed with me – Slits it was called. One way an' another I must 'ave punished a good few bottles of it while we was in the bay – comin' ashore every night or so. Chaffin' across the bar like, once when we were alone, "Mrs B.," I said, "when next I call I want you to remember that this is my particular – just as you're my particular." (She'd let you go *that* far!) "Just as you're my particular," I said. "Oh, thank you, Sergeant Pritchard," she says, an' put 'er hand up to the curl be'ind 'er ear. Remember that way she had, Pye?'

'I think so,' said the sailor.

'Yes, "Thank you, Sergeant Pritchard," she says. "The least I can do is to mark it for you in case you change your mind. There's no great demand for it in the Fleet," she says, "but to make sure I'll put it at the back o' the shelf," an' she snipped off a piece of her hair ribbon with that old dolphin cigar-cutter on the bar – remember it, Pye? – an' she tied a bow round what was left – just four bottles. That was '97 no, '96. In '98 I was in the *Resilient* – China Station – full commission. In Nineteen One, mark you, I was in the *Carthusian*, back in Auckland Bay again. Of course I went up to Mrs B.'s with the rest of us to see how things were goin'. They were the same as ever. (Remember the big tree on the pavement by the side-bar, Pye?) I never said anythin' in special (there was too many of us talkin' to her), but she saw me at once.'

'That wasn't difficult?' I ventured.

'Ah, but wait. I was comin' up to the bar, when, "Ada," she says to her niece, "get me Sergeant Pritchard's particular," and, gentlemen all, I tell you before I could shake 'ands with the lady, there were those four bottles o' Slits, with 'er 'air-ribbon in a bow round each o' their necks, set down in front o' me, an' as she drew the cork she looked at me under her eyebrows in that blindish way she had o' lookin', an', "Sergeant Pritchard," she says, "I do 'ope you 'aven't changed your mind about your particulars." That's the kind o' woman she was – after five years!'

'I don't *see* her yet somehow,' said Hooper, but with sympathy.

'She – she never scrupled to feed a lame duck or set 'er foot on a scorpion at any time of 'er life,' Pritchard added valiantly.

'That don't help me either. My mother's like that for one.'

The giant heaved inside his uniform and rolled his eyes at the car-roof. Said Pyecroft suddenly:

'How many women have you been intimate with all over the world, Pritch?'

Pritchard blushed plum-colour to the short hairs of his seventeen-inch neck.

' 'Undreds,' said Pyecroft. 'So've I. How many of 'em can you remember in your own mind, settin' aside the first – an' per'aps the last – *and one more*?'

'Few, wonderful few, now I tax myself,' said Sergeant Pritchard relievedly.

'An' how many times might you 'ave been at Auckland?'

'One – two,' he began – 'why, I can't make it more than three times in ten years. But I can remember every time that I ever saw Mrs B.'

'So can I – an' I've only been to Auckland twice – how she stood an' what she was sayin' an' what she looked like. That's the secret. 'Tisn't beauty, so to speak, nor good talk necessarily. It's just It. Some women'll stay in a man's memory if they once walk down a street, but most of 'em you can live with a month on end, an' next commission you'd be put to it to certify whether they talked in their sleep or not, as one might say.'

'Ah!' said Hooper. 'That's more the idea. I've known just two women of that nature.'

'An' it was no fault o' theirs?' asked Pritchard.

'None whatever. I know *that*!'

'An' if a man gets struck with that kind o' woman, Mr Hooper?' Pritchard went on.

'He goes crazy – or just saves himself,' was the slow answer.

'You've hit it,' said the Sergeant. 'You've seen an' known somethin' in the course o' your life, Mr Hooper. I'm lookin' at you!' He set down his bottle.

'And how often had Vickery seen her?' I asked.

'That's the dark an' bloody mystery,' Pyecroft answered. 'I'd never come across him till I come out in the *Hierophant* just now, an' there wasn't any one in the ship who knew much about him. You see, he was what you call a superior man. 'E spoke to me once or twice about Auckland and Mrs B. on the voyage out. I called that to mind subsequently. There must 'ave been a good deal between 'em, to my way o' thinkin'. Mind you, I'm only giving you my *résumé* of it all, because all I know is second-hand so to speak, or rather I should say more than second-'and.'

'How?' said Hooper peremptorily. 'You must have seen it or heard it.'

'Ye-es,' said Pyecroft. 'I used to think seein' and hearin' was the only regulation aids to ascertainin' facts, but as we get older we get more accommodatin'. The cylinders work easier, I suppose.... Were you in Cape Town last December when Phyllis's Circus came?'

'No – up-country,' said Hooper, a little nettled at the change of venue.

'I ask because they had a new turn of a scientific nature called "Home and Friends for a Tickey".'

'Oh, you mean the cinematograph – the pictures of prize-fights and steamers. I've seen 'em up-country.'

'Biograph or cinematograph was what I was alludin' to. London Bridge with the omnibuses – a troopship goin' to the war – marines on parade at Portsmouth, an' the Plymouth Express arrivin' at Paddin'ton.'

'Seen 'em all. Seen 'em all,' said Hooper impatiently.

'We *Heirophants* came in just before Christmas week an' leaf was easy.'

'I think a man gets fed up with Cape Town quicker than anywhere else on the station. Why, even Durban's more like Nature. We was there for Christmas,' Pritchard put in.

'Not bein' a devotee of Indian *peeris*, as our Doctor said to the Pusser, I can't exactly say. Phyllis's was good enough after musketry practice at Mozambique. I couldn't get off the first two or three nights on account of what you might call an imbroglio with our Torpedo Lieutenant in the submerged flat, where some pride of the West Country had sugared up a gyroscope; but I remember Vickery went ashore with our Carpenter Rigdon – old Crocus we called him. As a general rule Crocus never left 'is ship unless an' until he was 'oisted out with a winch, but *when* 'e went 'e would return noddin' like a lily gemmed with dew. We smothered him down below that night, but the things 'e said about Vickery as a fittin' playmate for a Warrant Officer of 'is cubic capacity, before we got him quiet, was what I should call pointed.'

'I've been with Crocus – in the *Redoubtable*,' said the Sergeant. 'He's a character if there is one.'

'Next night I went into Cape Town with Dawson and Pratt; but just at the door of the Circus I came across Vickery. "Oh!" he says, "you're the man I'm looking for. Come and sit next me. This way to the shillin' places!" I went astern at once, protestin' because tickey seats better suited my so-called finances. "Come on," says Vickery, "I'm payin'." Naturally I abandoned Pratt and Dawson in anticipation o' drinks to match the seats. "No," he says, when this was 'inted – "not now. Not now. As many as you please afterwards, but I want you sober for the occasion." I caught 'is face under a lamp just then, an' the appearance of it quite cured me of my thirst. Don't mistake. It didn't frighten me. It made me anxious. I can't tell you what it was like, but that was the effect which it 'ad on me. If you want to know, it reminded me of those things in bottles in those herbalistic shops at Plymouth – preserved in spirits of wine. White an' crumply things – previous to birth as you might say.'

'You 'ave a beastial mind, Pye,' said the Sergeant, relighting his pipe.

'Perhaps. We were in the front row, an' "Home an' Friends" came on early. Vickery touched me on the knee when the number went up. "If you see anything that strikes you," he says, "drop me a hint"; then he went on clicking. We saw London Bridge an' so forth an' so on, an' it was most interestin'. I'd never seen it before. You 'eard a little dynamo like buzzin', but the pictures were the real thing – alive an' movin'.'

'I've seen 'em,' said Hooper. 'Of course they are taken from the very thing itself – you see.'

'Then the Western Mail came in to Paddin'ton on the big magic-lantern sheet. First we saw the platform empty an' the porters standin' by. Then the engine come in, head on, an' the women in the front row jumped: she headed so straight. Then the doors opened and the passengers came out and the porters got the luggage – just like life. Only – only when any one came down too far towards us that was watchin', they walked right out o' the picture, so to speak. I was 'ighly interested, I can tell you. So were all of us. I watched an old man with a rug 'oo'd dropped a book an' was tryin' to pick it up, when quite slowly, from be'ind two porters – carryin' a little reticule an' lookin' from side to side – comes our Mrs Bathurst. There was no mistakin' the walk in a hundred thousand. She come forward – right forward – she looked out straight at us with that blindish look which Pritch alluded to. She walked on and on till she melted out of the picture – like – like a shadow jumpin' over a candle, an' as she went I 'eard Dawson in the tickey seats be'ind sing out: "Christ! there's Mrs B.!" '

Hooper swallowed his spittle and leaned forward intently.

'Vickery touched me on the knee again. He was clickin' his four false teeth with his jaw down like an enteric at the last kick. "Are you sure?" says he. "Sure," I says, "didn't you 'ear Dawson give tongue? Why, it's the woman herself." "I was sure before," he says, "but I brought you to make sure. Will you come again with me tomorrow?"

' "Willingly," I says, "it's like meetin' old friends."

' "Yes," he says, openin' his watch, "very like. It will be four-and-twenty hours less four minutes before I see her again. Come and have a drink," he says. "It may amuse you, but it's no sort of earthly use to me." He went out shaking his head an' stumblin' over people's feet as if he was drunk already. I anticipated a swift drink an' a speedy return, because I wanted to see the performin' elephants. Instead o' which Vickery began to navigate the town at the rate o' lookin' in at a bar every three minutes approximate Greenwich time. I'm not a drinkin' man, though there are those present' – he cocked his unforgettable eye at me – 'who may have seen me more or less imbued with the fragrant spirit. None the less when I drink I like to do it at anchor an' not at an average speed of eighteen knots on the measured mile. There's a tank as you might say at the back o' that big hotel up the hill – what do they call it?'

'The Molteno Reservoir,' I suggested, and Hooper nodded.

'That was his limit o' drift. We walked there an' we come down through the Gardens – there was a South-Easter blowin' – an' we finished up by the Docks. Then we bore up the road to Salt River, and wherever there was a pub Vickery put in sweatin'. He didn't look at what he drunk – he didn't look at the change. He walked an' he drunk an' he perspired rivers. I understood why old Crocus 'ad come back in the condition 'e did, because Vickery an' I 'ad two an' a half hours o' this gipsy manoeuvre, an' when we got back to the station there wasn't a dry atom on or in me.'

'Did he say anything?' Pritchard asked.

'The sum total of 'is conversation from 7.45 p.m. till 11.15

p.m. was "Let's have another". Thus the mornin' an' the evenin' were the first day, as Scripture says.... To abbreviate a lengthy narrative, I went into Cape Town for five consecutive nights with Master Vickery, and in that time I must 'ave logged about fifty knots over the ground an' taken in two gallon o' all the worst spirits south the Equator. The evolution never varied. Two shilling seats for us two; five minutes o' the pictures, an' perhaps forty-five seconds o' Mrs B. walking down towards us with that blindish look in her eyes an' the reticule in her hand. Then out – walk – and drink till train time.'

'What did you think?' said Hooper, his hand fingering his waistcoat-pocket.

'Several things,' said Pyecroft. 'To tell you the truth, I aren't quite done thinkin' about it yet. Mad? The man was a dumb lunatic – must 'ave been for months – years p'raps. I know somethin' o' maniacs, as every man in the Service must. I've been shipmates with a mad skipper – an' a lunatic Number One, but never both together, I thank 'Eaven. I could give you the names o' three captains now 'oo ought to be in an asylum, but you don't find me interferin' with the mentally afflicted till they begin to lay about 'em with rammers an' winch-handles. Only once I crept up a little into the wind towards Master Vickery. "I wonder what she's doin' in England," I says. "Don't it seem to you she's lookin' for somebody?" That was in the Gardens again, with the South-Easter blowin' as we were makin' our desperate round. "She's lookin' for me," he says, stoppin' dead under a lamp an' clickin'. When he wasn't drinkin', in which case all 'is teeth clicked on the glass, 'e was clickin' 'is four false teeth like a Marconi ticker. "Yes! lookin' for me," he said, an' he went on very softly an' as you might say affectionately. "*But,*" he went on, "in future, Mr Pyecroft, I should take it kindly of you if you'd confine your remarks to the drinks set before you. Otherwise," he says, "with the best will in the world towards you, I may find myself guilty of murder! Do you understand?" he says. "Perfectly," I says, "but would it at all soothe you to know that in such a case the chances o' your being killed are precisely equivalent to the chances o' me being outed." "Why, no," he said, "I'm almost afraid that 'ud be a temptation." Then I said – we was right under the lamp by that arch at the end o' the Gardens where the trams come round – "Assumin' murder was done – or attempted murder – I put it to you that you would still be left so badly crippled, as one might say, that your subsequent capture by the police – to 'oom you would 'ave to explain – would be largely inevitable." "That's better," 'e says, passin' 'is hands over his forehead. "That's much better, because," he says, "do you know, as I am now, Pye, I'm not so sure if I could explain anything much." Those were the only particular words I had with 'im in our walks as I remember.'

'What walks!' said Hooper. 'Oh my soul, what walks!'

'They were chronic,' said Pyecroft gravely, 'but I didn't anticipate any danger till the Circus left. Then I anticipated that, bein' deprived of 'is stimulant, he might react on me, so to say, with a hatchet. Consequently, after the final performance an' the ensuin' wet walk, I kep' myself aloof from my superior officer on board in the execution of 'is duty, as you might put it. Consequently, I was interested when the sentry informs me while I was passin' on my lawful occasions that Click had asked to see the captain. As a general rule warrant-officers don't dissipate much of the owner's time, but Click put in an hour and more be'ind that door. My duties kep' me within eyeshot of it. Vickery came out first, an' 'e actually nodded at me an' smiled. This knocked me out o' the boat, because, havin' seen 'is face for five consecutive nights, I didn't anticipate any change there more than a condenser in hell, so to speak. The owner emerged later. His face didn't read off at all, so I fell back on his cox, 'oo'd been eight years with him and knew him better than boat signals. Lamson – that was the cox's name – crossed 'is bows once or twice at low speeds an' dropped down to me visibly concerned. "He's shipped 'is court-martial face," says Lamson. "Some one's goin' to be 'ung. I've never seen that look but once before, when they chucked the gun-sights overboard in the *Fantastic.*" Throwin' gun-sights overboards, Mr Hooper, is the equivalent for mutiny in these degenerate days. It's done to attract the notice of the authorities an' the *Western Mornin' News* – generally by a stoker. Naturally, word went round the lower deck an' we had a private over'aul of our little consciences. But, barrin' a shirt which a second-class stoker said 'ad walked into 'is bag from the marines' flat by itself, nothin' vital transpired. The owner went about flyin' the signal for "attend public execution", so to say, but there was no corpse at the yard-arm. 'E lunched on the beach an' 'e returned with 'is regulation harbour-routine face about 3 p.m. Thus Lamson lost prestige for raising false alarms. The only person 'oo might 'ave connected the epicycloidal gears correctly was one Pyecroft, when he was told that Mr Vickery would go up-country that same evening to take over certain naval ammunition left after the war in Bloemfontein Fort. No details was ordered to accompany Master Vickery. He was told off first person singular – as a unit – by himself.'

The marine whistled penetratingly.

'That's what I thought,' said Pyecroft. 'I went ashore with him in the cutter an' 'e asked me to walk through the station. He was clickin' audibly, but otherwise seemed happy-ish.

' "You might like to know," he says, stoppin' just opposite the Admiral's front gate, "that Phyllis's Circus will be performin' at Worcester tomorrow night. So I shall see 'er yet once again. You've been very patient with me," he says.

' "Look here, Vickery," I said, "this thing's come to be just as much as I can stand. Consume your own smoke. I don't want to know any more."

' "You!" he said. "What have you got to complain of? – you've only 'ad to watch. I'm *it,*" he says, "but that's neither here nor there," he says. "I've one thing to say before shakin' 'ands. Remember," 'e says – we were just by the Admiral's garden-gate then – "remember that I am *not* a murderer, because my lawful wife died in childbed six weeks after I came out. That much at least I am clear of," 'e says.

'"Then what have you done that signifies?" I said. "What's the rest of it?"

'"The rest," 'e says, "is silence," an' he shook 'ands and went clickin' into Simonstown station.'

'Did he stop to see Mrs Bathurst at Worcester?' I asked.

'It's not known. He reported at Bloemfontein, saw the ammunition into the trucks, and then 'e disappeared. Went out – deserted, if you care to put it so – within eighteen months of his pension, an' if what 'e said about 'is wife was true he was a free man as 'e then stood. How do you read it off?'

'Poor devil!' said Hooper. 'To see her that way every night! I wonder what it was.'

'I've made my 'ead ache in that direction many a long night.'

'But I'll swear Mrs B. 'ad no 'and in it,' said the Sergeant, unshaken.

'No. Whatever the wrong or deceit was, he did it, I'm sure o' that. I 'ad to look at 'is face for five consecutive nights. I'm not so fond o' navigatin' about Cape Town with a South-Easter blowin' these days. I can hear those teeth click, so to say.'

'Ah, those teeth,' said Hooper, and his hand went to his waistcoat-pocket once more. 'Permanent things false teeth are. You read about 'em in all the murder trials.'

'What d'you suppose the captain knew – or did?' I asked.

'I've never turned my searchlight that way,' Pyecroft answered unblushingly.

We all reflected together, and drummed on empty beer bottles as the picnic-party, sunburned, wet, and sandy, passed our door singing 'The Honeysuckle and the Bee'.

'Pretty girl under that kapje,' said Pyecroft.

'They never circulated his description?' said Pritchard.

'I was askin' you before these gentlemen came,' said Hooper to me, 'whether you knew Wankies – on the way to the Zambesi – beyond Bulawayo?'

'Would he pass there – tryin' get to that Lake what's 'is name?' said Pritchard.

Hooper shook his head and went on: 'There's a curious bit o' line there, you see. It runs through solid teak forest – a sort o' mahogany really – seventy-two miles without a curve. I've had a train derailed there twenty-three times in forty miles. I was up there a month ago relievin' a sick inspector, you see. He told me to look out for a couple of tramps in the teak.'

'Two?' Pyecroft said. 'I don't envy that other man if –'

'We get heaps of tramps up there since the war. The inspector told me I'd find 'em at M'Bindwe siding waiting to go North. He'd given 'em some grub and quinine, you see. I went up on a construction train. I looked out for 'em. I saw them miles ahead along the straight, waiting in the teak. One of 'em was standin' up by the dead-end of the siding an' the other was squattin' down lookin' up at 'im, you see.'

'What did you do for 'em?' said Pritchard.

'There wasn't much I could do, except bury 'em. There'd been a bit of a thunderstorm in the teak, you see, and they were both stone dead and as black as charcoal. That's what they really were, you see – charcoal. They fell to bits when we tried to shift 'em. The man who was standin' up had the false teeth. I saw 'em shinin' against the black. Fell to bits he did too, like his mate squatting down an' watchin' him, both of 'em all wet in the rain. Both burned to charcoal, you see. And – that's what made me ask about marks just now – the false-toother was tattooed on the arms and chest – a crown and foul anchor with M. V. above.'

'I've seen that,' said Pyecroft quickly. 'It was so.'

'But if he was all charcoal-like?' said Pritchard, shuddering.

'You know how writing shows up white on a burned letter? Well, it was like that, you see. We buried 'em in the teak and I kept. ... But he was a friend of you two gentlemen, you see.'

Mr Hooper brought his hand away from his waistcoat-pocket – empty.

Pritchard covered his face with his hands for a moment, like a child shutting out an ugliness.

'And to think of her at Hauraki!' he murmured – 'with 'er 'air-ribbon on my beer. "Ada," she said to her niece.... Oh, my Gawd!'...

'On a summer afternoon, when the honeysuckle blooms,
And all Nature seems at rest,
Underneath the bower, 'mid the perfume of the flower,
Sat a maiden with the one she loves the best –'

sang the picnic-party waiting for their train at Glengariff.

'Well, I don't know how you feel about it,' said Pyecroft, 'but 'avin' seen 'is face for five consecutive nights on end, I'm inclined to finish what's left of the beer an' thank Gawd he's dead!'

'They'

(1904)

ONE view called me to another; one hill-top to its fellow, half across the county, and since I could answer at no more trouble than the snapping forward of a lever, I let the county flow under my wheels. The orchid-studded flats of the East gave way to the thyme, ilex, and grey grass of the Downs; these again to the rich cornland and fig-trees of the lower coast, where you carry the beat of the tide on your left hand for fifteen level miles; and when at last I turned inland through a huddle of rounded hills and woods I had run myself clean out of my known marks. Beyond that precise hamlet which stands godmother to the capital of the United States, I found hidden villages where bees, the only things awake, boomed in eighty-foot lindens that overhung grey Norman churches; miraculous brooks diving under stone bridges built for heavier traffic than would ever vex them again; tithe-barns larger than their churches, and an old smithy that cried out aloud how it had once been a hall of the Knights of the Temple. Gipsies I found on a common where the gorse, bracken, and heath fought it out together up a mile of Roman road; and a little farther on I disturbed a red fox rolling dog-fashion in the naked sunlight.

As the wooded hills closed about me I stood up in the car to take the bearings of that great Down whose ringed head is a landmark for fifty miles across the low countries. I judged that the lie of the country would bring me across some westward-running road that went to his feet, but I did not allow for the confusing veils of the woods. A quick turn plunged me first into a green cutting brim-full of liquid sunshine, next into a gloomy tunnel where last year's dead leaves whispered and scuffled about my tyres. The strong hazel stuff meeting overhead had not been cut for a couple of generations at least, nor had any axe helped the moss-cankered oak and beech to spring above them. Here the road changed frankly into a carpeted ride on whose brown velvet spent primrose-clumps showed like jade, and a few sickly, white-stalked bluebells nodded together. As the slope favoured I shut off the power and slid over the whirled leaves, expecting every moment to meet a keeper; but I only heard a jay, far off, arguing against the silence under the twilight of the trees.

Still the track descended. I was on the point of reversing and working my way back on the second speed ere I ended in some swamp, when I saw sunshine through the tangle ahead and lifted the brake.

It was down again at once. As the light beat across my face my fore-wheels took the turf of a great still lawn from which sprang horsemen ten feet high with levelled lances, monstrous peacocks, and sleek round-headed maids of honour – blue, black, and glistening – all of clipped yew. Across the lawn – the marshalled woods besieged it on three sides – stood an ancient house of lichened and weather-worn stone, with mullioned windows and roofs of rose-red tile. It was flanked by semi-circular walls, also rose-red, that closed the lawn on the fourth side, and at their feet a box hedge grew man-high. There were doves on the roof about the slim brick chimneys, and I caught a glimpse of an octagonal dove-house behind the screening wall.

Here, then, I stayed; a horseman's green spear laid at my breast; held by the exceeding beauty of that jewel in that setting.

'If I am not packed off for a trespasser, or if this knight does not ride a wallop at me,' thought I, 'Shakespeare and Queen Elizabeth at least must come out of that half-open garden door and ask me to tea.'

A child appeared at an upper window, and I thought the little thing waved a friendly hand. But it was to call a companion, for presently another bright head showed. Then I heard a laugh among the yew-peacocks, and turning to make sure (till then I had been watching the house only) I saw the silver of a fountain behind a hedge thrown up against the sun. The doves on the roof cooed to the cooing water; but between the two notes I caught the utterly happy chuckle of a child absorbed in some light mischief.

The garden door – heavy oak sunk deep in the thickness of the wall – opened further: a woman in a big garden hat set foot slowly on the time-hollowed stone step and as slowly walked across the turf. I was forming some apology when she lifted up her head and I saw that she was blind.

'I heard you,' she said. 'Isn't that a motor car?'

'I'm afraid I've made a mistake in my road. I should have turned off up above – I never dreamed – ' I began.

'But I'm very glad. Fancy a motor car coming into the garden! It will be such a treat – ' She turned and made as though looking about her. 'You – you haven't seen any one, have you – perhaps?'

'No one to speak to, but the children seemed interested at a distance.'

'Which?'

'I saw a couple up at the window just now, and I think I heard a little chap in the grounds.'

'Oh, lucky you!' she cried, and her face brightened. 'I hear them, of course, but that's all. You've seen them and heard them?'

'Yes,' I answered. 'And if I know anything of children, one of them's having a beautiful time by the fountain yonder. Escaped, I should imagine.'

'You're fond of children?'

I gave her one or two reasons why I did not altogether hate them.

'Of course, of course,' she said. 'Then you understand. Then you won't think it foolish if I ask you to take your car through the gardens, once or twice – quite slowly. I'm sure they'd like to see it. They see so little, poor things. One tries to make their life pleasant, but – ' she threw out her hands towards the woods. 'We're so out of the world here.'

'That will be splendid,' I said. 'But I can't cut up your grass.'

She faced to the right. 'Wait a minute,' she said. 'We're at the South gate, aren't we? Behind those peacocks there's a flagged path. We call it the Peacocks' Walk. You can't see it from here, they tell me, but if you squeeze along by the edge of the wood you can turn at the first peacock and get on to the flags.'

It was sacrilege to wake that dreaming house-front with the clatter of machinery, but I swung the car to clear the turf, brushed along the edge of the wood and turned in on the broad stone path where the fountain-basin lay like one star-sapphire.

'May I come too?' she cried. 'No, please don't help me. They'll like it better if they see me.'

She felt her way lightly to the front of the car, and with one foot on the step she called: 'Children, oh, children! Look and see what's going to happen!'

The voice would have drawn lost souls from the Pit, for the yearning that underlay its sweetness, and I was not surprised to hear an answering shout beyond the yews. It must have been the child by the fountain, but he fled at our approach, leaving a little toy boat in the water. I saw the glint of his blue blouse among the still horsemen.

Very disposedly we paraded the length of the walk and at her request backed again. This time the child had got the better of his panic, but stood far off and doubting.

'The little fellow's watching us,' I said. 'I wonder if he'd like a ride.'

'They're very shy still. Very shy. But, oh, lucky you to be able to see them! Let's listen.'

I stopped the machine at once, and the humid stillness, heavy with the scent of box, cloaked us deep. Shears I could hear where some gardener was clipping; a mumble of bees and broken voices that might have been the doves.

'Oh, unkind!' she said weariedly.

'Perhaps they're only shy of the motor. The little maid at the window looks tremendously interested.'

'Yes?' She raised her head. 'It was wrong of me to say that.

They are really fond of me. It's the only thing that makes life worth living – when they're fond of you, isn't it? I daren't think what the place would be without them. By the way, is it beautiful?'

'I think it is the most beautiful place I have ever seen.'

'So they all tell me. I can feel it, of course, but that isn't quite the same thing.'

'Then have you never – ?' I began, but stopped abashed.

'Not since I can remember. It happened when I was only a few months old, they tell me. And yet I must remember something, else how could I dream about colours. I see light in my dreams, and colours, but I never see *them*. I only hear them just as I do when I'm awake.'

'It's difficult to see faces in dreams. Some people can, but most of us haven't the gift,' I went on, looking up at the window where the child stood all but hidden.

'I've heard that too,' she said. 'And they tell me that one never sees a dead person's face in a dream. Is that true?'

'I believe it is – now I come to think of it.'

'But how is it with yourself – yourself?' The blind eyes turned towards me.

'I have never seen the faces of my dead in any dream,' I answered.

'Then it must be as bad as being blind.'

The sun had dipped behind the woods and the long shades were possessing the insolent horsemen one by one. I saw the light die from off the top of a glossy-leafed lance and all the brave hard green turn to soft black. The house, accepting another day at end, as it had accepted an hundred thousand gone, seemed to settle deeper into its rest among the shadows.

'Have you ever wanted to?' she said after the silence.

'Very much sometimes,' I replied. The child had left the window as the shadows closed upon it.

'Ah! So've I, but I don't suppose it's allowed. ... Where d'you live?'

'Quite the other side of the county – sixty miles and more,

and I must be going back. I've come without my big lamps.'

'But it's not dark yet. I can feel it.'

'I'm afraid it will be by the time I get home. Could you lend me someone to set me on my road at first? I've utterly lost myself.'

'I'll send Madden with you to the cross-roads. We are so out of the world, I don't wonder you were lost! I'll guide you round to the front of the house; but you will go slowly, won't you, till you're out of the grounds? It isn't foolish, do you think?'

'I promise you I'll go like this,' I said, and let the car start herself down the flagged path.

We skirted the left wing of the house, whose elaborately cast lead guttering alone was worth a day's journey; passed under a great rose-grown gate in the red wall, and so round to the high front of the house, which in beauty and stateliness as much excelled the back as that all others I had seen.

'Is it so very beautiful?' she said wistfully when she heard my raptures. 'And you like the lead figures too? There's the old azalea garden behind. They say that this place must have been made for children. Will you help me out, please? I should like to come with you as far as the cross-roads, but I mustn't leave them. Is that you, Madden? I want you to show this gentleman the way to the cross-roads. He has lost his way, but – he has seen them.'

A butler appeared noiselessly at the miracle of old oak that must be called the front door, and slipped aside to put on his hat. She stood looking at me with open blue eyes in which no sight lay, and I saw for the first time that she was beautiful.

'Remember,' she said quietly, 'if you are fond of them you will come again,' and disappeared within the house.

The butler in the car said nothing till we were nearly at the lodge gates, where catching a glimpse of a blue blouse in a shrubbery I swerved amply lest the devil that leads little boys to play should drag me into child-murder.

'Excuse me,' he asked of a sudden, 'but why did you do that, Sir?'

'The child yonder.'

'Our young gentleman in blue?'

'Of course.'

'He runs about a good deal. Did you see him by the fountain, Sir?'

'Oh, yes, several times. Do we turn here?'

'Yes, Sir. And did you 'appen to see them upstairs too?'

'At the upper window? Yes.'

'Was that before the mistress come out to speak to you, Sir?'

'A little before that. Why d'you want to know?'

He paused a little. 'Only to make sure that – that they had seen the car, Sir, because with children running about, though I'm sure you're driving particularly careful, there might be an accident. That was all, Sir. Here are the cross-roads. You can't miss your way from now on. Thank you, Sir, but that isn't *our* custom, not with –'

'I beg your pardon,' I said, and thrust away the British silver.

'Oh, it's quite right with the rest of 'em as a rule. Good-bye, Sir.'

He retired into the armour-plated conning-tower of his caste and walked away. Evidently a butler solicitous for the honour of his house, and interested, probably through a maid, in the nursery.

Once beyond the signposts at the cross-roads I looked back, but the crumpled hills interlaced so jealously that I could not see where the house had lain. When I asked its name at a cottage along the road, the fat woman who sold sweetmeats there gave me to understand that people with motor cars had small right to live – much less to 'go about talking like carriage folk'. They were not a pleasant-mannered community.

When I retraced my route on the map that evening I was little wiser. Hawkin's Old Farm appeared to be the Survey title of the place, and the old *County Gazetteer*, generally so ample, did not allude to it. The big house of those parts was Hodnington Hall, Georgian with early Victorian embellishments, as an atrocious steel engraving attested. I carried my difficulty to a neighbour – a deep-rooted tree of that soil – and he gave me a name of a family which conveyed no meaning.

A month or so later – I went again, or it may have been that my car took the road of her own volition. She over-ran the fruitless Downs, threaded every turn of the maze of lanes below the hills, drew through the high-walled woods, impenetrable in their full leaf, came out at the cross-roads where the butler had left me, and a little farther on developed an internal trouble which forced me to turn her in on a grass way-waste that cut into a summer-silent hazel wood. So far as I could make sure by the sun and a six-inch Ordnance map, this should be the road flank of that wood which I had first explored from the heights above. I made a mighty serious business of my repairs and a glittering shop of my repair kit, spanners, pump, and the like, which I spread out orderly upon a rug. It was a trap to catch all childhood, for on such a day, I argued, the children would not be far off. When I paused in my work I listened, but the wood was so full of the noises of summer (though the birds had mated) that I could not at first distinguish these from the tread of small cautious feet stealing across the dead leaves. I rang my bell in an alluring manner, but the feet fled, and I repented, for to a child a sudden noise is very real terror. I must have been at work half an hour when I heard in the wood the voice of the blind woman crying: 'Children, oh, children! Where are you?' and the stillness made slow to close on the perfection of that cry. She came towards me, half feeling her way between the tree boles, and though a child, it seemed, clung to her skirt, it swerved into the leafage like a rabbit as she drew nearer.

'Is that you?' she said, 'from the other side of the county?'

'Yes, it's me from the other side of the county.'

'Then why didn't you come through the upper woods? They were there just now.'

'They were here a few minutes ago. I expect they knew my car had broken down, and came to see the fun.'.

'Nothing serious, I hope? How do cars break down?'

'In fifty different ways. Only mine has chosen the fifty-first.'

She laughed merrily at the tiny joke, cooed with delicious laughter, and pushed her hat back.

'Let me hear,' she said.

'Wait a moment,' I cried, 'and I'll get you a cushion.'

She set her foot on the rug all covered with spare parts, and stooped above it eagerly. 'What delightful things!' The hands through which she saw glanced in the chequered sunlight. 'A box here – another box! Why, you've arranged them like playing shop!'

'I confess now that I put it out to attract them. I don't need half those things really.'

'How nice of you! I heard your bell in the upper wood. You say they were here before that?'

'I'm sure of it. Why are they so shy? That little fellow in blue who was with you just now ought to have got over his fright. He's been watching me like a Red Indian.'

'It must have been your bell,' she said. 'I heard one of them go past me in trouble when I was coming down. They're shy – so shy even with me.' She turned her face over her shoulder and cried again: 'Children, oh, children! Look and see!'

'They must have gone off together on their own affairs,' I suggested, for there was a murmur behind us of lowered voices broken by the sudden squeaking giggles of childhood. I returned to my tinkerings and she leaned forward, her chin on her hand, listening interestedly.

'How many are they?' I said at last. The work was finished, but I saw no reason to go.

Her forehead puckered a little in thought. 'I don't quite know,' she said simply. 'Sometimes more – sometimes less.

They come and stay with me because I love them, you see.'

'That must be very jolly,' I said, replacing a drawer, and as I spoke I heard the inanity of my answer.

'You – you aren't laughing at me?' she cried. 'I – I haven't any of my own. I never married. People laugh at me sometimes about them because – because – '

'Because they're savages,' I returned. 'It's nothing to fret for. That sort laugh at everything that isn't in their own fat lives.'

'I don't know. How should I? I only don't like being laughed at about *them*. It hurts; and when one can't see. . . . I don't want to seem silly,' her chin quivered like a child's as she spoke, 'but we blindies have only one skin, I think. Everything outside hits straight at our souls. It's different with you. You've such good defences in your eyes – looking out – before anyone can really pain you in your soul. People forget that with us.'

I was silent, reviewing that inexhaustible matter – the more than inherited (since it is also carefully taught) brutality of the Christian peoples, besides which the mere heathendom of the West Coast nigger is clean and restrained. It led me a long distance into myself.

'Don't do that!' she said of a sudden, putting her hands before her eyes.

'What?'

She made a gesture with her hand.

'That! It's – it's all purple and black. Don't! That colour hurts.'

'But how in the world do you know about colours?' I exclaimed, for here was a revelation indeed.

'Colours as colours?' she asked.

'No. *Those* Colours which you saw just now.'

'You know as well as I do,' she laughed, 'else you wouldn't have asked that question. They aren't in the world at all. They're in *you* – when you went so angry.'

'D'you mean a dull purplish patch, like port wine mixed with ink?' I said.

'I've never seen ink or port wine, but the colours aren't mixed. They can separate – all separate.'

'Do you mean black streaks and jags across the purple?'

She nodded. 'Yes – if they are like this,' and zig-zagged her finger again, 'but it's more red than purple – that bad colour.'

'And what are the colours at the top of the – whatever you see?'

Slowly she leaned forward and traced on the rug the figure of the Egg itself.

'I see them so,' she said, pointing with a grass stem, 'white, green, yellow, red, purple, and when people are angry or bad, black across the red – as you were just now.'

'Who told you anything about it – in the beginning?' I demanded.

'About the colours? No one. I used to ask what colours were when I was little – in tablecovers and curtains and carpets you see – because some colours hurt me and some made me happy. People told me; and when I got older that was how I saw people.' Again she traced the outline of the Egg which it is given to very few of us to see.

'All by yourself?' I repeated.

'All by myself. There wasn't anyone else. I only found out afterwards that other people did not see the Colours.'

She leaned against the tree-bole plaiting and unplaiting chance-plucked grass stems. The children in the wood had drawn nearer. I could see them with the tail of my eye frolicking like squirrels.

'Now I am sure you will never laugh at me,' she went on after a long silence. 'Nor at *them.*'

'Goodness! No!' I cried, jolted out of my train of thought. 'A man who laughs at a child – unless the child is laughing too – is a heathen!'

'I didn't mean that, of course. You'd never laugh *at* children, but I thought – I used to think – that perhaps you might laugh about *them*. So now I beg your pardon. ... What are you going to laugh at?'

I had made no sound, but she knew.

'At the notion of your begging my pardon. If you had done your duty as a pillar of the State and a landed proprietress you ought to have summoned me for trespass when I barged through your woods the other day. It was disgraceful of me – inexcusable.'

She looked at me, her head against the tree-trunk – long and steadfastly – this woman who could see the naked soul.

'How curious,' she half whispered. 'How very curious.'

'Why, what have I done?'

'You don't understand . . . and yet you understood about the Colours. Don't you understand?'

She spoke with a passion that nothing had justified, and I faced her bewilderedly as she rose. The children had gathered themselves in a roundel behind a bramble bush. One sleek head bent over something smaller, and the set of the little shoulders told me that fingers were on lips. They, too, had some child's tremendous secret. I alone was hopelessly astray there in the broad sunlight.

'No,' I said, and shook my head as though the dead eyes could note. 'Whatever it is, I don't understand yet. Perhaps I shall later – if you'll let me come again.'

'You will come again,' she answered. 'You will surely come again and walk in the wood.'

'Perhaps the children will know me well enough by that time to let me play with them – as a favour. You know what children are like.'

'It isn't a matter of favour but of right,' she replied, and while I wondered what she meant, a dishevelled woman plunged round the bend of the road, loose-haired, purple, almost lowing with agony as she ran. It was my rude, fat friend of the sweetmeat shop. The blind woman heard and stepped forward. 'What is it, Mrs Madehurst?' she asked.

The woman flung her apron over her head and literally grovelled in the dust, crying that her grandchild was sick to death, that the local doctor was away fishing, that Jenny the mother was at her wits' end, and so forth, with repetitions and bellowings.

'Where's the nearest doctor?' I asked between paroxysms.

'Madden will tell you. Go round to the house and take him with you. I'll attend to this. Be quick!' She half supported the fat woman into the shade. In two minutes I was blowing all the horns of Jericho under the front of the House Beautiful, and Madden, in the pantry, rose to the crisis like a butler and a man.

A quarter of an hour at illegal speeds caught us a doctor five miles away. Within the half-hour we had decanted him, much interested in motors, at the door of the sweetmeat shop, and drew up the road to await the verdict.

'Useful things, cars,' said Madden, all man and no butler. 'If I'd had one when mine took sick she wouldn't have died.'

'How was it?' I asked.

'Croup. Mrs Madden was away. No one knew what to do. I drove eight miles in a tax-cart for the doctor. She was choked when we came back. This car 'd ha' saved her. She'd have been close on ten now.'

'I'm sorry,' I said. 'I thought you were rather fond of children from what you told me going to the cross-roads the other day.'

'Have you seen 'em again, Sir – this mornin'?'

'Yes, but they're well broke to cars. I couldn't get any of them within twenty yards of it.'

He looked at me carefully as a scout considers a stranger – not as a menial should lift his eyes to his divinely appointed superior.

'I wonder why,' he said just above the breath that he drew.

We waited on. A light wind from the sea wandered up and down the long lines of the woods, and the wayside grasses, whitened already with summer dust, rose and bowed in sallow waves.

A woman, wiping the suds off her arms, came out of the cottage next the sweetmeat shop.

'I've be'n listenin' in de back-yard,' she said cheerily. 'He says Arthur's unaccountable bad. Did ye hear him shruck just now? Unaccountable bad. I reckon t'will come Jenny's turn to walk in de wood nex' week along, Mr Madden.'

'Excuse me, Sir, but your lap-robe is slipping,' said Madden deferentially. The woman started, dropped a curtsey, and hurried away.

'What does she mean by "walking in the wood"?' I asked.

'It must be some saying they use hereabouts. I'm from Norfolk myself,' said Madden. 'They're an independent lot in this county. She took you for a chauffeur, Sir.'

I saw the Doctor come out of the cottage followed by a draggle-tailed wench who clung to his arm as though he could make treaty for her with Death. 'Dat sort,' she wailed – 'dey're just as much to us dat has 'em as if dey was lawful born. Just as much – just as much! An' God he'd be just as pleased if you saved 'un, Doctor. Don't take it from me. Miss Florence will tell ye de very same. Don't leave 'im, Doctor!'

'I know, I know,' said the man; 'but he'll be quiet for a while now. We'll get the nurse and the medicine as fast as we can.' He signalled me to come forward with the car, and I strove not to be privy to what followed; but I saw the girl's face, blotched and frozen with grief, and I felt the hand without a ring clutching at my knees when we moved away.

The Doctor was a man of some humour, for I remember he claimed my car under the Oath of Aesculapius, and used it and me without mercy, First we convoyed Mrs Madehurst and the blind woman to wait by the sick-bed till the nurse should come. Next we invaded a neat county town for presciptions (the Doctor said the trouble was cerebro-spinal meningitis), and when the County Institute, banked and flanked with scared market cattle, reported itself out of nurses for the moment we literally flung ourselves loose upon the county. We conferred with the owners of great houses – magnates at the ends of overarching avenues whose big-boned womenfolk strode away from their tea-tables to listen to the imperious Doctor. At last a white-haired lady sitting under a cedar of Lebanon and surrounded by a court of magnificent Borzois – all hostile to motors – gave the Doctor, who received them as from a princess, written orders which we bore many miles at top speed, through a park, to a French nunnery, where we took over in exchange a pallid-faced and trembling Sister. She knelt at the bottom of the tonneau telling her beads without pause till, by short cuts of the Doctor's invention, we had her to the sweetmeat shop once more. It was a long afternoon crowded with mad episodes that rose and dissolved like the dust of our wheels; cross-sections of remote and incomprehensible lives through which we raced at right angles; and I went home in the dusk, wearied out, to dream of the clashing horns of cattle; round-eyed nuns walking in a garden of graves; pleasant tea-parties beneath shady trees; the carbolic-scented, grey-painted corridors of the County Institute; the steps of shy children in the wood, and the hands that clung to my knees as the motor began to move.

I had intended to return in a day or two, but it pleased Fate to hold me from that side of the county, on many pretexts, till the elder and the wild rose had fruited. There came at last a brilliant day, swept clear from the south-west, that brought the hills within hand's reach – a day of unstable airs and high filmy clouds. Through no merit of my own I was free, and set the car for the third time on that known road. As I reached the crest of the Downs I felt the soft air change, saw it glaze under the sun; and, looking down at the sea, in that instant beheld the blue of the Channel turn through polished silver and dulled steel to dingy pewter. A laden collier hugging the coast steered outward for deeper water, and, across copper-coloured haze, I saw sails rise one by one on the anchored fishing-fleet. In a deep dene behind me an eddy of sudden wind drummed through sheltered oaks, and spun aloft the first dry sample of autumn leaves. When I reached the beach road the sea-fog fumed over the brickfields, and the tide was telling all the groynes of the gale beyond Ushant. In less than an hour summer England vanished in chill grey. We were again the shut island of the North, all the ships of the world bellowing at our perilous gates; and between their outcries ran the piping of bewildered gulls. My cap dripped moisture, the folds of the rug held it in pools or sluiced it away in runnels, and the salt-rime stuck to my lips.

Inland the smell of autumn loaded the thickened fog among the trees, and the drip became a continuous shower. Yet the late flowers – mallow of the wayside, scabious of the field, and dahlia of the garden – showed gay in the mist, and beyond the sea's breath there was little sign of decay in the leaf. Yet in the villages the house doors were all open, and bare-legged, bare-headed children sat at ease on the damp doorsteps to shout 'pip-pip' at the stranger.

I made bold to call at the sweetmeat shop, where Mrs Madehurst met me with a fat woman's hospitable tears. Jenny's child, she said, had died two days after the nun had come. It was, she felt, best out of the way, even though insurance offices, for reasons which she did not pretend to follow, would not willingly insure such stray lives. 'Not but what Jenny didn't tend to Arthur as though he'd come all proper at de end of de first year – like Jenny herself.' Thanks to Miss Florence, the child had been buried with a pomp which, in Mrs Madehurst's opinion, more than covered the small irregularity of its birth. She described the coffin, within and without, the glass hearse, and the evergreen lining of the grave.

'But how's the mother?' I asked.

'Jenny? Oh, she'll get over it. I've felt dat way with one or two o' my own. She'll get over. She's walkin' in de wood now.'

'In this weather?'

Mrs Madehurst looked at me with narrowed eyes across the counter.

'I dunno but it opens de 'eart like. Yes, it opens de 'eart.

Dat's where losin' and bearin' comes so alike in de long run we do say.'

Now the wisdom of the old wives is greater than that of all the Fathers, and this last oracle sent me thinking so extendedly as I went up the road, that I nearly ran over a woman and a child at the wooded corner by the lodge gates of the House Beautiful.

'Awful weather!' I cried, as I slowed dead for the turn.

'Not so bad,' she answered placidly out of the fog. 'Mine's used to 'un. You'll find yours indoors, I reckon.'

Indoors, Madden received me with professional courtesy, and kind inquiries for the health of the motor, which he would put under cover.

I waited in a still, nut-brown hall, pleasant with late flowers and warmed with a delicious wood fire – a place of good influence and great peace. (Men and women may sometimes, after great effort, achieve a creditable lie; but the house, which is their temple, cannot say anything save the truth of those who have lived in it.) A child's cart and a doll lay on the black-and-white floor, where a rug had been kicked back. I felt that the children had only just hurried away – to hide themselves, most like – in the many turns of the great adzed staircase that climbed steadily out of the hall, or to crouch and gaze behind the lions and roses of the carven gallery above. Then I heard her voice above me, singing as the blind sing – from the soul:

'In the pleasant orchard-closes.'

And all my early summer came back at the call.

'In the pleasant orchard-closes,
God bless all our gains say we –
But may God bless all our losses,
Better suits with our degree.'

She dropped the marring fifth line, and repeated –

'Better suits with our degree!'

I saw her lean over the gallery, her linked hands white as pearl against the oak.

'Is that you – from the other side of the county?' she called.

'Yes, me – from the other side of the county,' I answered, laughing.

'What a long time before you had to come here again.' She ran down the stairs, one hand lightly touching the broad rail. 'It's two months and four days. Summer's gone!'

'I meant to come before, but Fate prevented.'

'I knew it. Please do something to that fire. They won't let me play with it, but I can feel it's behaving badly. Hit it!'

I looked on either side of the deep fireplace, and found but a half-charred hedge-stake with which I punched a black log into flame.

'It never goes out, day or night,' she said, as though explaining. 'In case any one comes in with cold toes, you see.'

'It's even lovelier inside than it was out,' I murmured. The red light poured itself along the age-polished dusky panels till the Tudor roses and lions of the gallery took colour and motion. An old eagle-topped convex mirror gathered the picture into its mysterious heart, distorting afresh the distorted shadows, and curving the gallery lines into the curves of a ship. The day was shutting down in half a gale as the fog turned to stringy scud. Through the uncurtained mullions of the broad window I could see the valiant horsemen of the lawn rear and recover against the wind that taunted them with legions of dead leaves.

'Yes, it must be beautiful,' she said. 'Would you like to go over it? There's still light enough upstairs.'

I followed her up the unflinching, wagon-wide staircase to the gallery whence opened the thin fluted Elizabethan doors.

'Feel how they put the latch low down for the sake of the children.' She swung a light door inward.

'By the way, where are they?' I asked. 'I haven't even heard them today.'

She did not answer at once. Then, 'I can only hear them,' she replied softly. 'This is one of their rooms – everything ready, you see.'

She pointed into a heavily-timbered room. There were little low gate tables and children's chairs. A doll's house, its hooked front half open, faced a great dappled rocking-horse, from whose padded saddle it was but a child's scramble to the broad window-seat overlooking the lawn. A toy gun lay in a corner beside a gilt wooden cannon.

'Surely they've only just gone,' I whispered. In the failing light a door creaked cautiously. I heard the rustle of a frock and the patter of feet – quick feet through a room beyond.

'I heard that,' she cried triumphantly. 'Did you? Children, oh, children! Where are you?'

The voice filled the walls that held it lovingly to the last perfect note, but there came no answering shout such as I had heard in the garden. We hurried on from room to oak-floored room; up a step here, down three steps there; among a maze of passages; always mocked by our quarry. One might as well have tried to work an unstopped warren with a single ferret. There were bolt-holes innumerable – recesses in walls, embrasures of deep-slitten windows now darkened, whence they could start up behind us; and abandoned fire-places, six feet deep in the masonry, as well as the tangle of communicating doors. Above all, they had the twilight for their helper in our game. I had caught one or two joyous chuckles of evasion, and once or twice had seen the silhouette of a child's frock against some darkening window at the end of a passage; but we returned empty-handed to the gallery, just as a middle-aged woman was setting a lamp in its niche.

'No, I haven't seen her either this evening, Miss Florence,' I heard her say, 'but that Turpin he says he wants to see you about his shed.'

'Oh, Mr Turpin must want to see me very badly. Tell him to come to the hall, Mrs Madden.'

I looked down into the hall whose only light was the dulled

fire, and deep in the shadow I saw them at last. They must have slipped down while we were in the passages, and now thought themselves perfectly hidden behind an old gilt leather screen. By child's law, my fruitless chase was as good as an introduction, but since I had taken so much trouble I resolved to force them to come forward later by the simple trick, which children detest, of pretending not to notice them. They lay close, in a little huddle, no more than shadows except when a quick flame betrayed an outline.

'And now we'll have some tea,' she said. 'I believe I ought to have offered it you at first, but one doesn't arrive at manners somehow when one lives alone and is considered – h'm – peculiar.' Then with very pretty scorn, 'Would you like a lamp to see to eat by?'

'The firelight's much pleasanter, I think.' We descended into that delicious gloom and Madden brought tea.

I took my chair in the direction of the screen ready to surprise or be surprised as the game should go, and at her permission, since a hearth is always sacred, bent forward to play with the fire.

'Where do you get these beautiful short faggots from?' I asked idly. 'Why, they are tallies!'

'Of course,' she said. 'As I can't read or write I'm driven back on the early English tally for my accounts. Give me one and I'll tell you what it meant.'

I passed her an unburned hazel-tally, about a foot long, and she ran her thumb down the nicks.

'This is the milk-record for the home farm for the month of April last year, in gallons,' said she. 'I don't know what I should have done without tallies. An old forester of mine taught me the system. It's out of date now for every one else; but my tenants respect it. One of them's coming now to see me. Oh, it doesn't matter. He has no business here out of office hours. He's a greedy, ignorant man – very greedy, or – he wouldn't come here after dark.'

'Have you much land then?'

'Only a couple of hundred acres in hand, thank goodness.

The other six hundred are nearly all let to folk who knew my folk before me, but this Turpin is quite a new man – and a highway robber.'

'But are you sure I shan't be – ?'

'Certainly not. You have the right. He hasn't any children.'

'Ah, the children!' I said, and slid my low chair back till it nearly touched the screen that hid them. 'I wonder whether they'll come out for me.'

There was a murmur of voices – Madden's and a deeper note – at the low, dark side door, and a ginger-headed, canvas-gaitered giant of the unmistakable tenant-farmer type stumbled or was pushed in.

'Come to the fire, Mr Turpin,' she said.

'If – if you please, Miss, I'll – I'll be quite as well by the door.' He clung to the latch as he spoke like a frightened child. Of a sudden I realized that he was in the grip of some almost overpowering fear.

'Well?'

'About that new shed for the young stock – that was all. These first autumn storms settin' in ... but I'll come again, Miss.' His teeth did not chatter much more than the door-latch.

'I think not,' she answered levelly. 'The new shed – m'm. What did my agent write you on the 15th?'

'I – fancied p'raps that if I came to see you – ma – man to man like, Miss. But – '

His eyes rolled into every corner of the room wide with horror. He half opened the door through which he had entered, but I noticed it shut again – from without and firmly.

'He wrote what I told him,' she went on. 'You are overstocked already. Dunnett's Farm never carried more than fifty bullocks – even in Mr Wright's time. And *he* used cake. You've sixty-seven and you don't cake. You've broken the lease in that respect. You're dragging the heart out of the farm.'

'I'm – I'm getting some minerals – superphosphates – next week. I've as good as ordered a truck-load already. I'll go down to the station tomorrow about 'em. Then I can come and see you man to man like, Miss, in the daylight. . . . That gentleman's not going away, is he?' He almost shrieked.

I had only slid the chair a little farther back, reaching behind me to tap on the leather of the screen, but he jumped like a rat.

'No. Please attend to me, Mr Turpin.' She turned in her chair and faced him with his back to the door. It was an old and sordid little piece of scheming that she forced from him – his plea for the new cow-shed at his landlady's expense, that he might with the covered manure pay his next year's rent out of the valuation after, as she made clear, he had bled the enriched pastures to the bone. I could not but admire the intensity of his greed, when I saw him outfacing for its sake whatever terror it was that ran wet on his forehead.

I ceased to tap the leather – was, indeed, calculating the cost of the shed – when I felt my relaxed hand taken and turned softly between the soft hands of a child. So at last I had triumphed. In a moment I would turn and acquaint myself with those quick-footed wanderers . . .

The little brushing kiss fell in the centre of my palm – as a gift on which the fingers were, once, expected to close: as the all-faithful half-reproachful signal of a waiting child not used to neglect even when grown-ups were busiest – a fragment of the mute code devised very long ago.

Then I knew. And it was as though I had known from the first day when I looked across the lawn at the high window.

I heard the door shut. The woman turned to me in silence, and I felt that she knew.

What time passed after this I cannot say. I was roused by the fall of a log, and mechanically rose to put it back. Then I returned to my place in the chair very close to the screen.

'Now you understand,' she whispered, across the packed shadows.

'Yes, I understand – now. Thank you.'

'I – I only hear them.' She bowed her head in her hands. 'I have no right, you know – no other right. I have neither borne nor lost – neither borne nor lost!'

'Be very glad then,' said I, for my soul was torn open within me.

'Forgive me!'

She was still, and I went back to my sorrow and my joy.

'It was because I loved them so,' she said at last, brokenly. '*That* was why it was, even from the first – even before I knew that they – they were all I should ever have. And I loved them so!'

She stretched out her arms to the shadows and the shadows within the shadow.

'They came because I loved them – because I needed them. I – I must have made them come. Was that wrong, think you?'

'No – no.'

'I – I grant you that the toys and – and all that sort of thing were nonsense, but – but I used to so hate empty rooms myself when I was little.' She pointed to the gallery. 'And the passages all empty.... And how could I ever bear the garden door shut? Suppose – '

'Don't! For pity's sake, don't!' I cried. The twilight had brought a cold rain with gusty squalls that plucked at the leaded windows.

'And the same thing with keeping the fire in all night. *I* don't think it so foolish – do you?'

I looked at the broad brick hearth, saw, through tears, I believe, that there was no unpassable iron on or near it, and bowed my head.

'I did all that and lots of other things – just to make believe. Then they came. I heard them, but I didn't know that they were not mine by right till Mrs Madden told me – '

'The butler's wife? What?'

'One of them – I heard – she saw. And knew Hers! *Not* for me. I didn't know at first. Perhaps I was jealous. Afterwards, I began to understand that it was only because I loved them, not because – . . . Oh, you *must* bear or lose,' she said piteously. 'There is no other way – and yet they love me. They must! Don't they?'

There was no other sound in the room except the lapping voices of the fire, but we two listened intently, and she at least took comfort from what she heard. She recovered herself and half rose. I sat still in my chair by the screen.

'Don't think me a wretch to whine about myself like this, but – but I'm all in the dark, you know, and *you* can see.'

In truth I could see, and my vision confirmed me in my resolve, though that was like the very parting of spirit and flesh. Yet a little longer I would stay since it was the last time.

'You think it is wrong, then?' she cried sharply, though I had said nothing.

'Not for you. A thousand times no. For you it is right. . . . I am grateful to you beyond words. For me it would be wrong. For me only . . .'

'Why?' she said, but passed her hand before her face as she had done at our second meeting in the wood. 'Oh, I see,' she went on simply as a child. 'For you it would be wrong.' Then with a little indrawn laugh. 'And, d'you remember, I called you lucky – once – at first. You who must never come here again!'

She left me to sit a little longer by the screen, and I heard the sound of her feet die out along the gallery above.

An Habitation Enforced

(1905)

> **My friend, if cause doth wrest thee,**
> **Ere folly hath much oppressed thee,**
> **Far from acquaintance kest thee**
> **Where country may digest thee . . .**
> **Thank God that so hath blessed thee,**
> **And sit down, Robin, and rest thee.**
>
> THOMAS TUSSER

IT came without warning, at the very hour his hand was outstretched to crumple the Holtz and Gunsberg Combine. The New York doctors called it overwork, and he lay in a darkened room, one ankle crossed above the other, tongue pressed into palate, wondering whether the next brain-surge of prickly fires would drive his soul from all anchorages. At last they gave judgement. With care he might in two years return to the arena, but for the present he must go across the water and do no work whatever. He accepted the terms. It was capitulation; but the Combine that had shivered beneath his knife gave him all the honours of war. Gunsberg himself, full of condolences, came to the steamer and filled the Chapins' suite of cabins with overwhelming flower-works.

'Smilax,' said George Chapin when he saw them. 'Fitz is right. I'm dead; only I don't see why he left out the "In Memoriam" on the ribbons!'

'Nonsense!' his wife answered, and poured him his tincture. 'You'll be back before you can think.'

He looked at himself in the mirror, surprised that his face had not been branded by the hells of the past three months. The noise of the decks worried him, and he lay down, his tongue only a little pressed against his palate.

An hour later he said: 'Sophie, I feel sorry about taking

you away from everything like this. I – I suppose we're the two loneliest people on God's earth tonight.'

Said Sophie his wife, and kissed him: 'Isn't it something to you that we're going together?'

They drifted about Europe for months – sometimes alone, sometimes with chance-met gipsies of their own land. From the North Cape to the Blue Grotto at Capri they wandered, because the next steamer headed that way, or because some one had set them on the road. The doctors had warned Sophie that Chapin was not to take interest even in other men's interests; but a familiar sensation at the back of the neck after one hour's keen talk with a Nauheimed railway magnate saved her any trouble. He nearly wept.

'And I'm over thirty,' he cried. 'With all I meant to do!'

'Let's call it a honeymoon,' said Sophie. 'D'you know, in all the six years we've been married, you've never told me what you meant to do with your life?'

'With my life? What's the use? It's finished now.' Sophie looked up quickly from the Bay of Naples. 'As far as my business goes, I shall have to live on my rents like that architect at San Moritz.'

'You'll get better if you don't worry; and even if it takes time, there are worse things than – How much have you?'

'Between four and five million. But it isn't the money. You know it isn't. It's the principle. How could you respect me? You never did, the first year after we married, till I went to work like the others. Our tradition and upbringing are against it. We can't accept *those* ideals.'

'Well, I suppose I married you for some sort of ideal,' she answered, and they returned to their forty-third hotel.

In England they missed the alien tongues of Continental streets that reminded them of their own polyglot cities. In England all men spoke one tongue, speciously like American to the ear, but on cross-examination unintelligible.

'Ah, but you have not seen England,' said a lady with iron-grey hair. They had met her in Vienna, Bayreuth and Florence, and were grateful to find her again at Claridge's, for she commanded situations, and knew where prescriptions are most carefully made up. 'You ought to take an interest in the home of our ancestors – as I do.'

'I've tried for a week, Mrs Shonts,' said Sophie, 'but I never get any further than tipping German waiters.'

'These are not the true type,' Mrs Shonts went on. 'I know where you should go.'

Chapin pricked up his ears, anxious to run anywhere from the streets on which quick men something of his kidney did the business denied to him.

'We hear and we obey, Mrs Shonts,' said Sophie, feeling his unrest as he drank the loathed British tea.

Mrs Shonts smiled, and took them in hand. She wrote widely and telegraphed far on their behalf, till, armed with her letter of introduction, she drove them into that wilderness which is reached from an ash-barrel of a station called Charing Cross. They were to go to Rocketts – the farm of one Cloke, in the southern counties – where, she assured them, they would meet the genuine England of folklore and song.

Rocketts they found after some hours, four miles from a station, and, so far as they could judge in the bumpy darkness, twice as many from a road. Trees, kine, and the outlines of barns showed shadowy about them when they alighted, and Mr and Mrs Cloke, at the open door of a deep stone-floored kitchen, made them slowly welcome. They lay in an attic beneath a wavy, whitewashed ceiling, and because it rained, a wood fire was made in an iron basket on a brick hearth, and they fell asleep to the chirping of mice and the whimper of flames.

When they woke it was a fair day, full of the noises of birds, the smell of box, lavender, and fried bacon, mixed with an elemental smell they had never met before.

'This,' said Sophie, nearly pushing out the thin casement in an attempt to see round the corner, 'is – what did the hack – cabman say to the railway porter about my trunk – quite "on the top"?'

'No; "a little bit of all right". I feel further away from

anywhere than I've ever felt in my life. We must find out where the telegraph office is.'

'Who cares?' said Sophie, wandering about, hair-brush in hand, to admire the illustrated weekly pictures pasted on door and cupboard.

But there was no rest for the alien soul till he had made sure of the telegraph office. He asked the Clokes' daughter, laying breakfast, while Sophie plunged her face in the lavender bush outside the low window.

'Go to the stile a-top o' the Barn field,' said Mary, 'and look across Pardons to the next spire. It's directly under. You can't miss it – not if you keep to the footpath. My sister's the telegraphist there. But you're in the three-mile radius, sir. The boy delivers telegrams directly to this door from Pardons village.'

'One has to take a good deal on trust in this country,' he murmured.

Sophie looked at the close turf, scarred only with last night's wheels; at two ruts which wound round a rickyard; and at the circle of still orchard about the half-timbered house.

'What's the matter with it?' she said. 'Telegrams delivered to the Vale of Avalon, of course,' and she beckoned in an earnest-eyed hound of engaging manners and no engagements, who answered, at times, to the name of Rambler. He led them, after breakfast, to the rise behind the house where the stile stood against the skyline, and, 'I wonder what we shall find now,' said Sophie, frankly prancing with joy on the grass.

It was a slope of gap-hedged fields possessed to their centres by clumps of brambles. Gates were not, and the rabbit-mined, cattle-rubbed posts leaned out and in. A narrow path doubled among the bushes, scores of white tails twinkled before the racing hound, and a hawk rose, whistling shrilly.

'No roads. No nothing!' said Sophie, her short skirt hooked by briers. 'I thought all England was a garden. There's your spire, George, across the valley. How curious!'

They walked towards it through an all-abandoned land. Here they found the ghost of a patch of lucerne that had refused to die; there a harsh fallow surrendered to yard-high thistles; and here a breadth of rampant kelk feigning to be lawful crop. In the ungrazed pastures swathes of dead stuff caught their feet, and the ground beneath glistened with sweat. At the bottom of the valley a little brook had undermined its footbridge, and frothed in the wreckage. But there stood great woods on the slopes beyond – old, tall, and brilliant, like unfaded tapestries against the walls of a ruined house.

'All this within a hundred miles of London,' he said. 'Looks as if it had had nervous prostration, too.' The footpath turned the shoulder of a slope, through a thicket of rank rhododendrons, and crossed what had once been a carriage-drive, which ended in the shadow of two gigantic holm-oaks.

'A house!' said Sophie, in a whisper. 'A colonial house!'

Behind the blue-green of the twin trees rose a dark-bluish brick Georgian pile, with a shell-shaped fan-light over its pillared door. The hound had gone off on his own foolish quests. Except for some stir in the branches and the flight of four startled magpies, there was neither life nor sound about the square house; but it looked out of its long windows most friendlily.

'Cha-armed to meet you, I'm sure,' said Sophie, and curtsied to the ground. 'George, this is history I can understand. *We* began here.' She curtsied again.

The June sunshine twinkled on all the lights. It was as though an old lady, wise in three generations' experience, but for the present sitting out, bent to listen to her flushed and eager grandchild.

'I *must* look!' Sophie tiptoed to a window, and shaded her eyes with her hand. 'Oh, this room's half-full of cotton-bales – wool, I suppose! But I can see a bit of the mantelpiece. George, do come! Isn't that some one?'

She fell back behind her husband. The front door opened slowly, to show the hound, his nose white with milk, in charge of an ancient of days clad in a blue linen ephod curiously gathered on breast and shoulders.

'Certainly,' said George, half aloud. 'Father Time himself. This is where he lives, Sophie.'

'We came – ,' said Sophie weakly. 'Can we see the house? I'm afraid that's our dog.'

'No, 'tis Rambler,' said the old man. 'He've been at my swillpail again. Staying at Rocketts, be ye? Come in. Ah! you runagate!'

The hound broke from him, and he tottered after him down the drive. They entered the hall – just such a high light hall as such a house should own. A slim-balustered staircase, wide and shallow and once creamy-white, climbed out of it under a long oval window. On either side delicately-moulded doors gave on to wool-lumbered rooms, whose sea-green mantelpieces were adorned with nymphs, scrolls, and Cupids in low relief.

'What's the firm that makes these things?' cried Sophie, enraptured. 'Oh, I forgot! These must be the originals. Adams, is it? I never dreamed of anything like that steel-cut fender. Does he mean us to go everywhere?'

'He's catching the dog,' said George, looking out. 'We don't count.'

They explored the first or ground floor, delighted as children playing burglars.

'This is like all England,' she said at last. 'Wonderful, but no explanation. You're expected to know it beforehand. Now let's try upstairs.'

The stairs never creaked beneath their feet. From the broad landing they entered a long, green-panelled room lighted by three full-length windows, which overlooked the forlorn wreck of a terraced garden, and wooden slopes beyond.

'The drawing-room, of course.' Sophie swam up and down it. 'That mantelpiece – Orpheus and Eurydice – is the best of them all. Isn't it marvellous? Why, the room seems furnished with nothing in it! How's that, George?'

'It's the proportions. I've noticed it.'

'I saw a Hepplewhite couch once' – Sophie laid her finger to her flushed cheek and considered. 'With two of them – one on each side – you wouldn't need anything else. Except – there must be one perfect mirror over that mantelpiece.'

'Look at that view. It's a framed Constable,' her husband cried.

'No; it's a Morland – a parody of a Morland. But about that couch, George. Don't you think Empire might be better than Hepplewhite? Dull gold against that pale green? It's a pity they don't make spinets nowadays.'

'I believe you can get them. Look at that oak wood behind the pines.'

' "While you sat and played toccatas stately at the clavichord," ' Sophie hummed, and, head on one side, nodded to where the perfect mirror should hang.

Then they found bedrooms with dressing-rooms and powdering-closets, and steps leading up and down – boxes of rooms, round, square, and octagonal, with enriched ceilings and chased door-locks.

'Now about servants. Oh!' She had darted up the last stairs to the chequered darkness of the top floor, where loose tiles lay among broken laths, and the walls were scrawled with names, sentiments, and hop-records. 'They've been keeping pigeons here,' she cried.

'And you could drive a buggy through the roof anywhere,' said George.

'That's what *I* say,' the old man cried below them on the stairs. 'Not a dry place for my pigeons at all.'

'But why was it allowed to get like this?' said Sophie.

' 'Tis with housen as teeth,' he replied. 'Let 'em go too far, and there's nothing *to* be done. Time was they was minded to sell her, but none would buy. She was too far-away-along any place. Time was they'd ha' lived there theyselves, but they took and died.'

'Here?' Sophie moved beneath the light of a hole in the roof.

'Nah – none dies here excep' falling off ricks and such. In London they died.' He plucked a lock of wool from his blue smock. 'They was no staple – neither the Elphicks nor the Moones. Shart and brittle all of 'em. Dead they be seventeen year, for I've been here caretakin' twenty-five.'

'Who does all the wool belong to downstairs?' George asked.

'To the estate. I'll show you the back parts if ye like. You're from America, ain't ye? I've had a son there once myself.' They followed him down the main stairway. He paused at the turn and swept one hand towards the wall. 'Plenty room here for your coffin to come down. Seven foot and three men at each end wouldn't brish the paint. If I die in my bed they'll 'ave to up-end me like a milk-can. 'Tis all luck, d'ye see?'

He led them on and on, through a maze of back-kitchens, dairies, larders, and sculleries, that melted along covered ways into a farm-house, visibly older than the main building which again, rambled out among barns, byres, pig-pens, stalls and stables to the dead fields behind.

'Somehow,' said Sophie, sitting exhausted on an ancient well-curb – 'somehow one wouldn't insult these lovely old things by filling them with hay.'

George looked at long stone walls upholding reaches of silvery oak weather-boarding; buttresses of mixed flint and bricks; outside stairs, stone upon arched stone; curves of thatch where grass sprouted; roundels of house-leeked tiles, and a huge paved yard populated by two cows and the repentant Rambler. He had not thought of himself or of the telegraph office for two and a half hours.

'But why,' said Sophie, as they went back through the crater of stricken fields, – 'why is one expected to know everything in England? Why do they never tell?'

'You mean about the Elphicks and the Moones?' he answered.

'Yes – and the lawyers and the estate. Who are they? I wonder whether those painted floors in the green room were real oak. Don't you like us exploring things together – better than Pompeii?'

George turned once more to look at the view. 'Eight hundred acres go with the house – the old man told me. Five farms altogether. Rocketts is one of 'em.'

'I like Mrs Cloke. But what is the old house called?'

George laughed. 'That's one of the things you're expected to know. He never told me.'

The Clokes were more communicative. That evening and thereafter for a week they gave the Chapins the official history, as one gives it to lodgers, of Friars Pardon the house and its five farms. But Sophie asked so many questions, and George was so humanly interested, that, as confidence in the strangers grew, they launched, with observed and acquired detail, into the lives and deaths and doings of the Elphicks and the Moones and their collaterals, the Haylings and the Torrells. It was a tale told serially by Cloke in the barn, or his wife in the dairy, the last chapters reserved for the kitchen o' nights by the big fire, when the two had been half the day exploring about the house, where old Iggulden, of the blue smock, cackled and chuckled to see them. The motives that swayed the characters were beyond their comprehension; the fates that shifted them were gods they had never met; the sidelights Mrs Cloke threw on act and incident were more amazing than anything in the record. Therefore the Chapins listened delightedly, and blessed Mrs Shonts.

'But why – why – *why* – did So-and-so do so-and-so?' Sophie would demand from her seat by the pothook; and Mrs Cloke would answer, smoothing her knees, 'For the sake of the place.'

'I give it up,' said George one night in their own room. 'People don't seem to matter in this country compared to the places they live in. The way *she* tells it, Friars Pardon was a sort of Moloch.'

'Poor old thing!' They had been walking round the farms as usual before tea. 'No wonder they loved it. Think of the sacrifices they made for it. Jane Elphick married the younger

Torrell to keep it in the family. The octagonal room with the moulded ceiling next to the big bedroom was hers. Now what did *he* tell you while he was feeding the pigs?' said Sophie.

'About the Torrell cousins and the uncle who died in Java. They lived at Burnt House – behind High Pardons, where that brook is all blocked up.'

'No; Burnt House is under High Pardons Wood, *before* you come to Gale Anstey,' Sophie corrected.

'Well, old man Cloke said –'

Sophie threw open the door and called down into the kitchen, where the Clokes were covering the fire: 'Mrs Cloke, isn't Burnt House under High Pardons?'

'Yes, my dear, of course, ' the soft voice answered absently. A cough. 'I beg your pardon, madam. What was it you said?'

'Never mind. I prefer it the other way,' Sophie laughed, and George retold the missing chapter as she sat on the bed.

'Here today an' gone tomorrow,' said Cloke warningly. 'They've paid their first month, but we've only that Mrs Shonts' letter for guarantee.'

'None she sent never cheated us yet. It slipped out before I thought. She's a most humane young lady. They'll be going away in a little. An' *you*'ve talked a lot too, Alfred.'

'Yes, but the Elphicks are all dead. No one can bring my loose talking home to me. But why do they stay on and stay on so?'

In due time George and Sophie asked each other that question, and put it aside. They argued that the climate – a pearly blend, unlike the hot and cold ferocities of their native land – suited them, as the thick stillness of the nights certainly suited George. He was saved even the sight of a metalled road, which, as presumably leading to business, wakes desire in a man; and the telegraph office at the village of Friars Pardon, where they sold picture post-cards and peg-tops, was two walking miles across the fields and woods. For all that touched his past among his fellows, or their remembrance of him, he might have been in another planet; and Sophie, whose life had been very largely spent among husbandless wives of lofty ideals, had no wish to leave this present of God. The unhurried meals, the foreknowledge of deliciously empty hours to follow, the breadths of soft sky under which they walked together and reckoned time only by their hunger or thirst; the good grass beneath their feet that cheated the miles; their discoveries, always together, amid the farms – Griffons, Rocketts, Burnt House, Gale Anstey, and the Home Farm, where Iggulden of the blue smock-frock would waylay them, and they would ransack the old house once more; the long wet afternoons when they tucked up their feet on the bedroom's deep window-sill over against the apple-trees, and talked together as never till then had they found time to talk – these things contented her soul, and her body throve.

'Have you realized,' she asked one morning, 'that we've been here absolutely alone for the last thirty-four days?'

'Have you counted them?' he asked.

'Did you like them?' she replied.

'I must have. I didn't think about them. Yes, I have. Six months ago I should have fretted myself sick. Remember at Cairo? I've only had two or three bad times. Am I getting better, or is it senile decay?'

'Climate, all climate,' Sophie swung her new-bought English boots, as she sat on the stile overlooking Friars Pardon, behind the Clokes' barn.

'One must take hold of things, though,' he said, 'if it's only to keep one's hand in.' His eyes did not flicker now as they swept the empty fields. 'Mustn't one?'

'Lay out a Morristown links over Gale Anstey? I dare say you could hire it.'

'No, I'm not as English as that – nor as Morristown. Clokes says all the farms here could be made to pay.'

'Well, I'm Anastasia in the *Treasure of Franchard.* I'm content to be alive and purr. There's no hurry.'

'No.' He smiled. 'All the same, I'm going to see after my mail.'

'You promised you wouldn't have any.'

'There's some business coming through that's amusing me. Honest. It doesn't get on my nerves at all.'

'Want a secretary?'

'No, thanks, old thing! Isn't that quite English?'

'Too English! Go away.' But none the less in broad daylight she returned the kiss. 'I'm off to Pardons. I haven't been to the house for nearly a week.'

'How've you decided to furnish Jane Elphick's bedroom?' he laughed, for it had come to be a permanent Castle in Spain between them.

'Black Chinese furniture and yellow silk brocade,' she answered, and ran downhill. She scattered a few cows at a gap with a flourish of a ground-ash that Iggulden had cut for her a week ago, and, singing as she passed under the holm-oaks, sought the farm-house at the back of Friars Pardon. The old man was not be found, and she knocked at his half-opened door, for she needed him to fill her idle forenoon. A blue-eyed sheep-dog, a new friend, and Rambler's old enemy, crawled out and besought her to enter.

Iggulden sat in his chair by the fire, a thistle-spud between his knees, his head drooped. Though she had never seen death before, her heart, that missed a beat, told her that he was dead. She did not speak or cry, but stood outside the door and the dog licked her hand. When he threw up his nose, she heard herself saying: 'Don't howl! Please don't begin to howl, Scottie, or I shall run away!'

She held her ground while the shadows in the rickyard moved toward noon; sat after a while on the steps by the door, her arms round the dog's neck, waiting till someone should come. She watched the smokeless chimneys of Friars Pardon slash its roofs with shadow, and the smoke of Iggulden's last lighted fire gradually thin and cease. Against her will she fell to wondering how many Moones, Elphicks, and Torrells had been swung round the turn of the broad hall stairs. Then she remembered the old man's talk of being 'up-ended like a milk-can', and buried her face on Scottie's neck. At last a horse's feet clinked upon flags, rustled in the old grey straw of the rickyard, and she found herself facing the Vicar – a figure she had seen at church declaiming impossibilities (Sophie was a Unitarian) in an unnatural voice.

'He's dead,' she said, without preface.

'Old Iggulden? I was coming for a talk with him.' The Vicar passed in uncovered. 'Ah!' she heard him say. 'Heart-failure! How long have you been here?'

'Since a quarter to eleven.' She looked at her watch earnestly and saw that her hand did not shake.

'I'll sit with him now till the doctor comes. D'you think you could tell him, and – yes, Mrs Betts in the cottage with the wistaria next the blacksmith's? I'm afraid this has been rather a shock to you.'

Sophie nodded, and fled towards the village. Her body failed her for a moment; she dropped beneath a hedge, and looked back at the great house. In some fashion its silence and stolidity steadied her for her errand.

Mrs Betts, small, black-eyed and dark, was almost as unconcerned as Friars Pardon.

'Yiss, yiss, of course. Dear me! Well, Iggulden he had had his day in my father's time. Muriel, get me my little blue bag, please. Yiss, ma'am. They come down like ellum-branches in still weather. No warnin' *at* all. Muriel, my bicycle's be'ind the fowl-house. I'll tell Dr Dallas, ma'am.'

She trundled off on her wheel like a brown bee, while Sophie – heaven above and earth beneath changed – walked stiffly home, to fall over George at his letters, in a muddle of laughter and tears.

'It's all quite natural for *them*,' she gasped. ' "They come down like ellum-branches in still weather. Yiss, ma'am." No, there wasn't anything in the least horrible, only – only – Oh, George, that poor shiny stick of his between his poor, thin knees! I couldn't have borne it if Scottie had howled. I didn't know the Vicar was so – so sensitive. He said he was afraid it was ra – rather a shock. Mrs Betts told me to go home, and I wanted to collapse on her floor. But I didn't disgrace myself. I – I couldn't have left him – could I?'

'You're sure you've took no 'arm?' cried Mrs Cloke, who had heard the news by farm-telegraphy, which is older but swifter than Marconi's.

'No. I'm perfectly well,' Sophie protested.

'You lay down till tea-time.' Mrs Cloke patted her shoulder. '*They*'ll be very pleased, though she 'as 'ad no proper understandin' for twenty years.'

'They' came before twilight – a black-bearded man in moleskins, and a little palsied old woman, who chirruped like a wren.

'I'm his son,' said the man to Sophie, among the lavender bushes. 'We 'ad a difference – twenty year back – and didn't speak since. But I'm his son all the same, and we thank you for the watching.'

'I'm only glad I happened to be there,' she answered, and from the bottom of her heart she meant it.

'We heard he spoke a lot o' you – one time an' another since you came. We thank you kindly,' the man added.

'Are you the son that was in America?' she asked.

'Yes, ma'am. On my uncle's farm, in Connecticut. He was what they call road-master there.'

'Whereabouts in Connecticut?' asked George over her shoulder.

'Veering Holler was the name. I was there six year with my uncle.'

'How small the world is!' Sophie cried. 'Why, all my mother's people come from Veering Hollow. There must be some there still – the Lashmars. Did you ever hear of them?'

'I remember hearing that name, seems to me,' he answered, but his face was blank as the back of a spade.

A little before dusk a woman in grey, striding like a foot-soldier, and bearing on her arm a long pole, crashed through the orchard calling for food. George, upon whom the unannounced English worked mysteriously, fled to the parlour; but Mrs Cloke came forward beaming. Sophie could not escape.

'We've only just heard of it,' said the stranger, turning on her. 'I've been out with the otterhounds all day. It was a splendidly sportin' thing – '

'Did you – er – kill?' said Sophie. She knew from books she could not go far wrong here.

'Yes, a dry bitch – seventeen pounds,' was the answer. 'A splendidly sportin' thing of you to do. Poor old Iggulden – '

'Oh – that!' said Sophie, enlightened.

'If there had been any people at Pardons it would never have happened. He'd have been looked after. But what can you expect from a parcel of London solicitors?'

Mrs Cloke murmured something.

'No. I'm soaked from the knees down. If I hang about I shall get chilled. A cup of tea, Mrs Cloke, and I can eat one of your sandwiches as I go.' She wiped her weather-worn face with a green-and-yellow silk handkerchief.

'Yes, my lady!' Mrs Cloke ran and returned swiftly.

'Our land marches with Pardons for a mile on the south,' she explained, waving the full cup, 'but one has quite enough to do with one's own people without poachin'. Still, if I'd known, I'd have sent Dora, of course. Have you seen her this afternoon, Mrs Cloke? No? I wonder whether that girl *did* sprain her ankle. Thank you.' It was a formidable hunk of bread and bacon that Mrs Cloke presented. 'As I was sayin', Pardons is a scandal! Lettin' people die like dogs. There ought to be people there who do their duty. You've done yours, though there wasn't the faintest call upon you. Good night. Tell Dora, if she comes, I've gone on.'

She strode away, munching her crust, and Sophie reeled breathless into the parlour, to shake the shaking George.

'Why did you keep catching my eye behind the blind? Why didn't you come out and do your duty?'

'Because I should have burst. Did you see the mud on its cheek?' he said.

'Once. I daren't look again. Who is she?'

'God. A local deity then. Anyway, she's another of the things you're expected to know by instinct.'

Mrs Cloke, shocked at their levity, told them that it was Lady Conant, wife of Sir Walter Conant, Baronet, a large landholder in the neighbourhood, and if not God, at least His visible Providence.

George made her talk of that family for an hour.

'Laughter,' said Sophie afterwards in their own room, 'is the mark of the savage. Why couldn't you control your emotions? It's all real to *her*.'

'It's all real to *me*. That's my trouble,' he answered in an altered tone. 'Anyway, it's real enough to mark time with. Don't you think so?'

'What d'you mean?' she asked quickly, though she knew his voice.

'That I'm better. I'm well enough to kick.'

'What at?'

'This!' He waved his hand round the one room. 'I must have something to play with till I'm fit for work again.'

'Ah!' She sat on the bed and leaned forward, her hands clasped. 'I wonder if it's good for you.'

'We've been better here than anywhere,' he went on slowly. 'One could always sell it again.'

She nodded gravely, but her eyes sparkled.

'The only thing that worries me is what happened this morning. I want to know how you feel about it. If it's on your nerves in the least we can have the old farm at the back of the house pulled down, or perhaps it has spoiled the notion for you?'

'Pull it down?' she cried. 'You've no business faculty. Why, that's where we could live while we're putting the big house in order. It's almost under the same roof. No! What happened this morning seemed to be more of – of a leading than anything else. There *ought* to be people at Pardons. Lady Conant's quite right.'

'I was thinking more of the woods and the roads. I could double the value of the place in six months.'

'What do they want for it?' She shook her head, and her loosened hair fell glowingly about her cheeks.

'Seventy-five thousand dollars. They'll take sixty-eight.'

'Less than half what we paid for our old yacht when we married. And we didn't have a good time in her. You were –'

'Well, I discovered I was too much of an American to be content to be a rich man's son. You aren't blaming me for that?'

'Oh no. Only it was a very businesslike honeymoon. How far are you along with the deal, George?'

'I can mail the deposit on the purchase money tomorrow morning, and we can have the thing completed in a fortnight or three weeks – if you say so.'

'Friars Pardon – Friars Pardon!' Sophie chanted rapturously, her dark-grey eyes big with delight. 'All the farms? Gale Anstey, Burnt House, Rocketts, the Home Farm, and Griffons? Sure you've got 'em all?'

'Sure.' He smiled.

'And the woods? High Pardons Wood, Lower Pardons, Suttons, Dutton's Shaw, Reuben's Ghyll, Maxey's Ghyll, and both the Oak Hangers? Sure you've got 'em all?'

'Every last stick. Why, you know them as well as I do.' He laughed. 'They say there's five thousand – a thousand pounds' worth of lumber – timber they call it – in the Hangers alone.'

'Mrs Cloke's oven must be mended first thing, *and* the kitchen roof. I think I'll have all this whitewashed.' Sophie broke in, pointing to the ceiling. 'The whole place is a scandal. Lady Conant is quite right. George, when did you begin to fall in love with the house? In the green room – that first day? I did.'

'I'm not in love with it. One must do something to mark time till one's fit for work.'

'Or when we stood under the oaks, and the door opened? Oh! Ought I to go to poor Iggulden's funeral?' She sighed with utter happiness.

'Wouldn't they call it a liberty – *now*?' said he.

'But I liked him.'

'But you didn't own him at the date of his death.'

'That wouldn't keep me away. Only, they made such a fuss about the watching' – she caught her breath – 'it might be ostentatious from that point of view, too. Oh, George,' – she reached for his hand – 'we're two little orphans moving in worlds not realized, and we shall make some bad breaks. But we're going to have the time of our lives.'

'We'll run up to London tomorrow and see if we can hurry those English law-solicitors. I want to get to work.'

They went. They suffered many things ere they returned across the fields in a fly one Saturday night, nursing a two by two-and-a-half box of deeds and maps – lawful owners of Friars Pardon and the five decayed farms therewith.

'I do most sincerely 'ope and trust you'll be 'appy, madam,' Mrs Cloke gasped, when she was told the news by the kitchen fire.

'Goodness! It isn't a marriage!' Sophie exclaimed, a little awed; for to them the joke, which to an American means work, was only just beginning.

'If it's took in a proper spirit' – Mrs Cloke's eye turned towards her oven.

'Send and have that mended tomorrow,' Sophie whispered.

'We couldn't 'elp noticing,' said Cloke slowly, 'from the times you walked there, that you an' your lady was drawn to it, but – but I don't know as we ever precisely thought – ' His wife's glance checked him.

'That we were that sort of people,' said George. 'We aren't sure of it ourselves yet.'

'Perhaps,' said Cloke, rubbing his knees, just for the sake of saying something, 'perhaps you'll park it?'

'What's that?' said George.

'Turn it all into a fine park like Violet Hill' – he jerked a thumb to westward – 'that Mr Sangres bought. It was four farms, and Mr Sangres made a fine park of them, with a herd of faller deer.'

'Then it wouldn't be Friars Pardon,' said Sophie. 'Would it?'

'I don't know as I've ever heard Pardons was ever anything but wheat an' wool. Only some gentlemen say that parks are less trouble than tenants.' He laughed nervously. 'But the gentry, o' course, they keep on pretty much as they was used to.'

'I see,' said Sophie. 'How did Mr Sangres make his money?'

'I never rightly heard. It was pepper an' spices, or it may ha' been gloves. No. Gloves was Sir Reginald Liss at Marley End. Spices was Mr Sangres. He's a Brazilian gentleman – very sunburnt, like.'

'Be sure o' one thing. You won't 'ave any trouble,' said Mrs Cloke, just before they went to bed.

Now the news of the purchase was told to Mr and Mrs Cloke alone at 8 p.m. of a Saturday. None left the farm till they set out for church next morning. Yet when they reached the church and were about to slip aside into their usual seats, a little beyond the font, where they could see the red-furred tails of the bell-ropes waggle and twist at ringing-time, they were swept forward irresistibly, a Cloke on either flank (and yet they had not walked with the Clokes), upon the ever-retiring bosom of a black-gowned verger, who ushered them into a room of a pew at the head of the left aisle, under the pulpit.

'This,' he sighed reproachfully, 'is the Pardons' Pew,' and shut them in.

They could see little more than the choir-boys in the chancel, but to the roots of the hair of their necks they felt the congregation behind mercilessly devouring them by look.

'*When the wicked man turneth away.*' The strong alien voice of the priest vibrated under the hammer-beam roof, and a loneliness unfelt before swamped their hearts, as they searched for places in the unfamiliar Church of England service. The Lord's Prayer – 'Our Father, *which* art' – set the seal on that desolation. Sophie found herself thinking how in other lands their purchase would long ere this have been discussed from every point of view in a dozen prints, forgetting that George for months had not been allowed to glance at those black and bellowing head-lines. Here was nothing but silence – not even hostility! The game was up to them. The other players hid their cards and waited. Suspense, she felt, was in the air, and when her sight cleared, she saw indeed a mural tablet of a footless bird brooding upon the carven motto, 'Wayte awhyle – wayte awhyle.'

At the Litany George had trouble with an unstable hassock, and drew the slip of carpet under the pew-seat. Sophie pushed her end back also, and shut her eyes against a burning that felt like tears. When she opened them she was looking at her mother's maiden name, fairly carved on a blue flagstone on the pew floor:

Ellen Lashmar. ob. 1796. aetat. 27.

She nudged George and pointed. Sheltered, as they kneeled, they looked for more knowledge, but the rest of the slab was blank.

'Ever hear of her?' he whispered.

'Never knew any of us came from here.'

'Coincidence?'

'Perhaps. But it makes me feel better,' and she smiled and winked away a tear on her lashes, and took his hand while they prayed for 'all women labouring of child' – not 'in the perils of childbirth'; and the sparrows who had found their way through the guards behind the stained-glass windows chirped above the faded gilt-and-alabaster family tree of the Conants.

The baronet's pew was on the right of the aisle. After service its inhabitants moved forth without haste, but so as to effectively block a dusky person with a large family who champed in their rear.

'Spices, I think,' said Sophie, deeply delighted as the Sangres closed up after the Conants. 'Let 'em get away, George.'

But when they came out many folk whose eyes were one still lingered by the lych-gate.

'I want to see if any more Lashmars are buried here,' said Sophie.

'Not now. This seems to be show day. Come home quickly,' he replied.

A group of families, the Clokes a little apart, opened to let them through. The men saluted with jerky nods, the women with remnants of a curtsey. Only Iggulden's son, his mother on his arm, lifted his hat as Sophie passed.

'Your people?' said the clear voice of Lady Conant in her ear.

'I suppose so,' said Sophie, blushing, for they were within two yards of her; but it was not a question.

'Then that child looks as if it were coming down with mumps. You ought to tell the mother she shouldn't have brought it to church.'

'I can't leave 'er be'ind, my lady,' the woman said. 'She'd set the 'ouse afire in a minute, she's that forward with the matches. Ain't you, Maudie dear?'

'Has Dr Dallas seen her?'

'Not yet, my lady.'

'He must. You can't get away, of course. M – m! My idiotic maid is coming in for her teeth tomorrow at twelve. She shall pick her up – at Gale Anstey, isn't it? – at eleven.'

'Yes. Thank you very much, my lady.'

'I oughtn't to have done it,' said Lady Conant apologetically, 'but there has been no one at Pardons for so long that you'll forgive my poachin'. Now, can't you lunch with us? The Vicar usually comes too. I don't use the horses on a Sunday,' – she glanced at the Brazilian's silver-plated chariot. 'It's only a mile across the fields.'

'You – you're very kind,' said Sophie, hating herself because her lip trembled.

'My dear' – the compelling tone dropped to a soothing

gurgle – 'd'you suppose I don't know how it feels to come to a strange county – country, I should say – away from one's own people? When I first left the Shires – I'm Shropshire, you know – I cried for a day and a night. But fretting doesn't make loneliness any better. Oh, here's Dora. She *did* sprain her leg that day.'

'I'm as lame as a tree still,' said the tall maiden frankly. 'You ought to go out with the otter-hounds, Mrs Chapin. I believe they're drawing your water next week.'

Sir Walter had already led off George, and the Vicar came up on the other side of Sophie. There was no escaping the swift procession or the leisurely lunch, where talk came and went in low-voiçed eddies that had the village for their centre. Sophie heard the Vicar and Sir Walter address her husband lightly as Chapin! (She also remembered many women known in a previous life who habitually addressed their husbands as Mr Such-an-one.) After lunch Lady Conant talked to her explicitly of maternity as that is achieved in cottages and farm-houses remote from aid, and of the duty thereto of the mistress of Pardons.

A gate in a beech hedge, reached across triple lawns, let them out before tea-time into the unkempt south side of their land.

'I want your hand, please,' said Sophie as soon as they were safe among the beech-boles and the lawless hollies. 'D'you remember the old maid in *Providence and the Guitar* who heard the Commissary swear, and hardly reckoned herself a maiden lady afterwards? Because I'm a relative of hers. Lady Conant is – '

'Did you find out anything about the Lashmars?' he interrupted.

'I didn't ask. I'm going to write to Aunt Sydney about it first. Oh, Lady Conant said something at lunch about their having bought some land from some Lashmars a few years ago. I found it was at the beginning of last century.'

'What did you say?'

'I said, "Really, how interesting!" Like that. I'm not going to push myself forward. I've been hearing about Mr Sangres' efforts in that direction. And you? I couldn't see you behind the flowers. Was it very deep water, dear?'

George mopped a brow already browned by outdoor exposure.

'Oh no – dead easy,' he answered. 'I've bought Friars Pardon to prevent Sir Walter's birds straying.'

A cock pheasant scuttered through the dry leaves and exploded almost under their feet. Sophie jumped.

'That's one of 'em,' said George calmly.

'Well, your nerves are better, at any rate,' she said. 'Did you tell 'em you'd bought the thing to play with?'

'No. That was where my nerve broke down. I only made one bad break – I think. I said I couldn't see why hiring land to men to farm wasn't as much a business proposition as anything else.'

'And what did they say?'

'They smiled. I shall know what that smile means some day. They don't waste their smiles. D'you see that track by Gale Anstey?'

They looked down from the edge of the hanger over a cup-like hollow. People by twos and threes in their Sunday best filed slowly along the paths that connected farm to farm.

'I've never seen so many on our land before,' said Sophie. 'Why is it?'

'To show us we mustn't shut up their rights of way.'

'Those cow-tracks we've been using cross-lots?' said Sophie forcibly.

'Yes. Any one of 'em would cost us two thousand pounds each in legal expenses to close.'

'But we don't want to,' she said.

'The whole community would fight if we did.'

'But it's our land. We can do what we like.'

'It's *not* our land. We've only paid for it. We belong to it, and it belongs to the people – our people, they call 'em. *I've* been to lunch with the English too.'

They passed slowly from one bracken-dotted field to the

next – flushed with pride of ownership, plotting alterations and restorations at each turn; halting in their tracks to argue, spreading apart to embrace two views at once, or closing to consider one. Couples moved out of their way, but smiling covertly.

'We shall make some bad breaks,' he said at last.

'Together, though. You won't let anyone else in, will you?'

'Except the contractors. This syndicate handles this proposition by its little lone.'

'But you might feel the want of someone,' she insisted.

'I shall – but it will be you. It's business, Sophie, but it's going to be good fun.'

'Please God,' she answered, flushing, and cried to herself as they went back to tea. 'It's worth it. Oh, it's worth it.'

The repairing and moving into Friars Pardon was business of the most varied and searching, but all done English-fashion, without friction. Time and money alone were asked. The rest lay in the hands of beneficent advisers from London, or spirits, male and female, called up by Mr and Mrs Cloke from the wastes of the farms. In the centre stood George and Sophie, a little aghast, their interests reaching out on every side.

'I ain't sayin' anything against Londoners,' said Cloke, self-appointed Clerk of the outer works, consulting engineer, head of the immigration bureau, and superintendent of Woods and Forests; 'but your own people won't go about to make more than a fair profit out of you.'

'How is one to know?' said George.

'Five years from now, or so on, maybe, you'll be lookin' over your first year's accounts, and, knowin' what you'll know then, you'll say: "Well, Billy Beartup" – or Old Cloke as it might be – "did me proper when I was new." No man likes to have that sort of thing laid up against him.'

'I think I see,' said George. 'But five years is a long time to look ahead.'

'I doubt if that oak Billy Beartup throwed in Reuben's

Ghyll will be fit for her drawin'-room floor in less than seven,' Cloke drawled.

'Yes, that's *my* work,' said Sophie. (Billy Beartup of Griffons, a woodman by training and birth, a tenant farmer by misfortune of marriage, had laid his broad axe at her feet a month before.) 'Sorry if I've committed you to another eternity.'

'And we shan't even know where we've gone wrong with *your* new carriage-drive before that time either,' said Cloke, ever anxious to keep the balance true – with an ounce or two in Sophie's favour. The past four months had taught George better than to reply. The carriage-road winding up the hill was his present keen interest. They set off to look at it and the imported American scraper, which had blighted the none too sunny soul of 'Skim' Winsh, the carter. But young Iggulden was in charge now, and under his guidance Buller and Roberts, the great horses, moved mountains.

'You lif' her like that, an' you tip her like that,' he explained to the gang. 'My uncle he was road-master in Connecticut.'

'Are they roads yonder?' said Skim, sitting under the laurels.

'No better than accommodation-roads. Dirt, they call 'em. They'd suit you, Skim.'

'Why?' said the incautious Skim.

' 'Cause you'd take no hurt when you fall out of your cart drunk on a Saturday,' was the answer.

'I didn't last time neither,' Skim roared.

After a loud laugh, old Whybarne of Gale Anstey piped feebly, 'Well, dirt or no dirt, there's no denyin' Chapin knows a good job when he sees it. 'E don't build one day and deestroy the next, like that nigger Sangres.'

'*She*'s the one that knows her own mind,' said Pinky, brother to Skim Winsh, and a Napoleon among carters who had helped to bring the grand piano across the fields in the autumn rains.

'She had ought to,' said Iggulden. 'Whoa, Buller! She's a Lashmar. They never was double-thinking.'

'Oh, you found that? Has the answer come from your uncle?' said Skim, doubtful whether so remote a land as America had posts.

The others looked at him scornfully. Skim was always a day behind the fair.

Iggulden rested from his labours. 'She's a Lashmar right enough. I started up to write to my uncle at once – the month after she said her folks came from Veerin' Holler.'

'Where there ain't any roads?' Skim interrupted, but none laughed.

'My uncle he married an American woman for his second, and she took it up like a – like the coroner. She's a Lashmar out of the old Lashmar place, 'fore they sold to Conants. She ain't no Toot Hill Lashmar, nor any o' the Crayford lot. Her folk come out of the ground here, neither Chalk nor Forest, but Wildishers. They sailed over to America – I've got it all writ down by my uncle's woman – in eighteen hundred an' nothing. My uncle says they're all slow begetters, like.'

'Would they be gentry yonder now?' Skim asked.

'Nah – there's no gentry in America, no matter how long you're there. It's against their law. There's only rich and poor allowed. They've been lawyers and such-like over yonder for a hundred years – but she's a Lashmar for all that.'

'Lord! What's a hundred years?' said Whybarne, who had seen seventy-eight of them.

'An' they write too, from yonder – my uncle's woman writes – that you can still tell 'em by headmark. Their hair's foxy-red still – an' they throw out when they walk. *He*'s in-toed – treads like a gipsy; but you watch, an' you'll see 'er throw out – like a colt.'

'Your trace wants taking up.' Pinky's large ears had caught the sounds of voices, and as the two broke through the laurel the men were hard at work, their eyes on Sophie's feet.

She had been less fortunate in her inquiries than Iggulden, for her Aunt Sydney of Meriden (a badged and certificated Daughter of the Revolution to boot) answered her inquiries with a two-paged discourse on patriotism, the leaflets of a Village Improvement Society, of which she was president, and a demand for an overdue subscription to a Factory Girls' Reading Circle. Sophie burned it all in the Orpheus and Eurydice grate, and kept her own counsel.

'What *I* want to know,' said George, when spring was coming, and the gardens needed thought, 'is who will ever pay me for my labour? I've put in at least half a million dollars' worth already.'

'Sure you're not taking too much out of yourself?' his wife asked.

'Oh no; I haven't been conscious of myself all winter.' He looked at his brown English gaiters and smiled. 'It's all behind me now. I believe I could sit down and think of all that – those months before we sailed.'

'Don't – ah, don't!' she cried.

'But I must go back one day. You don't want to keep me out of business always – or do you?' He ended with a nervous laugh.

Sophie sighed as she drew her own ground-ash (of old Iggulden's cutting) from the hall rack.

'Aren't you overdoing it too? You look a little tired,' he said.

'You make me tired. I'm going to Rocketts to see Mrs Cloke about Mary.' (This was the sister of the telegraphist, promoted to be sewing-maid at Pardons.) 'Coming?'

'I'm due at Burnt House to see about the new well. By the way, there's a sore throat at Gale Anstey – '

'That's *my* province. Don't interfere. The Whybarne children always have sore throats. They do it for jujubes.'

'Keep away from Gale Anstey till I make sure, honey. Cloke ought to have told me.'

'These people don't tell. Haven't you learnt that yet? But I'll obey, me lord. See you later!'

She set off afoot, for within the three main roads that bounded the blunt triangle of the estate (even by night one could scarcely hear the carts on them), wheels were not used except for farm work. The footpaths served all other purposes. And though at first they had planned improvements, they had soon fallen in with the customs of their hidden kingdom, and moved about the soft-footed ways by woodland, hedgerow, and shaw as freely as the rabbits. Indeed, for the most part Sophie walked bareheaded beneath her helmet of chestnut hair; but she had been plagued of late by vague toothaches, which she explained to Mrs Cloke, who asked some questions. How it came about Sophie never knew, but after a while behold Mrs Cloke's arm was about her waist, and her head was on that deep bosom behind the shut kitchen door.

'My dear! my dear!' the elder woman almost sobbed. 'An' d'you mean to tell me you never suspicioned? Why – why – where *was* you ever taught anything at all? Of *course* it is. It's what we've been only waitin' for, all of us. Time and again I've said to Lady – ' She checked herself. 'An' now we shall be as we should be.'

'But – but – but – ' Sophie whimpered.

'An' to see you buildin' your nest so busy – pianos and books – an' never thinkin' of a nursery !'

'No more I did.' Sophie sat bolt upright, and began to laugh.

'Time enough yet.' The fingers tapped thoughtfully on the broad knee. 'But – they must be strange-minded folk over yonder with you! Have you thought to send for your mother? She dead? My dear, my dear! Never mind! She'll be happy where she knows. 'Tis God's work. An' we was only waitin' for it, for you've never failed in your duty yet. It ain't your way. *What* did you say about my Mary's doings?' Mrs Cloke's face hardened as she pressed her chin on Sophie's forehead. 'If any of your girls thinks to be'ave arbitrary now, I'll – But they won't, my dear. I'll see they do their duty too. Be sure you'll 'ave no trouble.'

When Sophie walked back across the fields, heaven and earth changed about her as on the day of old Iggulden's death. For an instant she thought of the wide turn of the staircase, and the new ivory-white paint that no coffin-corner could scar, but presently the shadow passed in a pure wonder and bewilderment that made her reel. She leaned against one of their new gates and looked over their lands for some other stay.

'Well,' she said resignedly, half aloud, 'we must try to make him feel that he isn't a third in our party,' and turned the corner that looked over Friars Pardon, giddy, sick, and faint.

Of a sudden the house they had bought for a whim stood up as she had never seen it before, low-fronted, broad-winged, ample, prepared by course of generations for all such things. As it had steadied her when it lay desolate, so now that it had meaning from their few months of life within, it soothed and promised good. She went alone and quickly into the hall, and kissed either door-post, whispering: 'Be good to me. *You* know! You've never failed in your duty yet.'

When the matter was explained to George, he would have sailed at once to their own land, but this Sophie forbade.

'I don't want science,' she said. 'I just want to be loved, and there isn't time for that at home. Besides,' she added, looking out of the window, 'it would be desertion.'

George was forced to soothe himself with linking Friars Pardon to the telegraph system of Great Britain by telephone – three-quarters of a mile of poles, put in by Whybarne and a few friends. One of these was a foreigner from the next parish. Said he when the line was being run: 'There's an old ellum right in our road. Shall us throw her?'

'Toot Hill parish folk, neither grace nor good luck, God help 'em.' Old Whybarne shouted the local proverb from three poles down the line. '*We* ain't goin' to lay any axe-iron to coffin-wood here – not till we know where we are yet awhile. Swing round 'er, swing round!'

To this day, then, that sudden kink in the straight line across the upper pasture remains a mystery to Sophie and

George. Nor can they tell why Skim Winsh, who came to his cottage under Dutton Shaw most musically drunk at 10.45 p.m. of every Saturday night, as his father had done before him, sang no more at the bottom of the garden steps, where Sophie always feared he would break his neck. The path was undoubtedly an ancient right of way, and at 10.45 p.m. on Saturdays Skim remembered it was his duty to posterity to keep it open – till Mrs Cloke spoke to him – once. She spoke likewise to her daughter Mary, sewing-maid at Pardons, and to Mary's best new friend, the five-foot-seven imported London house-maid, who taught Mary to trim hats, and found the country dullish.

But there was no noise – at no time was there any noise – and when Sophie walked abroad she met no one in her path unless she had signified a wish that way. Then they appeared to protest that all was well with them and their children, their chickens, their roofs, their water-supply, and their sons in the Police or the railway service.

'But don't you find it dull, dear?' said George, loyally doing his best not to worry as the months went by.

'I've been so busy putting my house in order I haven't had time to think,' said she. 'Do you?'

'No – no. If I could only be sure of *you.*'

She turned on the green drawing-room's couch (it was Empire, not Hepplewhite after all), and laid aside a list of linen and blankets.

'It has changed everything, hasn't it?' she whispered.

'Oh Lord, yes. But I still think if we went back to Baltimore – '

'And missed our first real summer together. No, thank you, me lord.'

'But we're absolutely alone.'

'Isn't that what I'm doing my best to remedy? Don't you worry. I like it – like it to the marrow of my little bones. You don't realize what her house means to a woman. We thought we were living in it last year, but we hadn't begun to. Don't you rejoice in your study, George?'

'I prefer being here with you.' He sat down on the floor by the couch and took her hand.

'Seven,' she said as the French clock struck. 'Year before last you'd just be coming back from business.'

He winced at the recollection, then laughed. 'Business! I've been at work ten solid hours today.'

'Where did you lunch? With the Conants?'

'No; at Dutton Shaw, sitting on a log, with my feet in a swamp. But we've found out where the old spring is, and we're going to pipe it down to Gale Anstey next year.'

'I'll come and see tomorrow. Oh, please open the door, dear. I want to look down the passage. Isn't that corner by the stair-head lovely where the sun strikes in?' She looked through half-closed eyes at the vista of ivory-white and pale green all steeped in liquid gold.

'There's a step out of Jane Elphick's bedroom,' she went on – 'and *his* first step in the world ought to be up. I shouldn't wonder if those people hadn't put it there on purpose. George, will it make any odds to you if he's a girl?'

He answered, as he had many times before, that his interest was his wife, not the child.

'Then you're the only person who thinks so.' She laughed. 'Don't be silly, dear. It's expected. *I* know. It's my duty. I shan't be able to look our people in the face if I fail.'

'What concern is it of theirs, confound 'em!'

'You'll see. Luckily the tradition of the house is boys, Mrs Cloke says, so I'm provided for. Shall you ever begin to understand these people? I shan't.'

'And we bought it for fun – for fun?' He groaned. 'And here we are held up for goodness knows how long!'

'Why? Were you thinking of selling it?' He did not answer. 'Do you remember the second Mrs Chapin?' she demanded.

This was a bold, brazen little black-browed woman – a widow for choice – who on Sophie's death was guilefully to marry George for his wealth and ruin him in a year. George being busy, Sophie had invented her some two years after her marriage, and conceived she was alone among wives in so doing.

'You aren't going to bring *her* up again?' he asked anxiously.

'I only want to say that I should hate anyone who bought Pardons ten times worse than I used to hate the second Mrs Chapin. Think what we've put into it of our two selves.'

'At least a couple of million dollars. I know I could have made – ' He broke off.

'The beasts!' she went on. 'They'd be sure to build a red-brick lodge at the gates, and cut the lawn up for bedding out. You must leave instructions in your will that *he*'s never to do that, George, won't you?'

He laughed and took her hand again but said nothing till it was time to dress. Then he muttered: 'What the devil use is a man's country to him when he can't do business in it?'

Friars Pardon stood faithful to its tradition. At the appointed time was born, not that third in their party to whom Sophie meant to be so kind, but a godling; in beauty, it was manifest, excelling Eros, as in wisdom Confucius; an enhancer of delights, a renewer of companionships and an interpreter of Destiny. This last George did not realize till he met Lady Conant striding through Dutton Shaw a few days after the event.

'My dear fellow,' she cried, and slapped him heartily on the back, 'I can't tell you how glad we all are. – Oh, *she*'ll be all right. (There's never been any trouble over the birth of an heir at Pardons.) Now where the dooce is it?' She felt largely in her leather-bound skirt and drew out a small silver mug. 'I sent a note to your wife about it, but my silly ass of a groom forgot to take this. You can save me a tramp. Give her my love.' She marched off amid her guard of grave Airedales.

The mug was worn and dented: above the twined initials, G. L., was the crest of a footless bird and the motto: 'Wayte awhyle – wayte awhyle'.

'That's the other end of the riddle,' Sophie whispered,

when he saw her that evening. 'Read her note. The English write beautiful notes.'

> The warmest of welcomes to your little man. I hope he will appreciate his native land now he has come to it. Though you have said nothing we cannot, of course, look on him as a little stranger, and so I am sending him the old Lashmar christening mug. It has been with us since Gregory Lashmar, your great-grandmother's brother –

George stared at his wife.

'Go on,' she twinkled from the pillows.

> – mother's brother, sold his place to Walter's family. We seem to have acquired some of your household goods at that time, but nothing survives except the mug and the old cradle, which I found in the potting-shed and am having put in order for you. I hope little George – Lashmar, he will be too, won't he? – will live to see his grandchildren cut their teeth on his mug.
>
> Affectionately yours,
>
> ALICE CONANT.
>
> P.S. – How quiet you've kept about it all!

'Well, I'm – '

'Don't swear,' said Sophie. 'Bad for the infant mind.'

'But how in the world did she get at it? Have you ever said a word about the Lashmars?'

'You know the only time – to young Iggulden at Rocketts – when Iggulden died.'

'Your great-grandmother's brother! She's traced the whole connection. More than your Aunt Sydney could do. What does she mean about our keeping quiet?'

Sophie's eyes sparkled. 'I've thought that out too. We've got back at the English at last. Can't you see that *she* thought that *we* thought my mother's being a Lashmar was one of those things we'd expect the English to find out for themselves, and that's impressed her?' She turned the mug in her white hands, and sighed happily. ' "Wayte awhyle –

wayte awhyle." That's not a bad motto, George. It's been worth it.'

'But still I don't quite see – '

'I shouldn't wonder if they don't think our coming here was part of a deep-laid scheme to be near our ancestors. *They*'d understand that. And look how they've accepted us, all of them.'

'Are we so undesirable in ourselves?' George grunted.

'Be just, me lord. That wretched Sangres man has twice our money. Can you see Marm Conant slapping him between the shoulders? Not by a jugful! The poor beast doesn't exist!'

'Do you think it's that then?' He looked towards the cot by the fire where the godling snorted.

'The minute I get well I shall find out from Mrs Cloke what every Lashmar gives in doles (that's nicer than tips) every time a Lashmite is born. I've done my duty thus far, but there's much expected of me.'

Entered here Mrs Cloke, and hung worshipping over the cot. They showed her the mug and her face shone. 'Oh, now Lady Conant's sent it, it'll be all proper, ma'am, won't it? "George" of course he'd have to be, but seein' what he is we was hopin' – all your people was hopin' – it 'ud be "Lashmar" too, and that 'ud just round it out. A very 'andsome mug – quite unique, I should imagine. "Wayte awhyle – wayte awhyle." That's true with the Lashmars, I've heard. Very slow to fill their houses, they are. Most like Master George won't open 'is nursery till he's thirty.'

'Poor lamb!' cried Sophie. 'But how did you know my folk were Lashmars?'

Mrs Cloke thought deeply. 'I'm sure I can't quite say, ma'am, but I've a belief likely that it was something you may have let drop to young Iggulden when you was at Rocketts. That *may* have been what give us an inkling. An' so it came out, one thing in the way o' talk leading to another, and those American people at Veering Holler was very obligin' with news, I'm told, ma'am.'

'Great Scott!' said George, under his breath. 'And this is the simple peasant!'

'Yiss,' Mrs Cloke went on. 'An' Cloke was only wonderin' this afternoon – your pillow's slipped, my dear, you mustn't lie that a-way – just for the sake o' sayin' something, whether you wouldn't think well now of getting the Lashmar farms back, sir. They don't rightly round off Sir Walter's estate. They come caterin' across us more. Cloke, 'e 'ud be glad to show you over any day.'

'But Sir Walter doesn't want to sell, does he?'

'We can find out from his bailiff, sir, but' – with cold contempt – 'I think that trained nurse is just comin' up from her dinner, so I'm afraid we'll 'ave to ask you, sir. . . . Now, Master George – Ai-ie! Wake a litty-minute, lammie!'

A few months later the three of them were down at the brook in the Gale Anstey woods to consider the rebuilding of a footbridge carried away by spring floods. George Lashmar wanted all the bluebells on God's earth that day to eat, and Sophie adored him in a voice like to the cooing of a dove; so business was delayed.

'Here's the place,' said his father at last among the water forget-me-nots. 'But where the deuce are the larch-poles, Cloke? I told you to have them down here ready.'

'We'll get 'em down *if* you say so,' Cloke answered, with a thrust of the underlip they both knew.

'But I *did* say so. What on earth have you brought that timber-tug here for? We aren't building a railway bridge. Why, in America, half-a-dozen two-by-four bits would be ample.'

'I don't know nothin' about that,' said Cloke. 'An' I've nothin' to say against larch – *if* you want to make a temp'ry job of it. I ain't 'ere to tell you what isn't so, sir; an' you can't say I ever come creepin' up on you, or tryin' to lead you farther in than you set out –'

A year ago George would have danced with impatience.

Now he scraped a little mud off his old gaiters with his spud, and waited.

'All I say is that you can put up larch and make a temp'ry job of it; and by the time the young master's married it'll have to be done again. Now, I've brought down a couple of as sweet six-by-eight oak timbers as we've ever drawed. You put 'em in an' it's off your mind for good an' all. T'other way – I don't say it ain't right, I'm only just sayin' what I think – but t'other way, he'll no sooner be married than we'll 'ave it *all* to do again. You've no call to regard my words, but you can't get out of *that*.'

'No,' said George after a pause; 'I've been realizing that for some time. Make it oak then. We can't get out of it.'

The Mother Hive

(1908)

If the stock had not been old and overcrowded, the Wax-moth would never have entered; but where bees are too thick on the comb there must be sickness or parasites. The heat of the hive had risen with the June honey-flow, and though the fanners worked until their wings ached, to keep people cool, everybody suffered.

A young bee crawled up the greasy, trampled alighting-board. 'Excuse me,' she began, 'but it's my first honey-flight. Could you kindly tell me if this is my –'

' – own hive?' the Guard snapped. 'Yes! Buzz in, and be foul-brooded to you! Next!'

'Shame!' cried half-a-dozen old workers with worn wings and nerves, and there was a scuffle and a hum.

The little grey Wax-moth, pressed close in a crack in the alighting-board, had waited this chance all day. She scuttled in like a ghost, and, knowing the senior bees would turn her out at once, dodged into a brood-frame, where youngsters who had not yet seen the winds blow or the flowers nod discussed life. Here she was safe, for young bees will tolerate any sort of stranger. Behind her came the bee who had been slanged by the Guard.

'What is the world like, Melissa?' said a companion.

'Cruel! I brought in a full load of first-class stuff, and the Guard told me to go and be foul-brooded!' She sat down in the cool draught across the combs.

'If you'd only heard,' said the Wax-moth silkily, 'the insolence of the Guard's tone when she cursed our sister! It aroused the Entire Community.' She laid an egg. She had stolen in for that purpose.

'There *was* a bit of a fuss on the Gate,' Melissa chuckled. 'You were there, Miss – ?'

She did not know how to address the slim stranger.

'Don't call me "Miss". I'm a sister to all in affliction – just a working sister. My heart bled for you beneath your burden.' The Wax-moth caressed Melissa with her soft feelers and laid another egg.

'You mustn't lay here,' cried Melissa. 'You aren't a Queen.'

'My dear child, I give you my most solemn word of honour those aren't eggs. Those are my principles, and I am ready to die for them.' She raised her voice a little above the rustle and tramp round her. 'If you'd like to kill me, pray do.'

'Don't be unkind, Melissa,' said a young bee, impressed by the chaste folds of the Wax-moth's wing, which hid her ceaseless egg-dropping.

'*I* haven't done anything,' Melissa answered. 'She's doing it all.'

'Ah, don't let your conscience reproach you later, but when you've killed me, write me, at least, as one that loved her fellow-workers.'

Laying at every sob, the Wax-moth backed into a crowd of young bees, and left Melissa bewildered and annoyed. So she lifted up her little voice in the darkness and cried, 'Stores!' till a gang of cell-fillers hailed her, and she left her load with them.

'I'm afraid I foul-brooded you just now,' said a voice over her shoulder. 'I'd been on the Gate for three hours, and one would foul-brood the Queen herself after that. No offence meant.'

'None taken,' Melissa answered cheerily. 'I shall be on guard myself, some day. What's next to do?'

'There's a rumour of Death's Head Moths about. Send a gang of youngsters to the Gate, and tell them to narrow it in with a couple of stout scrap-wax pillars. It'll make the Hive hot, but we can't have Death's Headers in the middle of the honey-flow.'

'My Only Wings! I should think not!' Melissa had all a sound bee's hereditary hatred against the big, squeaking, feathery Thief of the Hives. 'Tumble out!' she called across the youngsters' quarters. 'All you who aren't feeding babies, show a leg. Scrap-wax pillars for the Ga-ate!' She chanted the order at length.

'That's nonsense,' a downy, day-old bee answered. 'In the first place, *I* never heard of a Death's Header coming into a hive. People don't *do* such things. In the second, building pillars to keep 'em out is purely a Cypriote trick, unworthy of British bees. In the third, if you trust a Death's Head, he will trust you. Pillar-building shows lack of confidence. Our dear sister in grey says so.'

'Yes. Pillars are un-English and provocative, and a waste of wax that is needed for higher and more practical ends,' said the Wax-moth from an empty store-cell.

'The safety of the Hive is the highest thing I've ever heard of. You mustn't teach us to refuse work,' Melissa began.

'You misunderstand me as usual, love. Work's the essence of life; but to expend precious unreturning vitality and real labour against imaginary danger, *that* is heartbreakingly absurd! If I can only teach a – a little toleration – a little ordinary kindness here towards that absurd old bogey you call the Death's Header, I shan't have lived in vain.'

'She *hasn't* lived in vain, the darling!' cried twenty bees together. 'You should see her saintly life, Melissa! She just devotes herself to spreading her principles, and – and – she looks lovely!'

An old, baldish bee came up the comb.

'Pillar-workers for the Gate! Get out and chew scraps. Buzz off!' she said. The Wax-moth slipped aside.

The young bees trooped down the frame, whispering.

'What's the matter with 'em?' said the oldster. 'Why do they call each other "ducky" and "darling"? Must be the weather.' She sniffed suspiciously. 'Horrid stuffy smell here. Like stale quilts. Not Wax-moth, I hope, Melissa?'

'Not to my knowledge,' said Melissa, who, of course, only knew the Wax-moth as a lady with principles, and had never thought to report her presence. She had always imagined Wax-moths to be like blood-red dragon-flies.

'You had better fan out this corner for a little,' said the old bee and passed on. Melissa dropped her head at once, took firm hold with her fore-feet, and fanned obediently at the regulation stroke – three-hundred beats to the second. Fanning tries a bee's temper, because she must always keep in the same place where she never seems to be doing any good, and, all the while, she is wearing out her only wings. When a bee cannot fly, a bee must not live; and a bee knows it. The Wax-moth crept forth, and caressed Melissa again.

'I see,' she murmured, 'that at heart you are one of Us.'

'I work with the Hive,' Melissa answered briefly.

'It's the same thing. We and the Hive are one.'

'Then why are your feelers different from ours? Don't cuddle so.'

'Don't be provincial, *carissima*. You can't have all the world alike – yet.'

'But why do you lay eggs?' Melissa insisted. 'You lay 'em like a Queen – only you drop them in patches all over the place. I've watched you.'

'Ah, Brighteyes, so you've pierced my little subterfuge? Yes, they *are* eggs. By and by they'll spread our principles. Aren't you glad?'

'You gave me your most solemn word of honour that they were not eggs.'

'That was my little subterfuge, dearest – for the sake of the Cause. Now I must reach the young.' The Wax-moth tripped towards the fourth brood-frame, where the young bees were busy feeding the babies.

It takes some time for a sound bee to realize a malignant and continuous lie. 'She's very sweet and feathery,' was all that Melissa thought, 'but her talk sounds like ivy honey tastes. I'd better get to my field-work again.'

She found the Gate in a sulky uproar. The youngsters told off to the pillars had refused to chew scrap-wax because it made their jaws ache, and were clamouring for virgin stuff.

'Anything to finish the job!' said the badgered Guards.

'Hang up, some of you, and make wax for these slack-jawed sisters.'

Before a bee can make wax she must fill herself with honey. Then she climbs to safe foothold and hangs, while other gorged bees hang on to her in a cluster. There they wait in silence till the wax comes. The scales are either taken out of the makers' pockets by the workers, or tinkle down on the workers while they wait. The workers chew them (they are useless unchewed) into the all-supporting, all-embracing Wax of the Hive.

But now, no sooner was the wax-cluster in position than the workers below broke out again.

'Come down!' they cried. 'Come down and work! Come on, you Levantine parasites! Don't think to enjoy yourselves up there while we're sweating down here!'

The cluster shivered, as from hooked fore-foot to hooked hind-foot it telegraphed uneasiness. At last a worker sprang up, grabbed the lowest wax-maker, and swung, kicking, above her companions.

'I can make wax too!' she bawled. 'Give me a full gorge and I'll make tons of it.'

'Make it, then,' said the bee she had grappled. The spoken word snapped the current through the cluster. It shook and glistened like a cat's fur in the dark. 'Unhook!' it murmured. 'No wax for anyone today.'

'You lazy thieves! Hang up at once and produce our wax,' said the bees below.

'Impossible! The sweat's gone. To make your wax we must have stillness, warmth, and food. Unhook! Unhook!'

They broke up as they murmured, and disappeared among the other bees, from whom, of course, they were undistinguishable.

'Seems as if we'd have to chew scrap-wax for these pillars, after all,' said a worker.

'Not by a whole comb,' cried the young bee who had broken the cluster. 'Listen here! I've studied the question more than twenty minutes. It's as simple as falling off a daisy. You've heard of Cheshire, Root and Langstroth?'

They had not, but they shouted 'Good old Langstroth!' just the same.

'Those three know all that there is to be known about making hives. One or t'other of 'em must have made ours, and if they've made it, they're bound to look after it. Ours is a "Guaranteed Patent Hive". You can see it on the label behind.'

'Good old guarantee! Hurrah for the label behind!' roared the bees.

'Well, such being the case, *I* say that when we find they've betrayed us, we can exact from them a terrible vengeance.'

'Good old vengeance! Good old Root! 'Nuff said! Chuck it!' The crowd cheered and broke away as Melissa dived through.

'D'you know where Langstroth, Root, and Cheshire live if you happen to want 'em?' she asked of the proud and panting orator.

'Gum me if I know they ever lived at all! But aren't they beautiful names to buzz about? Did you see how it worked up the sisterhood?'

'Yes, but it didn't defend the Gate,' she replied.

'Ah, perhaps that's true, but think how delicate *my* position is, sister. I've a magnificent appetite, and I don't like working. It's bad for the mind. My instinct tells me that I can act as a restraining influence on others. They would have been worse, but for me.'

But Melissa had already risen clear, and was heading for a breadth of virgin white clover, which to an over-tired bee is as soothing as plain knitting to a woman.

'I think I'll take this load to the nurseries,' she said, when she had finished. 'It was always quiet there in my day,' and she topped off with two little pats of pollen for the babies.

She was met on the fourth brood-comb by a rush of excited sisters all buzzing together.

'One at a time! Let me put down my load. Now, what is it, Sacharissa?' she said.

'Grey Sister – that fluffy one, I mean – she came and said we ought to be out in the sunshine gathering honey, because life was short. She said any old bee could attend to our babies, and some day old bees would. That isn't true, Melissa, is it? No old bees can take us away from our babies, can they?'

'Of course not. You feed the babies while your heads are soft. When your heads harden, you go on to field-work. Any one knows that.'

'We told her so. We *told* her so! But she only waved her feelers, and said we could all lay eggs like Queens if we chose. And I'm afraid lots of the weaker sisters believe her, and are trying to do it. *So* unsettling!'

Sacharissa sped to a sealed worker-cell whose lid pulsated, as the bee within began to cut its way out.

'Come along, precious!' she murmured, and thinned the frail top from the other side. A pale, damp, creased thing hoisted itself feebly on to the comb. Sacharissa's note changed at once. 'No time to waste! Go up the frame and preen yourself!' she said. 'Report for nursing-duty in my ward tomorrow evening at six. Stop a minute. What's the matter with your third right leg?'

The young bee held it out in silence – unmistakably a leg incapable of packing pollen.

'Thank you. You needn't report till the day after tomorrow.' Sacharissa turned to her companion. 'That's the fifth oddity hatched in my ward since noon. I don't like it.'

'There's always a certain number of 'em,' said Melissa. 'You can't stop a few working sisters from laying, now and then, when they overfeed themselves. They only raise dwarf drones.'

'But we're hatching out drones with workers' stomachs; workers with drones' stomachs; and albinos and mixed-leggers who can't pack pollen – like that poor little beast yonder. I don't mind dwarf drones any more than you do (they all die in July), but this steady hatch of oddities frightens me, Melissa!'

'How narrow of you! They are all so delightfully clever and unusual and interesting,' piped the Wax-moth from a crack above them. 'Come here, you dear, downy duck, and tell us all about your feelings.'

'I wish she'd go!' Sacharissa lowered her voice. 'She meets these – er – oddities as they dry out, and cuddles 'em in corners.'

'I suppose the truth is that we're over-stocked and too well fed to swarm,' said Melissa.

'That *is* the truth,' said the Queen's voice behind them. They had not heard the heavy royal footfall which sets empty cells vibrating. Sacharissa offered her food at once. She ate and dragged her weary body forward. 'Can you suggest a remedy?' she said.

'New principles!' cried the Wax-moth from her crevice. 'We'll apply them quietly – later.'

'Suppose we sent out a swarm?' Melissa suggested. 'It's a little late, but it might ease us off.'

'It would save us, but – I know the Hive! You shall see for yourself.' The old Queen cried the Swarming Cry, which to a bee of good blood should be what the trumpet was to Job's war-horse. In spite of her immense age (three years), it rang between the cañon-like frames as a pibroch rings in a mountain pass; the fanners changed their note, and repeated it up in every gallery; and the broad-winged drones, burly and eager, ended it on one nerve-thrilling outbreak of bugles: *'La Reine le veult! Swarm! Swar-rm! Swar-r-rm!'*

But the roar which should follow the Call was wanting. They heard a broken grumble like the murmur of a falling tide.

'Swarm? What for? Catch me leaving a good bar-frame Hive, with fixed foundations, for a rotten old oak out in the open where it may rain any minute! *We*'re all right! It's a "Patent Guaranteed Hive". Why do they want to turn us out? Swarming be gummed! Swarming was invented to cheat a worker out of her proper comforts. Come on off to bed!'

The noise died out as the bees settled in empty cells for the night.

'You hear?' said the Queen. 'I know the Hive!'

'Quite between ourselves, *I* taught them that,' cried the Wax-moth. 'Wait till my principles develop, and you'll see the light from a new quarter.'

'You speak truth for once,' the Queen said suddenly, for she recognized the Wax-moth. 'That Light will break into the top of the Hive. A Hot Smoke will follow it, and your children will not be able to hide in any crevice.'

'Is it possible?' Melissa whispered. 'I – we have sometimes heard a legend like it.'

'It is no legend,' the old Queen answered. 'I had it from my mother, and she had it from hers. After the Wax-moth has grown strong, a Shadow will fall across the Gate; a Voice will speak from behind a Veil; there will be Light, and Hot Smoke, and earthquakes, and those who live will see everything that they have done, all together in one place, burned up in one great Fire.' The old Queen was trying to tell what she had been told of the Bee Master's dealings with an infected hive in the apiary, two or three seasons ago; and, of course, from her point of view the affair was as important as the Day of Judgement.

'And then?' asked horrified Sacharissa.

'Then, I have heard that a little light will burn in a great darkness, and perhaps the world will begin again. Myself, I think not.'

'Tut! Tut!' the Wax-moth cried. 'You good, fat people always prophesy ruin if things don't go exactly your way. But I grant you there will be changes.'

There were. When her eggs hatched, the wax was riddled with little tunnels, coated with the dirty clothes of the caterpillars. Flannelly lines ran through the honey-stores, the pollen-larders, the foundations, and, worst of all, through the babies in their cradles, till the Sweeper Guards spent half their time tossing out useless little corpses. The lines ended in a maze of sticky webbing on the face of the comb. The caterpillars could not stop spinning as they walked, and as they walked everywhere, they smarmed and garmed everything. Even where it did not hamper the bees' feet, the stale, sour smell of the stuff put them off their work; though some of the bees who had taken to egg-laying said it encouraged them to be mothers and maintain a vital interest in life.

When the caterpillars became moths, they made friends with the ever-increasing Oddities – albinos, mixed-leggers, single-eyed composites, faceless drones, half-queens and laying-sisters; and the ever-dwindling band of the old stock worked themselves bald and fray-winged to feed their queer charges. Most of the Oddities would not, and many, on account of their malformations, could not, go through a day's field-work; but the Wax-moths, who were always busy on the brood-comb, found pleasant home occupations for them. One albino, for instance, divided the number of pounds of honey in stock by the number of bees in the Hive, and proved that if every bee only gathered honey for seven and three-quarter minutes a day, she would have the rest of the time to herself, and could accompany the drones on their mating flights. The drones were not at all pleased.

Another, an eyeless drone with no feelers, said that all brood-cells should be perfect circles, so as not to interfere with the grub or the workers. He proved that the old six-sided cell was solely due to the workers building against each other on opposite sides of the wall, and that if there were no interference, there would be no angles. Some bees tried the new plan for a while, and found it cost eight times more wax than the old six-sided specification; and, as they never allowed a cluster to hang up and make wax in peace, real wax was scarce. However, they eked out their task with varnish stolen from new coffins at funerals, and it made them rather sick. Then they took to cadging round sugar-factories and breweries, because it was easiest to get their material from those places. But the mixture of glucose and beer naturally fermented in store and blew the store-cells out of shape, besides smelling abominably. Some of the sound bees warned them that ill-gotten gains never prosper, but the Oddities at once surrounded them and balled them to death. That was a punishment they were almost as fond of as they were of eating, and they expected the sound bees to feed them. Curiously enough, the age-old instinct of loyalty and devotion towards the Hive made the sound bees do this, though their reason told them they ought to slip away and unite with some other healthy stock in the apiary.

'What about seven and three-quarter minutes' work now?' said Melissa one day as she came in. 'I've been at it for five hours, and I've only half a load.'

'Oh, the Hive subsists on the Hival Honey which the Hive produces,' said a blind Oddity squatting on a store-cell.

'But honey is gathered from flowers outside – two miles away sometimes,' cried Melissa.

'Pardon me,' said the blind thing, sucking hard. 'But this is the Hive, is it not?'

'It was. Worse luck, it is.'

'And the Hival Honey is here, is it not?' It opened a fresh store-cell to prove it.

'Ye-es, but it won't be long at this rate,' said Melissa.

'The rates have nothing to do with it. This Hive produces the Hival Honey. You people never seem to grasp the economic simplicity that underlies all life.'

'Oh, me!' said poor Melissa, 'haven't you ever been beyond the Gate?'

'Certainly not. A fool's eyes are in the ends of the earth. Mine are in my head.' It gorged till it bloated.

Melissa took refuge in her poorly paid field-work and told Sacharissa the story.

'Hut!' said that wise bee, fretting with an old maid of a thistle. 'Tell us something new. The Hive's full of such as him – it, I mean.'

'What's the end to be? All the honey going out and none coming in. Things *can't* last this way!' said Melissa.

'Who cares?' said Sacharissa. 'I know now how drones feel

the day before they're killed. A short life and a merry one for me!'

'If it only were merry! But think of those awful, solemn, lop-sided Oddities waiting for us at home – crawling and clambering and preaching – and dirtying things in the dark.'

'I don't mind that so much as their silly songs, after we've fed 'em, all about "work among the merry, merry blossoms",' said Sacharissa from the deeps of a stale Canterbury bell.

'I do. How's our Queen?' said Melissa.

'Cheerfully hopeless, as usual. But she lays an egg now and then.'

'Does she so?' Melissa backed out of the next bell with a jerk. 'Suppose, now, we sound workers tried to raise a Princess in some clean corner?'

'You'd be put to it to find one. The Hive's all Wax-moth and muckings. But – Well?'

'A Princess might help us in the time of the Voice behind the Veil that the Queen talks of. And anything is better than working for Oddities that chirrup about work that they can't do, and waste what we bring home.'

'Who cares?' said Sacharissa. 'I'm with you, for the fun of it. The Oddities would ball us to death, if they knew. Come home, and we'll begin.'

There is no room to tell how the experienced Melissa found a far-off frame so messed and mishandled by abandoned cell-building experiments that, for very shame, the bees never went there. How in that ruin she blocked out a Royal Cell of sound wax, but disguised by rubbish till it looked like a kopje among deserted kopjes. How she prevailed upon the hopeless Queen to make one last effort and lay a worthy egg. How the Queen obeyed and died. How her spent carcass was flung out on the rubbish-heap, and how a multitude of laying-sisters went about dropping drone-eggs where they listed, and said there was no more need of Queens. How, covered by this confusion, Sacharissa educated certain young bees to educate certain new-born bees in the almost lost art of making Royal Jelly. How the nectar for it was won out of hours in the teeth of chill winds. How the hidden egg hatched true – no drone, but Blood Royal. How it was capped, and how desperately they worked to feed and double-feed the now swarming Oddities, lest any break in the food-supplies should set them to instituting inquiries, which, with songs about work, was their favourite amusement. How in an auspicious hour, on a moonless night, the Princess came forth – a Princess indeed – and how Melissa smuggled her into a dark empty honey-magazine, to bide her time; and how the drones, knowing she was there, went about singing the deep disreputable love-songs of the old days – to the scandal of the laying-sisters, who do not think well of drones. These things are written in the Book of Queens, which is laid up in the hollow of the Great Ash Ygdrasil.

After a few days the weather changed again and became glorious. Even the Oddities would now join the crowd that hung out on the alighting-board, and would sing of work among the merry, merry blossoms till an untrained ear might have received it for the hum of a working hive. Yet, in truth, their store-honey had been eaten long ago. They lived from day to day on the efforts of the few sound bees, while the Wax-moths fretted and consumed again their already ruined wax. But the sound bees never mentioned these matters. They knew, if they did, the Oddities would hold a meeting and ball them to death.

'Now you see what we have done,' said the Wax-moths. 'We have created New Material, a New Convention, a New Type, as we said we would.'

'And new possibilities for us,' said the laying-sisters gratefully. 'You have given us a new life's work, vital and paramount.'

'More than that,' chanted the Oddities in the sunshine; 'you have created a new heaven and a new earth. Heaven, cloudless and accessible' (it was a perfect August evening), 'and Earth teeming with the merry, merry blossoms, waiting only our honest toil to turn them all to good. The – er – Aster, and the Crocus, and the – er – Ladies' Smock in her season, the Chrysanthemum after her kind, and the Guelder Rose bringing forth abundantly withal.'

'Oh, Holy Hymettus!' said Melissa, awestruck. 'I knew they didn't know how honey was made, but they've forgotten the Order of the Flowers! What will become of them?'

A Shadow fell across the alighting-board as the Bee Master and his son came by. The Oddities crawled in, and a Voice behind a Veil said: 'I've neglected the old Hive too long. Give me the smoker.'

Melissa heard and darted through the Gate. 'Come, oh, come!' she cried. 'It is the destruction the Old Queen foretold. Princess, come!'

'Really, you are too archaic for words,' said an Oddity in an alley-way. 'A cloud, I admit, may have crossed the sun; but why hysterics? Above all, why Princesses so late in the day? Are you aware it's the Hival Tea-Time? Let's sing grace.'

Melissa clawed past him with all six legs. Sacharissa had run to what was left of the fertile brood-comb. 'Down and out!' she called across the brown breadth of it. 'Nurses, guards, fanners, sweepers – out! Never mind the babies. They're better dead. Out, before the Light and the Hot Smoke!'

The Princess's first clear fearless call (Melissa had found her) rose and drummed through all the frames. '*La Reine le veult! Swarm! Swar-rm! Swar-r-r-m!*'

The Hive shook beneath the shattering thunder of a stuck-down quilt being torn back.

'Don't be alarmed, dears,' said the Wax-moths. 'That's our work. Look up, and you'll see the dawn of the New Day.'

Light broke in the top of the Hive as the Queen had prophesied – naked light on the boiling, bewildered bees.

Sacharissa rounded up her rearguard, which dropped headlong off the frame, and joined the Princess's detachment thrusting towards the Gate. Now panic was in full blast, and each sound bee found herself embraced by at least three Oddities. The first instinct of a frightened bee is to break into the stores and gorge herself with honey; but there were no stores left, so the Oddities fought the sound bees.

'You must feed us, or we shall die!' they cried, holding and clutching and slipping, while the silent scared earwigs and little spiders twisted between their legs. 'Think of the Hive, traitors! The Holy Hive!'

'You should have thought before!' cried the sound bees. 'Stay and see the dawn of your New Day.'

They reached the Gate at last over the soft bodies of many to whom they had ministered.

'On! Out! Up!' roared Melissa in the Princess's ear. 'For the Hive's sake! To the Old Oak!'

The Princess left the alighting-board, circled once, flung herself at the lowest branch of the Old Oak, and her little loyal swarm – you could have covered it with a pint mug – followed, hooked, and hung.

'Hold close!' Melissa gasped. 'The old legends have come true! Look!'

The Hive was half hidden by smoke, and Figures moved through the smoke. They heard a frame crack stickily, saw it heaved high and twirled round between enormous hands – a blotched, bulged, and perished horror of grey wax, corrupt brood, and small drone-cells, all covered with crawling Oddities, strange to the sun.

'Why, this isn't a hive! This is a museum of curiosities,' said the Voice behind the Veil. It was only the Bee Master talking to his son.

'Can you blame 'em, father?' said a second voice. 'It's rotten with Wax-moth. See here!'

Another frame came up. A finger poked through it, and it broke away in rustling flakes of ashy rottenness.

'Number Four Frame! That was your mother's pet comb once,' whispered Melissa to the Princess. 'Many's the good egg I've watched her lay there.'

'Aren't you confusing *post hoc* with *propter hoc*?' said the

Bee Master. 'Wax-moth only succeed when weak bees let them in.' A third frame crackled and rose into the light. 'All this is full of laying workers' brood. That never happens till the stock's weakened. Phew!'

He beat it on his knee like a tambourine, and it also crumbled to pieces.

The little swarm shivered as they watched the dwarf drone-grubs squirm feebly on the grass. Many sound bees had nursed on that frame, well knowing their work was useless; but the actual sight of even useless work destroyed disheartens a good worker.

'No, they have some recuperative power left,' said the second voice. 'Here's a Queen cell!'

'But it's tucked away among – What on earth *has* come to the little wretches? They seem to have lost the instinct of cell-building.' The father held up the frame where the bees had experimented in circular cell-work. It looked like the pitted head of a decaying toadstool.

'Not altogether,' the son corrected. 'There's one line, at least, of perfectly good cells.'

'My work,' said Sacharissa to herself. 'I'm glad Man does me justice before –'

That frame, too, was smashed out and thrown atop of the others and the foul earwiggy quilts.

As frame after frame followed it, the swarm beheld the upheaval, exposure, and destruction of all that had been well or ill done in every cranny of their Hive for generations past. There was black comb so old that they had forgotten where it hung; orange, buff, and ochre-varnished store-comb, built as bees were used to build before the days of artificial foundations; and there was a little, white, frail new work. There were sheets on sheets of level, even brood-comb that had held in its time unnumbered thousands of unnamed workers; patches of obsolete drone-comb, broad and high-shouldered, showing to what marks the male grub was expected to grow; and two-inch-deep honey-magazines, empty but still magnificent: the whole gummed and glued into twisted scrapwork, awry on the wires, half-cells, beginnings abandoned, or grandiose weak-walled, composite cells pieced out with rubbish and capped with dirt.

Good or bad, every inch of it was so riddled by the tunnels of the Wax-moth that it broke in clouds of dust as it was flung on the heap.

'Oh, see!' cried Sacharissa. 'The Great Burning that Our Queen foretold. Who can bear to look?'

A flame crawled up the pile of rubbish, and they smelt singeing wax.

The Figures stooped, lifted the Hive and shook it upside down over the pyre. A cascade of Oddities, chips of broken comb, scale, fluff, and grubs slid out, crackled, sizzled, popped a little, and then the flames roared up and consumed all that fuel.

'We must disinfect,' said a Voice. 'Get me a sulphur-candle, please.'

The shell of the Hive was returned to its place, a light was set in its sticky emptiness, tier by tier the Figures built it up, closed the entrance, and went away. The swarm watched the light leaking through the cracks all the long night. At dawn one Wax-moth came by, fluttering impudently.

'There has been a miscalculation about the New Day, my dears,' she began; 'one can't expect people to be perfect all at once. That was our mistake.'

'No, the mistake was entirely ours,' said the Princess.

'Pardon me,' said the Wax-moth. 'When you think of the enormous upheaval – call it good or bad – which our influence brought about, you will admit that we, and we alone – '

'You?' said the Princess. 'Our stock was not strong. So *you* came – as any other disease might have come. Hang close, all my people.'

When the sun rose, Veiled Figures came down, and saw their swarm at the bough's end waiting patiently within sight of the old Hive – a handful, but prepared to go on.

Little Foxes

A TALE OF THE GIHON HUNT

(1909)

A FOX came out of his earth on the banks of the Great River Gihon which waters Ethiopia. He saw a white man riding through the dry dhurra-stalks, and, that his destiny might be fulfilled, barked at him.

The rider drew rein among the villagers round his stirrup.

'What,' said he, 'is that?'

'That,' said the Sheikh of the village, 'is a fox, O Excellency Our Governor.'

'It is not then a jackal?'

'No jackal, but Abu Hussein, the Father of Cunning.'

'Also' – the white man spoke half aloud – 'I am Mudir of this Province.'

'It is true,' they cried. 'Ya, Saart el Mudir' (O Excellency Our Governor).

The Great River Gihon, well used to the moods of kings, slid between his mile-wide banks towards the sea, while the Governor praised God in a loud and searching cry never before heard by the River.

When he had lowered his right forefinger from behind his right ear, the villagers talked to him of their crops – barley, dhurra, millet, onions, and the like. The Governor stood up in his stirrups. North he looked at a strip of green cultivation a few hundred yards wide which lay like a carpet between the river and the tawny line of the desert. Sixty miles that strip stretched before him, and as many behind. At every half-mile a groaning waterwheel lifted the soft water from the river to the crops by way of a mud-built aqueduct. A foot or so wide was the water-channel; five foot or more high was the bank on which it ran, and its base was broad in proportion. Abu Hussein, misnamed the Father of Cunning, drank from the river below his earth, and his shadow was long in the low sun. He could not understand the loud cry which the Governor had cried.

The Sheikh of the village spoke of the crops from which the rulers of all lands draw revenue; but the Governor's eyes were fixed, between his horse's ears, on the nearest water-channel.

'Very like a ditch in Ireland,' he murmured, and smiled, dreaming of a razor-topped bank in distant Kildare.

Encouraged by that smile, the Sheikh continued. 'When crops fail it is necessary to remit taxation. Then it is a good thing, O Excellency Our Governor, that you should come and see the crops which have failed, and discover that we have not lied.'

'Assuredly.' The Governor shortened his reins. The horse cantered on, rose at the embankment of the water-channel, changed leg cleverly on top, and hopped down in a cloud of golden dust.

Abu Hussein from his earth watched with interest. He had never before seen such things.

'Assuredly,' the Governor repeated, and came back by the way he had gone. 'It is always best to see for one's self.'

An ancient and still bullet-speckled stern-wheel steamer, with a barge lashed to her side, came round the river bend. She whistled to tell the Governor his dinner was ready, and the horse, seeing his fodder piled on the barge, whinnied.

'Moreover,' the Sheikh added, 'in the Days of the Oppression the Emirs and their creatures dispossessed many people of their lands. All up and down the River our people are waiting to return to their lawful fields.'

'Judges have been appointed to settle that matter,' said the Governor. 'They will presently come in steamers and hear the witnesses.'

'Wherefore? Did the Judges kill the Emirs? We would rather be judged by the men who executed God's judgement on the Emirs. We would rather abide by *your* decision, O Excellency Our Governor.'

The Governor nodded. It was a year since he had seen the Emirs stretched close and still round the reddened sheepskin where lay El Mahdi, the Prophet of God. Now there remained no trace of their dominion except the old steamer, once part of a Dervish flotilla, which was his house and office. She sidled into the shore, lowered a plank, and the Governor followed his horse aboard.

Lights burned on her till late, dully reflected in the river that tugged at her mooring-ropes. The Governor read, not for the first time, the administration reports of one John Jorrocks, M.F.H.

'We shall need,' he said suddenly to his Inspector, 'about ten couple. I'll get 'em when I go home. You'll be Whip, Baker?'

The Inspector, who was not yet twenty-five, signified his assent in the usual manner, while Abu Hussein barked at the vast desert moon.

'Ha!' said the Governor, coming out in his pyjamas, 'we'll be giving you capivi in another three months, my friend.'

It was four, as a matter of fact, ere a steamer with a melodious bargeful of hounds anchored at that landing. The Inspector leaped down among them, and the homesick wanderers received him as a brother.

'Everybody fed 'em everything on board ship, but they're real dainty hounds at bottom,' the Governor explained. 'That's Royal you've got hold of – the pick of the bunch – and the bitch that's got hold of you – she's a little excited – is May Queen. Merriman, out of Cottesmore Maudlin, you know.'

'I know. "Grand old betch with the tan eye-brows,"' the Inspector cooed. 'Oh, Ben! I shall take an interest in life now. Hark to 'em! Oh, hark!'

Abu Hussein, under the high bank, went about his night's work. An eddy carried his scent to the barge, and three villages heard the crash of music that followed. Even then Abu Hussein did not know better than to bark in reply.

'Well, what about my Province?' the Governor asked.

'Not so bad,' the Inspector answered, with Royal's head between his knees. 'Of course, all the villages want remission of taxes, but, as far as I can see, the whole country's stinkin' with foxes. Our trouble will be choppin' -'em in cover. I've got a list of the only villages entitled to any remission. What d'you call this flat-sided, blue-mottled beast with the jowl?'

'Beagle-boy. I have my doubts about him. Do you think we can get two days a week?'

'Easy; and as many byes as you please. The Sheikh of this village here tells me that his barley has failed, and he wants a fifty per cent remission.'

'We'll begin with him tomorrow, and look at his crops as we go. Nothing like personal supervision,' said the Governor.

They began at sunrise. The pack flew off the barge in every direction, and, after gambols, dug like terriers at Abu Hussein's many earths. Then they drank themselves pot-bellied on Gihon water while the Governor and the Inspector chastised them with whips. Scorpions were added; for May Queen nosed one, and was removed to the barge lamenting. Mystery (a puppy, alas!) met a snake, and the blue-mottled Beagle-boy (never a dainty hound) ate that which he should have passed by. Only Royal, of the Belvoir tan head and the sad, discerning eyes, made any attempt to uphold the honour of England before the watching village.

'You can't expect everything,' said the Governor after breakfast.

'We got it, though – everything except foxes. Have you seen May Queen's nose?' said the Inspector.

'And Mystery's dead. We'll keep 'em coupled next time till we get well in among the crops. I say, what a babbling body-snatcher that Beagle-boy is! Ought to be drowned!'

'They bury people so dam' casual hereabouts. Give him another chance,' the Inspector pleaded, not knowing that he should live to repent most bitterly.

'Talkin' of chances,' said the Governor, 'this Sheikh lies

about his barley bein' a failure. If it's high enough to hide a hound at this time of year, it's all right. And he wants a fifty per cent remission, you said?'

'You didn't go on past the melon patch where I tried to turn Wanderer. It's all burned up from there on to the desert. His other waterwheel has broken down, too,' the Inspector replied.

'Very good. We'll split the difference and allow him twenty-five per cent off. Where'll we meet tomorrow?'

'There's some trouble among the villages down the river about their land-titles. It's good goin' about there too,' the Inspector said.

The next meet, then, was some twenty miles down the river, and the pack were not enlarged till they were fairly among the fields. Abu Hussein was there in force – four of him. Four delirious hunts of four minutes each – four hounds per fox – ended in four earths just above the river. All the village looked on.

'We forgot about the earths. The banks are riddled with 'em. This'll defeat us,' said the Inspector.

'Wait a moment!' The Governor drew forth a sneezing hound. 'I've just remembered I'm Governor of these parts.'

'Then turn out a black battalion to stop for us. We'll need 'em, old man.'

The Governor straightened his back. 'Give ear, O people!' he cried. 'I make a new Law!'

The villagers closed in. He called:

'Henceforward I will give one dollar to the man on whose land Abu Hussein is found. And another dollar' – he held up the coin – 'to the man on whose land these dogs shall kill him. But to the man on whose land Abu Hussein shall run into a hole such as is this hole, I will give not dollars, but a most immeasurable beating. Is it understood?'

'Our Excellency,' – a man stepped forth – 'on my land Abu Hussein was found this morning. Is it not so, brothers?'

None denied. The Governor tossed him over four dollars without a word.

'On my land they all went into their holes,' cried another. 'Therefore I must be beaten.'

'Not so. The land is mine, and mine are the beatings.'

This second speaker thrust forward his shoulders already bared, and the villagers shouted.

'Hullo! Two men anxious to be licked? There must be some swindle about the land,' said the Governor. Then in the local vernacular: 'What are your rights to the beating?'

As a river-reach changes beneath a slant of the sun, that which had been a scattered mob changed to a court of most ancient justice. The hounds tore and sobbed at Abu Hussein's hearthstone, all unnoticed among the legs of the witnesses, and Gihon, also accustomed to laws, purred approval.

'You will not wait till the Judges come up the river to settle the dispute?' said the Governor at last.

'No!' shouted all the village save the man who had first asked to be beaten. 'We will abide by Our Excellency's decision. Let Our Excellency turn out the creatures of the Emirs who stole our land in the Days of the Oppression.'

'And thou sayest?' the Governor turned to the man who had first asked to be beaten.

'I say *I* will wait till the wise Judges come down in the steamer. Then I will bring my many witnesses,' he replied.

'He is rich. He will bring many witnesses,' the village Sheikh muttered.

'No need. Thine own mouth condemns thee!' the Governor cried. 'No man lawfully entitled to his land would wait one hour before entering upon it. Stand aside!' The man fell back, and the village jeered him.

The second claimant stooped quickly beneath the lifted hunting-crop. The village rejoiced.

'O Such an one; Son of such an one,' said the Governor, prompted by the Sheikh, 'learn, from the day when I send the order, to block up all the holes where Abu Hussein may hide – on – thy – land!'

The light flicks ended. The man stood up triumphant. By

that accolade had the Supreme Government acknowledged his title before all men.

While the village praised the perspicacity of the Governor, a naked, pock-marked child strode forward to the earth, and stood on one leg, unconcerned as a young stork.

'Ha!' he said, hands behind his back. 'This should be blocked up with bundles of dhurra stalks – or, better, bundles of thorns.'

'Better thorns,' said the Governor. 'Thick ends innermost.'

The child nodded gravely and squatted on the sand.

'An evil day for thee, Abu Hussein,' he shrilled into the mouth of the earth. 'A day of obstacles to thy flagitious returns in the morning!'

'Who is it?' the Governor asked the Sheikh. 'It thinks.'

'Farag the Fatherless. His people were slain in the Days of the Oppression. The man to whom Our Excellency has awarded the land is, as it were, his maternal uncle.'

'Will it come with me and feed the big dogs?' said the Governor.

The other peering children drew back. 'Run!' they cried. 'Our Excellency will feed Farag to the big dogs.'

'I will come,' said Farag. 'And I will never go.' He threw his arm round Royal's neck, and the wise beast licked his face.

'Binjamin, by Jove!' the Inspector cried.

'No!' said the Governor. 'I believe he has the makings of James Pigg!'

Farag waved his hand to his uncle, and led Royal on to the barge. The rest of the pack followed.

Gihon, that had seen many sports, learned to know the Hunt barge well. He met her rounding his bends on grey December dawns to music wild and lamentable as the almost forgotten throb of Dervish drums, when, high above Royal's tenor bell, sharper even than lying Beagle-boy's falsetto break, Farag chanted deathless war against Abu Hussein and all his seed. At sunrise the River would shoulder her carefully into her place, and listen to the rush and scutter of the pack fleeing up the gang-plank, and the tramp of the Governor's Arab behind them. They would pass over the brow into the dewless crops, where Gihon, low and shrunken, could only guess what they were about when Abu Hussein flew down the bank to scratch at a stopped earth, and flew back into the barley again. As Farag had foretold, it was evil days for Abu Hussein ere he learned to take the necessary steps and to get away crisply. Sometimes Gihon saw the whole procession of the Hunt silhouetted against the morning blue, bearing him company for many merry miles. At every half mile the horses and the donkeys jumped the water-channels – up, on, change your leg, and off again – like figures in a zoetrope, till they grew small along the line of waterwheels. Then Gihon waited their rustling return through the crops, and took them to rest on his bosom at ten o'clock. While the horses ate, and Farag slept with his head on Royal's flank, the Governor and his Inspector worked for the good of the Hunt and his Province.

After a little time there was no need to beat any man for neglecting his earths. The steamer's destination was telegraphed from waterwheel to waterwheel, and the villagers stopped out and put to according. If an earth were overlooked, it meant some dispute as to the ownership of the land, and then and there the Hunt checked and settled it in this wise: The Governor and the Inspector side by side, but the latter half a horse's length to the rear; both bare-shouldered claimants well in front; the villagers half-mooned behind them, and Farag with the pack, who quite understood the performance, sitting down on the left. Twenty minutes were enough to settle the most complicated case, for, as the Governor said to a real Judge on the steamer, 'One gets at the truth in a hunting-field a heap quicker than in your law-courts.'

'But when the evidence is conflicting?' the Judge suggested.

'Watch the field. They'll throw tongue fast enough if

you're running a wrong scent. You've never had an appeal from one of my decisions yet.'

The Sheikhs on horseback – the lesser folk on clever donkeys – the children so despised by Farag – soon understood that villages which repaired their waterwheels and channels stood highest in the Governor's favour. He bought their barley for his horses.

'Channels,' he said, 'are necessary that we may all jump them. They are necessary, moreover, for the crops. Let there be many wheels and sound channels – and much good barley.'

'Without money,' replied an aged Sheikh, 'there can be no waterwheels.'

'I will lend the money,' said the Governor.

'At what interest, O Our Excellency?'

'Take you two of May Queen's puppies to bring up in your village in such a manner that they do not eat filth, nor lose their hair, nor catch fever from lying in the sun, but become wise hounds.'

'Like Ray-yal – not like Bigglebai?' (Already it was an insult along the River to compare a man to the shifty anthropophagous blue-mottled harrier.)

'Certainly, like Ray-yal – not in the least like Bigglebai. *That* shall be the interest on the loan. Let the puppies thrive and the waterwheel be built, and I shall be content,' said the Governor.

'The wheel shall be built, but, O Our Excellency, if by God's favour the pups grow to be well-smellers, not filth-eaters, not unaccustomed to their name, not lawless, who will do them and me justice at the time of judging the young dogs?'

'Hounds, man, hounds! Ha-wands, O Sheikh, we call them in their manhood.'

'The ha-wands when they are judged at the Sha-ho. I have unfriends down the river to whom Our Excellency has also entrusted ha-wands to bring up.'

'Puppies, man! Pah-peaz, we call them, O Sheikh, in their childhood.'

'Pah-peaz. My enemies may judge my pah-peaz unjustly at the Sha-ho. This must be thought of.'

'I see the obstacle. Hear now! If the new waterwheel is built in a month without oppression, thou, O Sheikh, shalt be named one of the judges to judge the pah-peaz at the Sha-ho. Is it understood?'

'Understood. We will build the wheel. I and my seed are responsible for the repayment of the loan. Where are my pah-peaz? If they eat fowls, must they on any account eat the feathers?'

'On no account must they eat the feathers. Farag in the barge will tell thee how they are to live.'

There is no instance of any default on the Governor's personal and unauthorized loans, for which they called him the Father of Waterwheels. But the first puppy-show at the capital needed enormous tact and the presence of a black battalion ostentatiously drilling in the barrack square to prevent trouble after the prize-giving.

But who can chronicle the glories of the Gihon Hunt – or their shames? Who remembers the kill in the market-place, when the Governor bade the assembled Sheikhs and warriors observe how the hounds would instantly devour the body of Abu Hussein; but how, when he had scientifically broken it up, the weary pack turned from it in loathing, and Farag wept because he said the world's face had been blackened? What men who have not yet ridden beyond the sound of any horn recall the midnight run which ended – Beagle-boy leading – among tombs; the hasty whip-off, and the oath, taken above bones, to forget the worry? That desert run, when Abu Hussein forsook the cultivation, and made a six-mile point to earth in a desolate khor – when strange armed riders on camels swooped out of a ravine, and, instead of giving battle, offered to take the tired hounds home on their beasts. Which they did, and vanished.

Above all, who remembers the death of Royal, when a certain Sheikh wept above the body of the stainless hound as it might have been his son's – and that day the Hunt rode no more? The badly-kept log-book says little of this, but at the end of their second season (forty-nine brace) appears the dark entry: 'New blood badly wanted. They are beginning to listen to Beagle-boy.'

The Inspector attended to the matter when his leave fell due.

'Remember,' said the Governor, 'you must get us the best blood in England – real, dainty hounds – expense no object, but don't trust your own judgement. Present my letters of introduction, and take what they give you.'

The Inspector presented his letters in a society where they make much of horses, more of hounds, and are tolerably civil to men who can ride. They passed him from house to house, mounted him according to his merits, and fed him, after five years of goat chop and Worcester sauce, perhaps a thought too richly.

The seat or castle where he made his great coup does not much matter. Four Masters of Foxhounds were at table, and in a mellow hour the Inspector told them stories of the Gihon Hunt. He ended: 'Ben said I wasn't to trust my own judgement about hounds; but *I* think there ought to be a special tariff for Empire-makers.'

As soon as his hosts could speak, they reassured him on this point.

'And now tell us about your first puppy-show all over again,' said one.

'And about the earth-stoppin'. Was that all Ben's own invention?' said another.

'Wait a moment,' said a large, clean-shaven man – not an M.F.H. – at the end of the table. 'Are your villagers habitually beaten by your Governor when they fail to stop foxes' holes?'

The tone and the phrase were enough, even if, as the Inspector confessed afterwards, the big, blue double-chinned man had not looked so like Beagle-boy. He took him on for the honour of Ethiopia.

'We only hunt twice a week – sometimes three times. I've

never known a man chastised more than four times a week – unless there's a bye.'

The large loose-lipped man flung his napkin down, came round the table, cast himself into the chair next to the Inspector, and leaned forward earnestly, so that he breathed in the Inspector's face.

'Chastized with what?' he said.

'With the *kourbash* – on the feet. A *kourbash* is a strip of old hippo-hide with a sort of keel on it, like the cutting edge of a boar's tusk. But we use the rounded side for a first offender.'

'And do any consequences follow this sort of thing? For the victim, I mean – not for you?'

'Ve-ry rarely. Let me be fair. I've never seen a man die under the lash, but gangrene may set up if the *kourbash* has been pickled.'

'Pickled in what?' All the table was still and interested.

'In copperas, of course. Didn't you know *that*?' said the Inspector.

'Thank God I didn't.' The large man sputtered visibly.

The Inspector wiped his face and grew bolder.

'You mustn't think we're careless about our earth-stoppers. We've a Hunt fund for hot tar. Tar's a splendid dressing if the toe-nails aren't beaten off. But huntin' as large a country as we do, we mayn't be back at that village for a month, and if the dressings ain't renewed, and gangrene sets in, often as not you find your man pegging about on his stumps. We've a well-known local name for 'em down the river. We call 'em the Mudir's Cranes. You see, I persuaded the Governor to bastinado only on one foot.'

'On one foot? The Mudir's Cranes!' The large man turned purple to the top of his bald head. 'Would you mind giving me the local word for Mudir's Cranes?'

From a too well stocked memory the Inspector drew one short adhesive word which surprises by itself even unblushing Ethiopia. He spelt it out, saw the large man write it down on his cuff and withdraw. Then the Inspector translated a few of its significations and implications to the four Masters of Foxhounds. He left three days later with eight couple of the best hounds in England – a free and a friendly and an ample gift from four packs to the Gihon Hunt. He had honestly meant to undeceive the large blue-mottled man, but somehow forgot about it.

The new draft marks a new chapter in the Hunt's history. From an isolated phenomenon in a barge it became a permanent institution with brick-built kennels ashore, and an influence, social, political, and administrative, coterminous with the boundaries of the Province. Ben, the Governor, departed to England, where he kept a pack of real dainty hounds, but never ceased to long for the old lawless lot. His successors were *ex-officio* Masters of the Gihon Hunt, as all Inspectors were Whips. For one reason, Farag, the kennel-huntsman, in khaki and puttees, would obey nothing under the rank of an Excellency, and the hounds would obey no one but Farag; for another, the best way of estimating crop returns and revenue was by riding straight to hounds; for a third, though Judges down the river issued signed and sealed land-titles to all lawful owners, yet public opinion along the river never held any such title valid till it had been confirmed, according to precedent, by the Governor's hunting-crop in the hunting-field, above the wilfully neglected earth. True, the ceremony had been cut down to three mere taps on the shoulder, but Governors who tried to evade that much found themselves and their office compassed about with a great cloud of witnesses who took up their time with lawsuits and, worse still, neglected the puppies. The older Sheikhs, indeed, stood out for the immeasurable beatings of the old days – the sharper the punishment, they argued, the surer the title; but here the hand of modern progress was against them, and they contented themselves with telling tales of Ben the first Governor, whom they called the Father of Waterwheels, and for that heroic age when men, horses, and hound were worth following.

This same Modern Progress which brought dog-biscuit

and brass water-taps to the kennels was at work all over the world. Forces, Activities, and Movements sprang into being, agitated themselves, coalesced, and, in one political avalanche, overwhelmed a bewildered, and not in the least intending it, England. The echoes of the New Era were borne into the Province on the wings of inexplicable cables. The Gihon Hunt read speeches and sentiments and policies which amazed them, and they thanked God, prematurely, that their Province was too far off, too hot, and too hard-worked to be reached by those speakers or their policies. But they, with others, underestimated the scope and purpose of the New Era.

One by one the Provinces of the Empire were hauled up and baited, hit and held, lashed under the belly, and forced back on their haunches for the amusement of their new masters in the parish of Westminster. One by one they fell away, sore and angry, to compare stripes with each other at the ends of the uneasy earth. Even so the Gihon Hunt, like Abu Hussein in the old days, did not understand. Then it reached them through the Press that they habitually flogged to death good revenue-paying cultivators who neglected to stop earths; but that the few, the very few, who did not die under hippo-wide whips soaked in copperas, walked about on their gangrenous ankle-bones, and were known in derision as the Mudir's Cranes. The charges were vouched for in the House of Commons by a Mr Lethabie Groombride, who had formed a Committee, and was disseminating literature. The Province groaned; the Inspector – now an Inspector of Inspectors – whistled. He had forgotten the gentleman who sputtered in people's faces.

'He shouldn't have looked so like Beagle-boy!' was his sole defence when he met the Governor at breakfast on the steamer after a meet.

'You shouldn't have joked with an animal of that class,' said Peter the Governor. 'Look what Farag has brought me!'

It was a pamphlet, signed on behalf of a Committee by a

lady secretary, but composed by some person who thoroughly understood the language of the Province. After telling the tale of the beatings, it recommended all the beaten to institute criminal proceedings against their Governor, and, as soon as might be, to rise against English oppression and tyranny. Such documents were new in Ethiopia in those days.

The Inspector read the last half-page. 'But – but,' he stammered, 'this is impossible. White men don't write this sort of stuff.'

'Don't they, just?' said the Governor. 'They get made Cabinet Ministers for doing it too. I went home last year. *I* know.'

'It'll blow over,' said the Inspector weakly.

'Not it. Groombride is coming down here to investigate the matter in a few days.'

'For himself?'

'The Imperial Government's behind him. Perhaps you'd like to look at my orders.' The Governor laid down an uncoded cable. The whiplash to it ran: 'You will afford Mr Groombride every facility for his inquiry, and will be held responsible that no obstacles are put in his way to the fullest possible examination of any witnesses which he may consider necessary. He will be accompanied by his own interpreter, who must not be tampered with.'

'That's to me – Governor of the Province!' said Peter the Governor.

'It seems about enough,' the Inspector answered.

Farag, kennel-huntsman, entered the saloon, as was his privilege.

'My uncle, who was beaten by the Father of Waterwheels, would approach, O Excellency,' he said, 'and there are also others on the bank.'

'Admit,' said the Governor.

There tramped aboard Sheikhs and villagers to the number of seventeen. In each man's hand was a copy of the pamphlet; in each man's eyes terror and uneasiness of the sort that Governors spend and are spent to clear away. Farag's uncle, now Sheikh of the village, spoke: 'It is written in this book, O Excellency, that the beatings whereby we hold our lands are all valueless. It is written that every man who received such a beating from the Father of Waterwheels who slew the Emirs should instantly begin a lawsuit, because the title to his land is not valid.'

'It is so written. We do not wish lawsuits. We wish to hold our land as it was given to us after the Days of the Oppression,' they cried all together.

The Governor glanced at the Inspector. This was serious. To cast doubt on the ownership of land means, in Ethiopia, the letting in of waters, and the getting out of troops.

'Your titles are good,' said the Governor. The Inspector confirmed with a nod.

'Then what is the meaning of these writings which come from down the river where the Judges are?' Farag's uncle waved his copy. 'By whose order are we ordered to slay *you*, O Excellency Our Governor'.

'It is not written that you are to slay me.'

'Not in those very words, but if we leave an earth unstopped, it is the same as though we wished to save Abu Hussein from the hounds. These writings say: "Abolish your rulers." How can we abolish except we kill? We hear rumours of one who comes from down the river soon to lead us to kill.'

'Fools!' said the Governor. 'Your titles are good. This is madness!'

'It is so written,' they answered like a pack.

'Listen,' said the Inspector smoothly. 'I know who caused the writings to be written and sent. He is a man of a blue-mottled jowl, in aspect like Bigglebai who ate unclean matters. He will come up the river and will give tongue about the beatings.'

'Will he impeach our land-titles? An evil day for him!'

'Go slow, Baker,' the Governor whispered. 'They'll kill him if they get scared about their land.'

'I tell a parable.' The Inspector lit a cigarette. 'Declare which of you took to walk the children of Milkmaid?'

'Melik-meid First or Second?' said Farag quickly.

'The second – the one which was lamed by the thorn.'

'No – no. Melik-meid the Second strained her shoulder leaping my water-channel,' a Sheikh cried. 'Melik-meid the First was lamed by the thorns on the day when Our Excellency fell thrice.'

'True – true. The second Melik-meid's mate was Malvolio, the pied hound,' said the Inspector.

'I had two of the second Melik-meid's pups,' said Farag's uncle. 'They died of the madness in their ninth month.'

'And how did they do before they died?' said the Inspector.

'They ran about in the sun and slavered at the mouth till they died.'

'Wherefore?'

'God knows. He sent the madness. It was no fault of mine.'

'Thine own mouth hath answered thee,' the Inspector laughed. 'It is with men as it is with dogs. God afflicts some with a madness. It is no fault of ours if such men run about in the sun and froth at the mouth. The man who is coming will emit spray from his mouth in speaking, and will always edge and push in towards his hearers. When ye see and hear him ye will understand that he is afflicted of God: being mad. He is in God's Hand.'

'But our titles! Are our titles to our lands good?' the crowd repeated.

'Your titles are in my hands – they are good,' said the Governor.

'And he who wrote the writings is an afflicted of God?' said Farag's uncle.

'The Inspector hath said it,' cried the Governor. 'Ye will see when the man comes. O Sheikhs and men, have we ridden together and walked puppies together, and bought and sold barley for the horses, that, after these years, we should run riot on the scent of a madman – an afflicted of God?'

'But the Hunt pays us to kill mad jackals,' said Farag's uncle. 'And he who questions my titles to my land – '

'Aahh! 'Ware riot!' The Governor's hunting-crop cracked like a three-pounder. 'By Allah,' he thundered, 'if the afflicted of God come to any harm at your hands, I myself will shoot every hound and every puppy, and the Hunt shall ride no more. On your heads be it. Go in peace, and tell the others.'

'The Hunt shall ride no more?' said Farag's uncle. 'Then how can the land be governed? No – no, O Excellency Our Governor, we will not harm a hair on the head of the afflicted of God. He shall be to us as is Abu Hussein's wife in her breeding season.'

When they were gone the Governor mopped his forehead.

'We must put a few soldiers in every village this Groombride visits, Baker. Tell 'em to keep out of sight, and have an eye on the villagers. He's trying 'em rather high.'

'O Excellency,' said the smooth voice of Farag, laying the *Field* and *Country Life* square on the table, 'is the afflicted of God who resembles Bigglebai one with the man whom the Inspector met in the great house in England, and to whom he told the tale of the Mudir's Cranes?'

'The same man, Farag,' said the Inspector.

'I have often heard the Inspector tell the tale to Our Excellency at feeding-time in the kennels: but since I am in the Government service I have never told it to my people. May I loose that tale among the villages?'

The Governor nodded. 'No harm,' said he.

The details of Mr Groombride's arrival, with his interpreter, who, he proposed, should eat with him at the Governor's table, his allocution to the Governor on the New Movement and the sins of Imperialism, I purposely omit. At three in the afternoon, Mr Groombride said: 'I will go out now and address your victims in this village.'

'Won't you find it rather hot?' said the Governor. 'They generally take a nap till sunset at this time of year.'

Mr Groombride's large, loose lips set. '*That*,' he replied pointedly, 'would be enough to decide me. I fear you have not quite mastered your instructions. May I ask you to send for my interpreter? I hope he has not been tampered with by your subordinates.'

He was a yellowish boy called Abdul, who had well eaten and drunk with Farag. The Inspector, by the way, was not present at the meal.

'At whatever risk, I shall go unattended,' said Mr Groombride. 'Your presence would cow them from giving evidence. Abdul, my good friend, would you very kindly open the umbrella?'

He passed up the gang-plank to the village, and with no more prelude than a Salvation Army picket in a Portsmouth slum, cried: 'Oh, my brothers!'

He did not guess how his path had been prepared. The village was widely awake. Farag, in loose, flowing garments, quite unlike a kennel-huntsman's khaki and puttees, leaned against the wall of his uncle's house. 'Come and see the afflicted of God,' he cried musically, 'whose face, indeed, resembles that of Bigglebai.'

The village came, and decided that on the whole Farag was right.

'I can't quite catch what they are saying,' said Mr Groombride.

'They saying they very much pleased to see you, sar,' Abdul interpreted.

'Then I do think they might have sent a deputation to the steamer; but I suppose they were frightened of the officials. Tell them not to be frightened, Abdul.'

'He says you are not to be frightened,' Abdul explained. A child here sputtered with laughter. 'Refrain from mirth,' Farag cried. 'The afflicted of God is the guest of The Excellency Our Governor. We are responsible for every hair of his head.'

'He has none,' a voice spoke. 'He has the white and the shining mange.'

'Now tell them what I have come for, Abdul, and please keep the umbrella well up. I think I shall reserve myself for my little vernacular speech at the end.'

'Approach! Look! Listen!' Abdul chanted. 'The afflicted of God will now make sport. Presently he will speak in your tongue, and will consume you with mirth. I have been his servant for three weeks. I will tell you about his under-garments and his perfumes for his head.'

He told them at length.

'And didst thou take any of his perfume bottles?' said Farag at the end.

'I am his servant. I took two,' Abdul replied.

'Ask him,' said Farag's uncle, 'what he knows about our land-titles. Ye young men are all alike.' He waved a pamphlet. Mr Groombride smiled to see how the seed sown in London had borne fruit by Gihon. Lo, all the seniors held copies of the pamphlet!

'He knows less than a buffalo. He told me on the steamer that he was driven out of his own land by Demah-Kerazi, which is a devil inhabiting crowds and assemblies,' said Abdul.

'Allah between us and Evil!' a woman cackled from the darkness of a hut. 'Come in, children, he may have the Evil Eye.'

'No, my aunt,' said Farag. 'No afflicted of God has an evil eye. Wait till ye hear his mirth-provoking speech which he will deliver. I have heard it twice from Abdul.'

'They seem very quick to grasp the point. How far have you got, Abdul?'

'All about the beatings, sar. They are highly interested.'

'Don't forget about the local self-government, and please hold the umbrella over me. It is hopeless to destroy unless one first builds up.'

'He may not have the Evil Eye,' Farag's uncle grunted, 'but his devil led him too certainly to question my land-title. Ask him whether he still doubts my land-title?'

'Or mine, or mine?' cried the elders.

'What odds? He is an afflicted of God,' Farag called. 'Remember the tale I told you.'

'Yes, but he is an Englishman, and doubtless of influence, or Our Excellency would not entertain him. Bid that down-country jackass ask him.'

'Sar,' said Abdul, 'these people much fearing they may be turned out of their land in consequence of your remarks. Therefore they ask you to make promise no bad consequences following your visit.'

Mr Groombride held his breath and turned purple. Then he stamped his foot.

'Tell them,' he cried, 'that if a hair of any one of their heads is touched by any official on any account whatever, all England shall ring with it. Good God! What callous oppression! The dark places of the earth are full of cruelty.' He wiped his face, and throwing out his arms cried: 'Tell them, oh! tell the poor serfs not to be afraid of me. Tell them I come to redress their wrongs – not, Heaven knows, to add to their burden.'

The long-drawn gurgle of the practised public speaker pleased them much.

'That is how the new water-tap runs out in the kennel,' said Farag. 'The Excellency Our Governor entertains him that he may make sport. Make him say the mirth-moving speech.'

'What did he say about my land-titles?' Farag's uncle was not to be turned.

'He says,' Farag interpreted, 'that he desires nothing better than that you should live on your lands in peace. He talks as though he believed himself to be Governor.'

'Well. We here are all witnesses to what he has said. Now go forward with the sport.' Farag's uncle smoothed his garments. 'How diversely hath Allah made His creatures! On one He bestows strength to slay Emirs. Another He causes to go mad and wander in the sun, like the afflicted sons of Melik-meid.'

'Yes, and to emit spray from the mouth, as the Inspector told us. All will happen as the Inspector foretold,' said Farag. 'I have never yet seen the Inspector thrown out during any run.'

'I think,' – Abdul plucked at Mr Groombride's sleeves, – 'I think perhaps it is better now, sar, if you give your fine little native speech. They not understanding English, but much pleased at your condescensions.'

'Condescensions?' Mr Groombride spun round. 'If they only knew how I felt towards them in my heart! If I could express a tithe of my feelings! I must stay here and learn the language. Hold up the umbrella, Abdul! I think my little speech will show them I know something of their *vie intime*.'

It was a short, simple, carefully learned address, and the accent, supervised by Abdul on the steamer, allowed the hearers to guess its meaning, which was a request to see one of the Mudir's Cranes; since the desire of the speaker's life, the object to which he would consecrate his days, was to improve the condition of the Mudir's Cranes. But first he must behold them with his own eyes. Would, then, his brethren, whom he loved, show him a Mudir's Crane whom he desired to love?

Once, twice, and again in his peroration he repeated his demand, using always – that they might see he was acquainted with their local argot – using always, I say, the word which the Inspector had given him in England long ago – the short adhesive word which, by itself, surprises even unblushing Ethiopia.

There are limits to the sublime politeness of an ancient people. A bulky, blue-chinned man in white clothes, his name red-lettered across his lower shirt-front, spluttering from under a green-lined umbrella almost tearful appeals to be introduced to the Unintroducible; naming loudly the Unnameable; dancing, as it seemed, in perverse joy at mere mention of the Unmentionable – found those limits. There was a moment's hush, and then such mirth as Gihon through his centuries had never heard – a roar like the roar of his own cataracts in flood. Children cast themselves on the ground, and rolled back and forth cheering and whooping; strong men, their faces hidden in their clothes, swayed in silence, till the agony became insupportable, and they threw up their heads and bayed at the sun; women, mothers and virgins, shrilled shriek upon mounting shriek, and slapped their thighs as it might have been the roll of musketry. When they tried to draw breath, some half-strangled voice would quack out the word, and the riot began afresh. Last to fall was the city-trained Abdul. He held on to the edge of apoplexy, then collapsed, throwing the umbrella from him.

Mr Groombride should not be judged too harshly. Exercise and strong emotion under a hot sun, the shock of public ingratitude, for the moment ruffled his spirit. He furled the umbrella, and with it beat the prostrate Abdul, crying that he had been betrayed.

In which posture the Inspector, on horseback, followed by the Governor, suddenly found him.

'That's all very well,' said the Inspector, when he had taken Adbul's dramatically dying depositions on the steamer, 'but you can't hammer a native merely because he laughs at you. I see nothing for it but for the law to take its course.'

'You might reduce the charge to – er – tampering with an interpreter,' said the Governor. Mr Groombride was too far gone to be comforted.

'It's the publicity that I fear,' he wailed. 'Is there no possible means of hushing up the affair? You don't know what a question – a single question in the House means to a man in my position – the ruin of my political career, I assure you.'

'I shouldn't have imagined it,' said the Governor thoughtfully.

'And, though perhaps I ought not to say it, I am not without honour in my own country – or influence. A word in season, as you know, Your Excellency. It might carry an official far.'

The Governor shuddered.

'Yes, *that* had to come too,' he said to himself. 'Well, look here. If I tell this man of yours to withdraw the charge against you, you can go to Gehenna for aught I care. The only condition I make is, that if you write – I suppose that's part of your business – about your travels, you don't praise *me*!'

So far Mr Groombride has loyally adhered to this understanding.

The House Surgeon

(1909)

On an evening after Easter Day, I sat at a table in a homeward-bound steamer's smoking-room, where half a dozen of us told ghost stories. As our party broke up, a man, playing Patience in the next alcove, said to me: 'I didn't quite catch the end of that last story about the Curse on the family's first-born.'

'It turned out to be drains,' I explained. 'As soon as new ones were put into the house the Curse was lifted, I believe. I never knew the people myself.'

'Ah! I've had *my* drains up twice; I'm on gravel too.'

'You don't mean to say you've a ghost in your house? Why didn't you join our party?'

'Any more orders, gentlemen, before the bar closes?' the steward interrupted.

'Sit down again and have one with me,' said the Patience player. 'No, it isn't a ghost. Our trouble is more depression than anything else.'

'How interesting! Then it's nothing any one can see?'

'It's – it's nothing worse than a little depression. And the odd part is that there hasn't been a death in the house since it was built – in 1863. The lawyer said so. That decided me – my good lady, rather – and he made me pay an extra thousand for it.'

'How curious! Unusual, too!' I said.

'Yes, ain't it? It was built for three sisters – Moultrie was the name – three old maids. They all lived together; the eldest owned it. I bought it from her lawyer a few years ago, and if I've spent a pound on the place first and last, I must have spent five thousand. Electric light, new servants' wing, garden – all that sort of thing. A man and his family ought to be happy after so much expense, ain't it?' He looked at me through the bottom of his glass.

'Does it affect your family much?'

'My good lady – she's a Greek by the way – and myself are middle-aged. We can bear up against depression; but it's hard on my little girl. I say little; but she's twenty. We send her visiting to escape it. She almost lived at hotels and hydros last year, but that isn't pleasant for her. She used to be a canary – a perfect canary – always singing. You ought to hear her. She doesn't sing now. That sort of thing's unwholesome for the young, ain't it?'

'Can't you get rid of the place?' I suggested.

'Not except at a sacrifice, and we are fond of it. Just suits us three. We'd love it if we were allowed.'

'What do you mean by not being allowed?'

'I mean because of the depression. It spoils everything.'

'What's it like exactly?'

'I couldn't very well explain. It must be seen to be appreciated, as the auctioneers say. Now, I was much impressed by the story you were telling just now.'

'It wasn't true,' I said.

'My tale is true. If you would do me the pleasure to come down and spend a night at my little place, you'd learn more than you would if I talked till morning. Very likely 'twouldn't touch your good self at all. You might be – immune, ain't it? On the other hand, if this influenza-influence *does* happen to affect you, why, I think it will be an experience.'

While he talked he gave me his card, and I read his name was L. Maxwell M'Leod, Esq., of Holmescroft. A City address was tucked away in a corner.

'My business,' he added, 'used to be furs. If you are interested in furs – I've given thirty years of my life to 'em.'

'You're very kind,' I murmured.

'Far from it, I assure you. I can meet you next Saturday afternoon anywhere in London you choose to name, and I'll be only too happy to motor you down. It ought to be a delightful run at this time of year – the rhododendrons will be out. I mean it. You don't know how truly I mean it. Very probably – it won't affect you at all. And – I think I may say I have the finest collection of narwhal tusks in the world. All the best skins and horns have to go through London, and L. Maxwell M'Leod, he knows where they come from, and where they go to. That's his business.'

For the rest of the voyage up-Channel Mr M'Leod talked to me of the assembling, preparation, and sale of the rarer furs; and told me things about the manufacture of fur-lined coats which quite shocked me. Somehow or other, when we landed on Wednesday, I found myself pledged to spend that week-end with him at Holmescroft.

On Saturday he met me with a well-groomed motor, and ran me out in an hour and a half to an exclusive residential district of dustless roads and elegantly designed country villas, each standing in from three to five acres of perfectly appointed land. He told me land was selling at eight hundred pounds the acre, and the new golf links, whose Queen Anne pavilion we passed, had cost nearly twenty-four thousand pounds to create.

Holmescroft was a large, two-storied, low, creeper-covered residence. A veranda at the south side gave on to a garden and two tennis courts, separated by a tasteful iron fence from a most park-like meadow of five or six acres, where two Jersey cows grazed. Tea was ready in the shade of a promising copper beech, and I could see groups on the lawn of young men and maidens appropriately clothed, playing lawn tennis in the sunshine.

'A pretty scene, ain't it?' said Mr M'Leod. 'My good lady's sitting under the tree, and that's my little girl in pink on the far court. But I'll take you to your room, and you can see 'em all later.'

He led me through a wide parquet-floored hall furnished in pale lemon, with huge cloisonné vases, an ebonized and gold grand piano, and banks of pot flowers in Benares brass bowls, up a pale oak staircase to a spacious landing, where there was a green velvet settee trimmed with silver. The blinds were down, and the light lay in parallel lines on the floors.

He showed me my room, saying cheerfully: 'You may be a little tired. One often is without knowing it after a run through traffic. Don't come down till you feel quite restored. We shall all be in the garden.'

My room was rather close, and smelt of perfumed soap. I threw up the window at once, but it opened so close to the floor and worked so clumsily that I came within an ace of pitching out, where I should certainly have ruined a rather lopsided laburnum below. As I set about washing off the journey's dust, I began to feel a little tired. But, I reflected, I had not come down here in this weather and among these new surroundings to be depressed, so I began to whistle.

And it was just then that I was aware of a little grey shadow, as it might have been a snowflake seen against the light, floating at an immense distance in the background of my brain. It annoyed me, and I shook my head to get rid of it. Then my brain telegraphed that it was the fore-runner of a swift-striding gloom which there was yet time to escape if I would force my thoughts away from it, as a man leaping for life forces his body forward and away from the fall of a wall. But the gloom overtook me before I could take in the meaning of the message. I moved towards the bed, every nerve already aching with the foreknowledge of the pain that was to be dealt it, and sat down, while my amazed and angry soul dropped, gulf by gulf, into that Horror of great darkness which is spoken of in the Bible, and which, as auctioneers say, must be experienced to be appreciated.

Despair upon despair, misery upon misery, fear after fear, each causing their distinct and separate woe, packed in upon me for an unrecorded length of time, until at last they blurred together, and I heard a click in my brain like the click in the ear when one descends in a diving-bell, and I knew that the pressures were equalized within and without, and that, for the moment, the worst was at an end. But I knew also that at any moment the darkness might come down anew; and while I dwelt on this speculation precisely as a man torments a raging tooth with his tongue, it ebbed away into the little grey shadow on the brain of its first coming, and once more I heard my brain, which knew what would recur, telegraph to every quarter for help, release, or diversion.

The door opened, and M'Leod reappeared. I thanked him politely, saying I was charmed with my room, anxious to meet Mrs M'Leod, much refreshed with my wash, and so on and so forth. Beyond a little stickiness at the corners of my mouth, it seemed to me that I was managing my words admirably, the while that I myself cowered at the bottom of unclimbable pits. M'Leod laid his hand on my shoulder, and said: 'You've got it now already, ain't it?'

'Yes,' I answered, 'it's making me sick!'

'It will pass off when you come outside. I give you my word it will then pass off. Come!'

I shambled out behind him, and wiped my forehead in the hall.

'You mustn't mind,' he said. 'I expect the run tired you. My good lady is sitting there under the copper beech.'

She was a fat woman in an apricot-coloured gown, with a heavily powdered face, against which her black long-lashed eyes showed like currants in dough. I was introduced to many fine ladies and gentlemen of those parts. Magnificently appointed landaus and covered motors swept in and out of the drive, and the air was gay with the merry outcries of the tennis-players.

As twilight drew on they all went away, and I was left alone with Mr and Mrs M'Leod, while tall men-servants and maid-servants took away the tennis and tea things. Miss M'Leod had walked a little down the drive with a light-haired young man, who apparently knew everything about every South American railway stock. He had told me at tea that these were the days of financial specialization.

'I think it went off beautifully, my dear,' said Mr M'Leod to his wife; and to me: 'You feel all right now, ain't it? Of course you do.'

Mrs M'Leod surged across the gravel. Her husband

skipped nimbly before her into the south veranda, turned a switch, and all Holmescroft was flooded with light.

'You can do that from your room also,' he said as they went in. 'There is something in money, ain't it?'

Miss M'Leod came up behind me in the dusk. 'We have not yet been introduced,' she said, 'but I suppose you are staying the night?'

'Your father was kind enough to ask me,' I replied.

She nodded. 'Yes, *I* know; and you know too, don't you? I saw your face when you came to shake hands with mamma. You felt the depression very soon? It is simply frightful in that bedroom sometimes. What do you think it is – bewitchment? In Greece, where I was a little girl, it might have been; but not in England, do you think? Or *do* you?'

'I don't know what to think,' I replied. 'I never felt anything like it. Does it happen often?'

'Yes, sometimes. It comes and goes.'

'Pleasant!' I said, as we walked up and down the gravel at the lawn edge. 'What has been your experience of it?'

'That is difficult to say, but – sometimes that – that depression is like as it were' – she gesticulated in most un-English fashion – 'a light. Yes, like a light turned into a room – only a light of blackness, do you understand? – into a happy room. For sometimes we are so happy, all we three, – so *very* happy. Then this blackness, it is turned on us just like – ah, I know what I mean now – like the headlamp of a motor, and we are eclip-sed. And there is another thing – '

The dressing-gong roared, and we entered the over-lighted hall. My dressing was a brisk athletic performance, varied with outbursts of song – careful attention paid to articulation and expression. But nothing happened. As I hurried downstairs, I thanked Heaven that nothing had happened.

Dinner was served breakfast-fashion; the dishes were placed on the sideboard over heaters, and we helped ourselves.

'We always do this when we are alone, so we talk better,' said Mr M'Leod.

'And we are always alone,' said the daughter.

'Cheer up, Thea. It will all come right,' he insisted.

'No, papa.' She shook her dark head. 'Nothing is right while *it* comes.'

'It is nothing that we ourselves have ever done in our lives – that I will swear to you,' said Mrs M'Leod suddenly. 'And we have changed our servants several times. So we know it is not *them*.'

'Never mind. Let us enjoy ourselves while we can,' said Mr M'Leod, opening the champagne.

But we did not enjoy ourselves. The talk failed. There were long silences.

'I beg your pardon,' I said, for I thought some one at my elbow was about to speak.

'Ah! That is the other thing!' said Miss M'Leod. Her mother groaned.

We were silent again, and, in a few seconds it must have been, a live grief beyond words – not ghostly dread or horror, but aching, helpless grief – overwhelmed us, each, I felt, according to his or her nature, and held steady like the beam of a burning-glass. Behind that pain I was conscious there was a desire on somebody's part to explain something on which some tremendously important issue hung.

Meantime I rolled bread pills and remembered my sins; M'Leod considered his own reflection in a spoon; his wife seemed to be praying, and the girl fidgeted desperately with hands and feet till the darkness passed on – as though the malignant rays of a burning-glass had been shifted from us.

'There,' said Miss M'Leod, half rising. 'Now you see what makes a happy home. Oh, sell it – sell it, father mine, and let us go away!'

'But I've spent thousands on it. You shall go to Harrogate next week, Thea dear.'

'I'm only just back from hotels. I am *so* tired of packing.'

'Cheer up, Thea. It is over. You know it does not often come here twice in the same night. I think we shall dare now to be comfortable.'

He lifted a dish-cover, and helped his wife and daughter.

His face was lined and fallen like an old man's after a debauch, but his hand did not shake, and his voice was clear. As he worked to restore us by speech and action, he reminded me of a grey-muzzled collie herding demoralized sheep.

After dinner we sat round the dining-room fire – the drawing-room might have been under the Shadow for aught we knew – talking with the intimacy of gipsies by the wayside, or of wounded comparing notes after a skirmish. By eleven o'clock the three between them had given me every name and detail they could recall that in any way bore on the house, and what they knew of its history.

We went to bed in a fortifying blaze of electric light. My one fear was that the blasting gust of depression would return – the surest way, of course, to bring it. I lay awake till dawn, breathing quickly and sweating lightly beneath what De Quincey inadequately describes as 'the oppression of inexpiable guilt'. Now as soon as the lovely day was broken, I fell into the most terrible of all dreams – that joyous one in which all past evil has not only been wiped out of our lives, but has never been committed; and in the very bliss of our assured innocence, before our loves shriek and change countenance, we wake to the day we have earned.

It was a coolish morning, but we preferred to breakfast in the south veranda. The forenoon we spent in the garden, pretending to play games that come out of boxes, such as croquet and clock-golf. But most of the time we drew together and talked. The young man who knew all about South American railways took Miss M'Leod for a walk in the afternoon, and at five M'Leod thoughtfully whirled us all up to dine in town.

'Now, don't say you will tell the Psychological Society, and that you will come again,' said Miss M'Leod, as we parted. 'Because I know you will not.'

'You should not say that,' said her mother. 'You should say, "Good-bye, Mr Perseus. Come again."'

'Not him!' the girl cried. 'He has seen the Medusa's head!'

Looking at myself in the restaurant's mirrors, it seemed to

me that I had not much benefited by my week-end. Next morning I wrote out all my Holmescroft notes at fullest length, in the hope that by so doing I could put it all behind me. But the experience worked on my mind, as they say certain imperfectly understood rays work on the body.

I am less calculated to make a Sherlock Holmes than any man I know, for I lack both method and patience, yet the idea of following up the trouble to its source fascinated me. I had no theory to go on, except a vague idea that I had come between two poles of a discharge, and had taken a shock meant for some one else. This was followed by a feeling of intense irritation. I waited cautiously on myself, expecting to be overtaken by horror of the supernatural, but my self persisted in being humanly indignant, exactly as though it had been the victim of a practical joke. It was in great pains and upheavals – that I felt in every fibre – but its dominant idea, to put it coarsely, was to get back a bit of its own. By this I knew that I might go forward if I could find the way.

After a few days it occurred to me to go to the office of Mr J. M. M. Baxter – the solicitor who had sold Holmescroft to M'Leod. I explained I had some notion of buying the place. Would he act for me in the matter?

Mr Baxter, a large, greyish, throaty-voiced man, showed no enthusiasm. 'I sold it to Mr M'Leod,' he said. 'It'ud scarcely do for me to start on the running-down tack now. But I can recommend –'

'I know he's asking an awful price,' I interrupted, 'and atop of it he wants an extra thousand for what he calls your clean bill of health.'

Mr Baxter sat up in his chair. I had all his attention.

'Your guarantee with the house. Don't you remember it?'

'Yes, yes. That no death had taken place in the house since it was built. I remember perfectiy.'

He did not gulp as untrained men do when they lie, but his jaws moved stickily, and his eyes, turning towards the deed-boxes on the wall, dulled. I counted seconds, one, two, three –

one, two, three – up to ten. A man, I knew, can live through ages of mental depression in that time.

'I remember perfectly.' His mouth opened a little as though it had tasted old bitterness.

'Of course *that* sort of thing doesn't appeal to me,' I went on. '*I* don't expect to buy a house free from death.'

'Certainly not. No one does. But it was Mr M'Leod's fancy – his wife's rather, I believe; and since we could meet it – it was my duty to my clients – at whatever cost to my own feelings – to make him pay.'

'That's really why I came to you. I understood from him you knew the place well.'

'Oh yes. Always did. It originally belonged to some connections of mine.'

'The Misses Moultrie, I suppose. How interesting! They must have loved the place before the country round about was built up.'

'They were very fond of it indeed.'

'I don't wonder. So restful and sunny. I don't see how they could have brought themselves to part with it.'

Now it is one of the most constant peculiarities of the English that in polite conversation – and I had striven to be polite – no one ever does or sells anything for mere money's sake.

'Miss Agnes – the youngest – fell ill' (he spaced his words a little), 'and, as they were very much attached to each other, that broke up the home.'

'Naturally. I fancied it must have been something of that kind. One doesn't associate the Staffordshire Moultries' (my Demon of Irresponsibility at that instant created 'em) 'with – with being hard up.'

'I don't know whether we're related to them,' he answered importantly. 'We may be, for our branch of the family comes from the Midlands.'

I give this talk at length, because I am so proud of my first attempt at detective work. When I left him, twenty minutes later, with instructions to move against the owner of

Holmescroft with a view to purchase. I was more bewildered than any Doctor Watson at the opening of a story.

Why should a middle-aged solicitor turn plover's-egg colour and drop his jaw when reminded of so innocent and festal a matter as that no death had ever occurred in a house that he had sold? If I knew my English vocabulary at all, the tone in which he said the youngest sister 'fell ill' meant that she had gone out of her mind. That might explain his change of countenance, and it was just possible that her demented influence still hung about Holmescroft. But the rest was beyond me.

I was relieved when I reached M'Leod's City office, and could tell him what I had done – not what I thought.

M'Leod was quite willing to enter into the game of the pretended purchase, but did not see how it would help if I knew Baxter.

'He's the only living soul I can get at who was connected with Holmescroft,' I said.

'Ah! Living soul is good,' said M'Leod. 'At any rate our little girl will be pleased that you are still interested in us. Won't you come down some day this week?'

'How is it there now?' I asked.

He screwed up his face. 'Simply frightful!' he said. 'Thea is at Droitwich.'

'I should like it immensely, but I must cultivate Baxter for the present. You'll be sure and keep him busy your end, won't you?'

He looked at me with quiet contempt. 'Do not be afraid. I shall be a good Jew. I shall be my own solicitor.'

Before a fortnight was over, Baxter admitted ruefully that M'Leod was better than most firms in the business. We buyers were coy, argumentative, shocked at the price of Holmescroft, inquisitive, and cold by turns, but Mr M'Leod the seller easily met and surpassed us; and Mr Baxter entered every letter, telegram, and consultation at the proper rates in a cinematograph-film of a bill. At the end of a month he said it looked as though M'Leod, thanks to him, were really going to listen to reason. I was some pounds out of pocket, but I had learned something of Mr Baxter on the human side. I deserved it. Never in my life have I worked to conciliate, amuse and flatter a human being as I worked over my solicitor.

It appeared that he golfed. Therefore, I was an enthusiastic beginner, anxious to learn. Twice I invaded his office with a bag (M'Leod lent it) full of the spelicans needed in this detestable game, and a vocabulary to match. The third time the ice broke, and Mr Baxter took me to his links, quite ten miles off, where in a maze of tramway-lines, rail-roads, and nursery-maids, we skelped our divoted way round nine holes like barges plunging through head seas. He played vilely and had never expected to meet any one worse; but as he realized my form, I think he began to like me, for he took me in hand by the two hours together. After a fortnight he could give me no more than a stroke a hole, and when, with this allowance, I once managed to beat him by one, he was honestly glad, and assured me that I should be a golfer if I stuck to it. I was sticking to it for my own ends, but now and again my conscience pricked me; for the man was a nice man. Between games he supplied me with odd pieces of evidence such as that he had known the Moultries all his life, being their cousin, and that Miss Mary, the eldest, was an unforgiving woman who would never let bygones be. I naturally wondered what she might have against him; and somehow connected him unfavourably with mad Agnes.

'People ought to forgive and forget,' he volunteered one day between rounds. 'Specially where, in the nature of things, they can't be sure of their deductions. Don't you think so?'

'It all depends on the nature of the evidence on which one forms one's judgement,' I answered.

'Nonsense!' he cried. 'I'm lawyer enough to know that there's nothing in the world so misleading as circumstantial evidence. Never was.'

'Why? Have you ever seen men hanged on it?'

'Hanged? People have been supposed to be eternally lost on it.' His face turned grey again. 'I don't know how it is with you, but my consolation is that God must know. He *must*! Things that seem on the face of 'em like murder, or say suicide, may appear different to God. Heh?'

'That's what the murderer and the suicide can always hope – I suppose.'

'I have expressed myself clumsily as usual. The facts as God knows 'em – may *be* different – even after the most clinching evidence. I've always said that – both as a lawyer and a man, but some people won't – I don't want to judge 'em – we'll say they can't – believe it; whereas *I* say there's always a working chance – a certainty – that the worst hasn't happened.' He stopped and cleared his throat. 'Now, let's come on! This time next week I shall be taking my holiday.'

'What links?' I asked carelessly, while twins in a perambulator got out of our line of fire.

'A potty little nine-hole affair at a Hydro in the Midlands. My cousins stay there. Always will. Not but what the fourth and the seventh holes take some doing. You could manage it, though,' he said encouragingly. 'You're doing much better. It's only your approach-shots that are weak.'

'You're right. I can't approach for nuts! I shall go to pieces while you're away – with no one to coach me,' I said mournfully.

'I haven't taught you anything,' he said, delighted with the compliment.

'I owe all I've learned to you, anyhow. When will you come back?'

'Look here,' he began. 'I don't know your engagements, but I've no one to play with at Burry Mills. Never have. Why couldn't you take a few days off and join me there? I warn you it will be rather dull. It's a throat and gout place – baths, massage, electricity, and so forth. But the fourth and the seventh holes really take some doing.'

'I'm for the game,' I answered valiantly, Heaven well knowing that I hated every stroke and word of it.

'That's the proper spirit. As their lawyer I must ask you not to say anything to my cousins about Holmescroft. It upsets 'em. Always did. But speaking as man to man, it would be very pleasant for me if you could see your way to –'

I saw it as soon as decency permitted, and thanked him sincerely. According to my now well-developed theory he had certainly misappropriated his aged cousins' monies under power of attorney, and had probably driven poor Moultrie out of her wits, but I wished that he was not so gentle, and good-tempered, and innocent-eyed.

Before I joined him at Burry Mills Hydro, I spent a night at Holmescroft. Miss M'Leod had returned from her Hydro, and first we made very merry on the open lawn in the sunshine over the manners and customs of the English resorting to such places. She knew dozens of Hydros, and warned me how to behave in them, while Mr and Mrs M'Leod stood aside and adored her.

'Ah! That's the way she always comes back to us,' he said. 'Pity it wears off so soon, ain't it? You ought to hear her sing "With mirth, thou pretty bird".'

We had the house to face through the evening, and there we neither laughed nor sang. The gloom fell on us as we entered, and did not shift till ten o'clock, when we crawled out, as it were, from beneath it.

'It has been bad this summer,' said Mrs M'Leod in a whisper after we realized that we were freed. 'Sometimes I think the house will get up and cry out – it is so bad.'

'How?'

'Have you forgotten what comes after the depression?'

So then we waited about the small fire, and the dead air in the room presently filled and pressed down upon us with the sensation (but words are useless here) as though some dumb and bound power were striving against gag and bond to deliver its soul of an articulate word. It passed in a few minutes, and I fell to thinking about Mr Baxter's conscience and Agnes Moultrie, gone mad in the well-lit bedroom that waited me. These reflections secured me a night during which I rediscovered how, from purely mental causes, a man can be physically sick. But the sickness was bliss compared with my dreams when the birds waked. On my departure, M'Leod gave me a beautiful narwhal's horn much as a nurse gives a child sweets for being brave at a dentist's.

'There's no duplicate of it in the world,' he said, 'else it would have come to old Max M'Leod,' and he tucked it into the motor. Miss M'Leod on the far side of the car whispered, 'Have you found out anything, Mr Perseus?'

I shook my head.

'Then I shall be chained to my rock all my life,' she went on. 'Only don't tell papa.'

I supposed she was thinking of the young gentleman who specialized in South American rails, for I noticed a ring on the third finger of her left hand.

I went straight from that house to Burry Mills Hydro, keen for the first time in my life on playing golf, which is guaranteed to occupy the mind, Baxter had taken me a room communicating with his own, and after lunch introduced me to a tall, horse-headed elderly lady of decided manners, who a white-haired maid pushed along in a bath-chair through the park-like grounds of the Hydro. She was Miss Mary Moultrie, and she coughed and cleared her throat just like Baxter. She suffered – she told me it was the Moultrie caste-mark – from some obscure form of chronic bronchitis, complicated with spasm of the glottis; and, in a dead flat voice, with a sunken eye that looked and saw not, told me what washes, gargles, pastilles, and inhalations she had proved most beneficial. From her I was passed on to her younger sister, Miss Elizabeth, a small and withered thing with twitching lips, victim, she told me, to very much the same sort of throat, but secretly devoted to another set of medicines. When she went away with Baxter and the bath-chair, I fell across a Major of the Indian Army with gout in his glassy eyes, and a stomach which he had taken all round the Continent. He laid everything before me; and him I escaped only to be confided in by a matron with a tendency to follicular tonsillitis and eczema. Baxter waited hand and foot on his cousins till five o'clock, trying, as I saw, to atone for his treatment of the dead sister. Miss Mary ordered him about like a dog.

'I warned you it would be dull,' he said when we met in the smoking-room.

'It's tremendously interesting,' I said. 'But how about a look round the links?'

'Unluckily damp always affects my eldest cousin. I've got to buy her a new bronchitis-kettle. Arthurs broke her old one yesterday.'

We slipped out to the chemist's shop in the town, and he bought a large glittering tin thing whose workings he explained.

'I'm used to this sort of work. I come up here pretty often,' he said. 'I've the family throat too.'

'You're a good man,' I said. 'A very good man.'

He turned towards me in the evening light among the beeches, and his face changed to what it might have been a generation before.

'You see,' he said huskily, 'there was the youngest – Agnes. Before she fell ill, you know. But she didn't like leaving her sisters. Never would.' He hurried on with his odd-shaped load and left me among the ruins of my black theories. The man with that face had done Agnes Moultrie no wrong.

We never played our game. I was waked between two and three in the morning from my hygienic bed by Baxter in an ulster over orange-and-white pyjamas, which I should never have suspected from his character.

'My cousin has had some sort of a seizure,' he said. 'Will you come? I don't want to wake the doctor. Don't want to make a scandal. Quick!'

So I came quickly, and, led by the white-haired Arthurs in a jacket and petticoat, entered a double-bedded room reeking with steam and Friar's Balsam. The electrics were all on. Miss Mary – I knew her by her height – was at the open window, wrestling with Miss Elizabeth, who gripped her round the knees. Her hand was at her throat, which was streaked with blood.

'She's done it. She's done it too!' Miss Elizabeth panted. 'Hold her! Help me!'

'Oh, I say! Women don't cut their throats,' Baxter whispered.

'My God! Has she cut her throat?' the maid cried, and with no warning rolled over in a faint. Baxter pushed her under the wash-basins, and leaped to hold the gaunt woman who crowed and whistled as she struggled towards the window. He took her by the shoulder, and she struck out wildly.

'All right! She's only cut her hand,' he said. 'Wet towel – quick!'

While I got that he pushed her backward. Her strength seemed almost as great as his. I swabbed at her throat when I could, and found no mark; then helped him to control her a little. Miss Elizabeth leaped back to bed, wailing like a child.

'Tie up her hand somehow,' said Baxter. 'Don't let it drip about the place. She' – he stepped on broken glass in his slippers – 'she must have smashed a pane.'

Miss Mary lurched towards the open window again, dropped on her knees, her head on the sill, and lay quiet, surrendering the cut hand to me.

'What did she do?' Baxter turned towards Miss Elizabeth in the far bed.

'She was going to throw herself out of the window,' was the answer. 'I stopped her, and sent Arthurs for you. Oh, we can never hold up our heads again!'

Miss Mary writhed and fought for breath. Baxter found a shawl which he threw over her shoulders.

'Nonsense!' said he. 'That isn't like Mary'; but his face worked when he said it.

'You wouldn't believe about Aggie, John. Perhaps you will now!' said Miss Elizabeth. 'I *saw* her do it, and she's cut her throat too!'

'She hasn't,' I said. 'It's only her hand.'

Miss Mary suddenly broke from us with an indescribable grunt, flew, rather than ran, to her sister's bed, and there shook her as one furious schoolgirl would shake another.

'No such thing,' she croaked. 'How dare you think so, you wicked little fool?'

'Get into bed, Mary,' said Baxter. 'You'll catch a chill.'

She obeyed, but sat up with the grey shawl round her lean shoulders, glaring at her sister. 'I'm better now,' she crowed. 'Arthurs let me sit out too long. Where's Arthurs? The kettle.'

'Never mind Arthurs,' said Baxter. '*You* get the kettle.' I hastened to bring it from the side-table. 'Now, Mary, as God sees you, tell me what you've done.'

His lips were dry, and he could not moisten them with his tongue.

Miss Mary applied herself to the mouth of the kettle, and between indraws of steam said: 'The spasm came on just now, while I was asleep. I was nearly choking to death. So I went to the window. I've done it often before, without waking any one. Bessie's such an old maid about draughts! I tell you I was choking to death. I couldn't manage the catch, and I nearly fell out. That window opens too low. I cut my hand trying to save myself. Who has tied it up in this filthy handkerchief? I wish you had had my throat, Bessie. I never was nearer dying!' She scowled on us all impartially, while her sister sobbed.

From the bottom of the bed we heard a quivering voice: 'Is she dead? Have they took her away? Oh, I never could bear the sight o' blood!'

'Arthurs,' said Miss Mary, 'you are an hireling. Go away!'

It is my belief that Arthurs crawled out on all fours, but I was busy picking up broken glass from the carpet.

Then Baxter, seated by the side of the bed, began to cross-examine in a voice I scarcely recognized. No one could for an instant have doubted the genuine rage of Miss Mary against her sister, her cousin, or her maid; and that the doctor should have been called in – for she did me the honour of calling me doctor – was the last drop. She was choking with her throat; had rushed to the window for air; had nearly pitched out, and in catching at the window-bars had cut her hand. Over and over she made this clear to the intent Baxter. Then she turned on her sister and tongue-lashed her savagely.

'You mustn't blame me,' Miss Bessie faltered at last. 'You know what we think of night and day.'

'I'm coming to that,' said Baxter. 'Listen to me. What *you* did, Mary, misled four people into thinking you – you meant to do away with yourself.'

'Isn't one suicide in the family enough? Oh, God, help and pity us! You *couldn't* have believed that!' she cried.

'The evidence was complete. Now, don't you think,' – Baxter's finger wagged under her nose – '*can't* you think that poor Aggie did the same thing at Holmescroft when she fell out of the window?'

'She had the same throat,' said Miss Elizabeth. 'Exactly the same symptoms. Don't you remember, Mary?'

'Which was her bedroom?' I asked of Baxter in an undertone.

'Over the south veranda, looking on to the tennis lawn.'

'I nearly fell out of that very window when I was at Holmescroft – opening it to get some air. The sill doesn't come much above your knees,' I said.

'You hear that, Mary? Mary, do you hear what this gentleman says? Won't you believe that what nearly happened to you must have happened to poor Aggie that night? For God's sake – for her sake – Mary, *won't* you believe?'

There was a long silence while the steam-kettle puffed.

'If I could have proof – if I could have proof,' said she, and broke into most horrible tears.

Baxter motioned to me, and I crept away to my room, and lay awake till morning, thinking more specially of the dumb Thing at Holmescroft which wished to explain itself. I hated

Miss Mary as perfectly as though I had known her for twenty years, but I felt that, alive or dead, I should not like her to condemn me.

Yet at midday, when I saw Miss Mary in her bath-chair, Arthurs behind and Baxter and Miss Elizabeth on either side, in the park-like grounds of the Hydro, I found it difficult to arrange my words.

'Now that you know all about it,' said Baxter aside, after the first strangeness of our meeting was over, 'it's only fair to tell you that my poor cousin did not die *in* Holmescroft at all. She was dead when they found her under the window in the morning. Just dead.'

'Under that laburnum outside the window?' I asked, for I suddenly remembered the crooked evil thing.

'Exactly. She broke the tree in falling. But no death has ever taken place *in* the house, so far as we were concerned. You can make yourself quite easy on that point. Mr M'Leod's extra thousand for what you called the "clean bill of health" was something towards my cousins' estate when we sold. It was my duty as their lawyer to get it for them – at any cost to my own feelings.'

I know better than to argue when the English talk about their duty. So I agreed with my solicitor.

'Their sister's death must have been a great blow to your cousins,' I went on. The bath-chair was behind me.

'Unspeakable,' Baxter whispered. 'They brooded on it day and night. No wonder. If their theory of poor Aggie making away with herself was correct, she was eternally lost.'

'Do you believe that she made away with herself?'

'No, thank God! Never have! And after what happened to Mary last night, I see perfectly what happened to poor Aggie. She had the family throat too. By the way, Mary thinks you are a doctor. Otherwise she wouldn't like your having been in her room.'

'Very good. Is she convinced now about her sister's death?'

'She'd give anything to be able to believe it, but she's a

hard woman, and brooding along certain lines makes one groovy. I have sometimes been afraid for her reason – on the religious side, don't you know. Elizabeth doesn't matter. Brain of a hen. Always had.'

Here Arthurs summoned me to the bath-chair, and the ravaged face, beneath its knitted Shetland wool hood, of Miss Mary Moultrie.

'I need not remind you, I hope, of the seal of secrecy – absolute secrecy – in your profession,' she began. 'Thanks to my cousin's and my sister's stupidity, you have found out – ' She blew her nose.

'Please don't excite her, sir,' said Arthurs at the back.

'But, my dear Miss Moultrie, I only know what I've seen, of course, but it seems to me that what you thought was a tragedy in your sister's case, turns out, on your own evidence, so to speak, to have been an accident – a dreadfully sad one – but absolutely an accident.'

'Do you believe that too?' she cried. 'Or are you only saying it to comfort me?'

'I believe it from the bottom of my heart. Come down to Holmescroft for an hour – for half an hour – and satisfy yourself.'

'Of what? You don't understand. I see the house every day – every night. I am always there in spirit – waking or sleeping. I couldn't face it in reality.'

'But you must,' I said. 'If you go there in the spirit the greater need for you to go there in the flesh. Go to your sister's room once more, and see the window – I nearly fell out of it myself. It's – it's awfully low and dangerous. That would convince you,' I pleaded.

'Yet Aggie had slept in that room for years,' she interrupted.

'You've slept in your room here for a long time, haven't you? But you nearly fell out of the window when you were choking.'

'That is true. That is one thing true,' she nodded. 'And I might have been killed as – perhaps – Aggie was killed.'

'In that case your own sister and cousin and maid would have said you had committed suicide, Miss Moultrie. Come down to Holmescroft, and go over the place just once.'

'You are lying,' she said quite quietly. 'You don't want me to come down to see a window. It is something else. I warn you we are Evangelicals. We don't believe in prayers for the dead. "As the tree falls – " '

'Yes. I daresay. But you persist in thinking that your sister committed suicide – '

'No! No! I have always prayed that I might have misjudged her.'

Arthurs at the bath-chair spoke up: 'Oh, Miss Mary! you *would* 'ave it from the first that poor Miss Aggie 'ad made away with herself; an', of course, Miss Bessie took the notion from you. Only Master – Mister John stood out, and – and I'd 'ave taken my Bible oath *you* was making away with yourself last night.'

Miss Mary leaned towards me, one finger on my sleeve.

'If going to Holmescroft kills me,' she said, 'you will have the murder of a fellow-creature on your conscience for all eternity.'

'I'll risk it,' I answered. Remembering what torment the mere reflection of her torments had cast on Holmescroft, and remembering, above all, the dumb Thing that filled the house with its desire to speak, I felt that there might be worse things.

Baxter was amazed at the proposed visit, but at a nod from that terrible woman went off to make arrangements. Then I sent a telegram to M'Leod bidding him and his vacate Holmescroft for that afternoon. Miss Mary should be alone with her dead, as I had been alone.

I expected untold trouble in transporting her, but to do her justice, her promise given for the journey, she underwent it without murmur, spasm, or unnecessary word. Miss Bessie, pressed in a corner by the window, wept behind her veil, and from time to time tried to take hold of her sister's hand. Baxter wrapped himself in his newly-found happiness as selfishly as a bridegroom, for he sat still and smiled.

'So long as I know that Aggie didn't make away with herself,' he explained, 'I tell you frankly I don't care what happened. She's as hard as a rock – Mary. Always was. *She* won't die.'

We led her out on to the platform like a blind woman, and so got her into the fly. The half-hour crawl to Holmescroft was the most racking experience of the day. M'Leod had obeyed my instructions. There was no one visible in the house or the gardens; and the front door stood open.

Miss Mary rose from beside her sister, stepped forth first, and entered the hall.

'Come, Bessie,' she cried.

'I daren't. Oh, I daren't.'

'Come!' Her voice had altered. I felt Baxter start. 'There's nothing to be afraid of.'

'Good heavens!' said Baxter. 'She's running up the stairs. We'd better follow.'

'Let's wait below. She's going to the room.'

We heard the door of the bedroom I knew open and shut, and we waited in the lemon-coloured hall, heavy with the scent of flowers.

'I've never been into it since it was sold,' Baxter sighed. 'What a lovely restful place it is! Poor Aggie used to arrange the flowers.'

'Restful?' I began, but stopped of a sudden, for I felt all over my bruised soul that Baxter was speaking the truth. It was a light, spacious, airy house, full of the sense of well-being and peace – above all things, of peace. I ventured into the dining-room where the thoughtful M'Leods had left a small fire. There was no terror there present or lurking; and in the drawing-room, which for good reasons we had never cared to enter, the sun and the peace and the scent of the flowers worked together as is fit in an inhabited house. When I returned to the hall, Baxter was sweetly asleep on a couch, looking most unlike a middle-aged solicitor who had spent a broken night with an exacting cousin.

There was ample time for me to review it all – to felicitate myself upon my magnificent acumen (barring some errors about Baxter as a thief and possibly a murderer), before the door above opened, and Baxter, evidently a light sleeper, sprang awake.

'I've had a heavenly little nap,' he said, rubbing his eyes with the backs of his hands like a child. 'Good Lord! That's not *their* step!'

But it was. I had never before been privileged to see the Shadow turned backward on the dial – the years ripped bodily off poor human shoulders – old sunken eyes filled and alight – harsh lips moistened and human.

'John,' Miss Mary called, 'I know now. Aggie didn't do it!' and 'She didn't do it!' echoed Miss Bessie, and giggled.

'I did not think it wrong to say a prayer,' Miss Mary continued. 'Not for her soul, but for our peace. Then I was convinced.'

'Then we got conviction,' the younger sister piped.

'We've misjudged poor Aggie, John. But I feel she knows now. Wherever she is, she knows that we know she is guiltless.'

'Yes, she knows. I felt it too,' said Miss Elizabeth.

'I never doubted,' said John Baxter, whose face was beautiful at that hour. 'Not from the first. Never have!'

'You never offered me proof, John. Now, thank God, it will not be the same any more. I can think henceforward of Aggie without sorrow.' She tripped, absolutely tripped, across the hall. 'What ideas these Jews have of arranging furniture!' She spied me behind a big cloisonné vase.

'I've seen the window,' she said remotely. 'You took a great risk in advising me to undertake such a journey However, as it turns out ... I forgive you, and I pray you may never know what mental anguish means! Bessie! Look at this peculiar piano! Do you suppose, Doctor, these people would offer one tea? I miss mine.'

'I will go and see,' I said, and explored M'Leod's new-built servants' wing. It was in the servants' hall that I unearthed the M'Leod family bursting with anxiety.

'Tea for three, quick,' I said. 'If you ask me any questions now, I shall have a fit!' So Mrs M'Leod got it, and I was butler, amid murmured apologies from Baxter, still smiling and self-absorbed, and the cold disapproval of Miss Mary, who thought the pattern of the china vulgar. However, she ate well, and even asked me whether I would not like a cup of tea for myself.

They went away in the twilight – the twilight that I had once feared. They were going to an hotel in London to rest after the fatigues of the day, and as their fly turned down the drive, I capered on the doorstep, with the all-darkened house behind me.

Then I heard the uncertain feet of the M'Leods, and bade them not to turn on the lights, but to feel – to feel what I had done; for the Shadow was gone, with the dumb desire in the air. They drew short, but afterwards deeper, breaths, like bathers entering chill water, separated one from the other, moved about the hall, tiptoed upstairs, raced down, and then Miss M'Leod, and I believe her mother, though she denies this, embraced me. I know M'Leod did.

It was a disgraceful evening. To say we rioted through the house is to put it mildly. We played a sort of Blind Man's Buff along the darkest passages, in the unlighted drawing-room, and the little dining-room, calling cheerily to each other after each exploration that here, and here, and here, the trouble had removed itself. We came up to *the* bedroom – mine for the night again – and sat, the women on the bed, and we men on chairs, drinking in blessed draughts of peace and comfort and cleanliness of soul, while I told them my tale in full, and received fresh praise, thanks, and blessing.

When the servants, returned from their day's outing, gave us a supper of cold fried fish, M'Leod had sense enough to open no wine. We had been practically drunk since nightfall, and grew incoherent on water and milk.

'I like that Baxter,' said M'Leod. 'He's a sharp man. The

death wasn't *in* the house, but he ran it pretty close, ain't it?'

'And the joke of it is that he supposes I want to buy the place from you,' I said. 'Are you selling?'

'Not for twice what I paid for it – now,' said M'Leod. 'I'll keep you in furs all your life; but not our Holmescroft.'

'No – never our Holmescroft,' said Miss M'Leod. 'We'll ask *him* here on Tuesday, mamma.' They squeezed each other's hands.

'Now tell me,' said Mrs M'Leod – 'that tall one I saw out of the scullery window – did *she* tell you she was always here in the spirit? I hate her. She made all this trouble. It was *not* her house after she had sold it. What do you think?'

'I suppose,' I answered, 'she brooded over what she believed was her sister's suicide night and day – she confessed she did – and her thoughts being concentrated on this place, they felt like a – like a burning-glass.'

'Burning-glass is good,' said M'Leod.

'I said it was like a light of blackness turned on us,' cried the girl, twiddling her ring. 'That must have been when the tall one thought worst about her sister and the house.'

'Ah, the poor Aggie!' said Mrs M'Leod. 'The poor Aggie, trying to tell every one it was not so! No wonder we felt Something wished to say Something. Thea, Max, do you remember that night – '

'We need not remember any more,' M'Leod interrupted. 'It is not our trouble. They have told each other now.'

'Do you think, then,' said Miss M'Leod, 'that those two, the living ones, were actually told something – upstairs – in your – in the room?'

'I can't say. At any rate they were made happy, and they ate a big tea afterwards. As your father says, it is not our trouble any longer – thank God!'

'Amen!' said M'Leod. 'Now, Thea, let us have some music after all these months. "With mirth, thou pretty bird", ain't it? You ought to hear that.'

And in the half-lighted hall, Thea sang an old English song that I had never heard before:

'With mirth, thou pretty bird, rejoice
  Thy Maker's praise enhancèd;
Lift up thy shrill and pleasant voice,
  Thy God is high advancèd!
Thy food before He did provide,
And gives it in a fitting side,
  Wherewith be thou sufficèd!
Why shouldst thou now unpleasant be,
  Thy wrath against God venting,
That He a little bird made thee,
  Thy silly head tormenting,
Because He made thee not a man?
Oh, Peace! He hath well thought thereon,
  Therewith be thou sufficèd!'

As Easy as A.B.C.

(1912)

The A.B.C., that semi-elected, semi-nominated body of a few score persons, controls the Planet. Transportation is Civilization, our motto runs. Theoretically we do what we please, so long as we do not interfere with the traffic **and all it implies.** ***Practically, the A.B.C. confirms or annuls all international arrangements, and, to judge from its last report, finds our tolerant, humorous, lazy little Planet only too ready to shift the whole burden of public administration on its shoulders.***

'With the Night Mail.'*

ISN'T it almost time that our Planet took some interest in the proceedings of the Aerial Board of Control? One knows that easy communications nowadays, and lack of privacy in the past, have killed all curiosity among mankind, but as the Board's Official Reporter I am bound to tell my tale.

At 9.30 a.m. August 26, A.D. 2065, the Board, sitting in London, was informed by De Forest that the District of Northern Illinois had riotously cut itself out of all systems and would remain disconnected till the Board should take over and administer it direct.

Every Northern Illinois freight and passenger tower was, he reported, out of action; all District main, local, and guiding lights had been extinguished; all General Communications were dumb, and through traffic had been diverted. No reason had been given, but he gathered unofficially from the Mayor of Chicago that the District complained of 'crowd-making and invasion of privacy'.

As a matter of fact, it is of no importance whether Northern Illinois stay in or out of planetary circuit; as a matter of policy, any complaint of invasion of privacy needs immediate investigation, lest worse follow.

By 9.45 a.m. De Forest, Dragomiroff (Russia), Takahira

* ***Actions and Reactions.***

(Japan), and Pirolo (Italy) were empowered to visit Illinois and 'to take such steps as might be necessary for the resumption of traffic and *all that that implies*'. By 10 a.m. the Hall was empty, and the four Members and I were aboard what Pirolo insisted on calling 'my leetle godchild' – that is to say, the new *Victor Pirolo*. Our Planet prefers to know Victor Pirolo as a gentle, grey-haired enthusiast who spends his time near Foggia, inventing or creating new breeds of Spanish-Italian olive-trees; but there is another side to his nature – the manufacture of quaint inventions, of which the *Victor Pirolo* is, perhaps, not the least surprising. She and a few score sister-craft of the same type embody his latest ideas. But she is not comfortable. An A.B.C. boat does not take the air with the level-keeled lift of a liner, but shoots up rocket-fashion like the 'aeroplane' of our ancestors, and makes her height at top-speed from the first. That is why I found myself sitting suddenly on the large lap of Eustace Arnott, who commands the A.B.C. Fleet. One knows vaguely that there is such a thing as a Fleet somewhere on the Planet, and that, theoretically, it exists for the purposes of what used to be known as 'war'. Only a week before, while visiting a glacier sanatorium behind Gothaven, I had seen some squadrons making false auroras far to the north while they manoeuvred round the Pole; but, naturally, it had never occurred to me that the things could be used in earnest.

Said Arnott to De Forest as I staggered to a seat on the chart-room divan: 'We're tremendously grateful to 'em in Illinois. We've never had a chance of exercising all the Fleet together. I've turned in a General Call, and I expect we'll have at least two hundred keels aloft this evening.'

'Well aloft?' De Forest asked.

'Of course, sir. Out of sight till they're called for.'

Arnott laughed as he lolled over the transparent chart-table where the map of the summer-blue Atlantic slid along, degree by degree, in exact answer to our progress. Our dial already showed 320 m.p.h. and we were two thousand feet above the uppermost traffic lines.

'Now, where is this Illinois District of yours?' said Dragomiroff. 'One travels so much, one sees so little. Oh, I remember! It is in North America.'

De Forest, whose business it is to know the out districts, told us that it lay at the foot of Lake Michigan, on a road to nowhere in particular, was about half an hour's run from end to end, and, except in one corner, as flat as the sea. Like most flat countries nowadays, it was heavily guarded against invasion of privacy by forced timber – fifty-foot spruce and tamarack, grown in five years. The population was close on two millions, largely migratory between Florida and California, with a backbone of small farms (they call a thousand acres a farm in Illinois) whose owners come into Chicago for amusements and society during the winter. They were, he said, noticeably kind, quiet folk, but a little exacting, as all flat countries must be, in their notions of privacy. There had, for instance, been no printed news-sheet in Illinois for twenty-seven years. Chicago argued that engines for printed news sooner or later developed into engines for invasion of privacy, which in turn might bring the old terror of Crowds and blackmail back to the Planet. So news-sheets were not.

'And that's Illinois,' De Forest concluded. 'You see, in the Old Days, she was in the forefront of what they used to call "progress", and Chicago –'

'Chicago?' said Takahira. 'That's the little place where there is Salati's Statue of the Nigger in Flames? A fine bit of old work.'

'When did you see it?' asked De Forest quickly. 'They only unveil it once a year.'

'I know. At Thanksgiving. It was then,' said Takahira, with a shudder. 'And they sang MacDonough's Song, too.'

'Whew!' De Forest whistled. 'I did not know that! I wish you'd told me before. MacDonough's Song may have had its uses when it was composed, but it was an infernal legacy for any man to leave behind.'

'It's protective instinct, my dear fellows,' said Pirolo, rolling a cigarette. 'The Planet, she has had her dose of popular government. She suffers from inherited agrophobia. She has no – ah – use for crowds.'

Dragomiroff leaned forward to give him a light. 'Certainly,' said the white-bearded Russian, 'the Planet has taken all precautions against crowds for the past hundred years. What is our total population today? Six hundred million, we hope; five hundred, we think; but – but if next year's census shows more than four hundred and fifty, I myself will eat all the extra little babies. We have cut the birth-rate out – right out! For a long time we have said to Almighty God, "Thank You, Sir, but we do not much like Your game of life, so we will not play."'

'Anyhow,' said Arnott defiantly, 'men live a century apiece on the average now.'

'Oh, that is quite well! I am rich – you are rich – we are all rich and happy because we are so few and we live so long. Only *I* think Almighty God He will remember what the Planet was like in the time of Crowds and the Plague. Perhaps He will send us nerves. Eh, Pirolo?'

The Italian blinked into space. 'Perhaps,' he said, 'He has sent them already. Anyhow, you cannot argue with the Planet. She does not forget the Old Days, and – what can you do?'

'For sure we can't remake the world.' De Forest glanced at the map flowing smoothly across the table from west to east. 'We ought to be over our ground by nine tonight. There won't be much sleep afterwards.'

On which hint we dispersed, and I slept till Takahira waked me for dinner. Our ancestors thought nine hours' sleep ample for their little lives. We, living thirty years longer, feel ourselves defrauded with less than eleven out of the twenty-four.

By ten o'clock we were over Lake Michigan. The west shore was lightless, except for a dull ground-glare at Chicago, and a single traffic-directing light – its leading beam pointing north – at Waukegan on our starboard bow. None of the Lake villages gave any sign of life; and inland, westward, so far as we could see, blackness lay unbroken on the level earth.

We swooped down and skimmed low across the dark, throwing calls county by county. Now and again we picked up the faint glimmer of a house-light, or heard the rap and rend of a cultivator being played across the fields, but Northern Illinois as a whole was one inky, apparently uninhabited, waste of high, forced woods. Only our illuminated map, with its little pointer switching from county to county, as we wheeled and twisted, gave us any idea of our position. Our calls, urgent, pleading, coaxing or commanding, through the General Communicator brought no answer. Illinois strictly maintained her own privacy in the timber which she grew for that purpose.

'Oh, this is absurd!' said De Forest. 'We're like an owl trying to work a wheat-field. Is this Bureau Creek? Let's land, Arnott, and get hold of some one.'

We brushed over a belt of forced woodland – fifteen-year-old maple sixty feet high – grounded on a private meadow-dock, none too big, where we moored to our own grapnels, and hurried out through the warm dark night towards a light in a verandah. As we neared the garden gate I could have sworn we had stepped knee-deep in quicksand, for we could scarcely drag our feet against the prickling currents that clogged them. After five paces we stopped, wiping our foreheads, as hopelessly stuck on dry smooth turf as so many cows in a bog.

'Pest!' cried Pirolo angrily. 'We are ground-circuited. And it is my own system of ground-circuits too! I know the pull.'

'Good evening,' said a girl's voice from the verandah. 'Oh, I'm sorry! We've locked up. Wait a minute.'

We heard the click of a switch, and almost fell forward as the currents round our knees were withdrawn.

The girl laughed, and laid aside her knitting. An old-fashioned Controller stood at her elbow, which she reversed from time to time, and we could hear the snort and clank of the obedient cultivator half a mile away, behind the guardian woods.

'Come in and sit down,' she said. 'I'm only playing a

plough. Dad's gone to Chicago to – Ah! Then it was *your* call I heard just now!'

She had caught sight of Arnott's Board uniform, leaped to the switch, and turned it full on.

We were checked, gasping, waist-deep in current this time, three yards from the verandah.

'We only want to know what's the matter with Illinois,' said De Forest placidly.

'Then hadn't you better go to Chicago and find out?' she answered. 'There's nothing wrong here. We own ourselves.'

'How can we go anywhere if you won't loose us?' De Forest went on, while Arnott scowled. Admirals of Fleets are still quite human when their dignity is touched.

'Stop a minute – you don't know how funny you look!' She put her hands on her hips and laughed mercilessly.

'Don't worry about that,' said Arnott, and whistled. A voice answered from the *Victor Pirolo* in the meadow.

'Only a single-fuse ground-circuit!' Arnott called. 'Sort it out gently, please.'

We heard the ping of a breaking lamp; a fuse blew out somewhere in the verandah roof, frightening a nest full of birds. The ground-circuit was open. We stooped and rubbed our tingling ankles.

'How rude – how very rude of you!' the Maiden cried.

'Sorry, but we haven't time to look funny,' said Arnott. 'We've got to go to Chicago; and if I were you, young lady, I'd go into the cellars for the next two hours, and take mother with me.'

Off he strode, with us at his heels, muttering indignantly, till the humour of the thing struck and doubled him up with laughter at the foot of the gangway ladder.

'The Board hasn't shown what you might call a fat spark on this occasion,' said De Forest, wiping his eyes. 'I hope I didn't look as big a fool as you did, Arnott! Hullo! What on earth is that? Dad coming home from Chicago?'

There was a rattle and a rush, and a five-plough cultivator, blades in air like so many teeth, trundled itself at us round the edge of the timber, fuming and sparking furiously.

'Jump!' said Arnott, as we bundled ourselves through the none-too-wide door. 'Never mind about shutting it. Up!'

The *Victor Pirolo* lifted like a bubble, and the vicious machine shot just underneath us, clawing high as it passed.

'There's a nice little spit-kitten for you!' said Arnott, dusting his knees. 'We ask her a civil question. First she circuits us and then she plays a cultivator at us!'

'And then we fly,' said Dragomiroff. 'If I were forty years more young, I would go back and kiss her. Ho! Ho!'

'I,' said Pirolo, 'would smack her! My pet ship has been chased by a dirty plough; a – how do you say? – agricultural implement.'

'Oh, that is Illinois all over,' said De Forest. 'They don't content themselves with talking about privacy. They arrange to have it. And now, where's your alleged fleet, Arnott? We must assert ourselves against this wench.'

Arnott pointed to the black heavens.

'Waiting on – up there,' said he. 'Shall I give them the whole installation, sir?'

'Oh, I don't think the young lady is quite worth that,' said De Forest. 'Get over Chicago, and perhaps we'll see something.'

In a few minutes we were hanging at two thousand feet over an oblong block of incandescence in the centre of the little town.

'That looks like the old City Hall. Yes, there's Salati's Statue in front of it,' said Takahira. 'But what on earth are they doing to the place? I thought they used it for a market nowadays! Drop a little, please.'

We could hear the sputter and crackle of road-surfacing machines – the cheap Western type which fuse stone and rubbish into lava-like ribbed glass for their rough country roads. Three or four surfacers worked on each side of a square of ruins. The brick and stone wreckage crumbled, slid forward, and presently spread out into white-hot pools of sticky slag, which the levelling-rods smoothed more or less flat. Already a third of the big block had been so treated, and was cooling to dull red before our astonished eyes.

'It is the Old Market,' said De Forest. 'Well, there's nothing to prevent Illinois from making a road through a market. It doesn't interfere with traffic, that I can see.'

'Hsh!' said Arnott, gripping me by the shoulder. 'Listen! They're singing. Why on the earth are they singing?'

We dropped again till we could see the black fringe of people at the edge of that glowing square.

At first they only roared against the roar of the surfacers and levellers. Then the words came up clearly – the words of the Forbidden Song that all men knew, and none let pass their lips – poor Pat MacDonough's Song, made in the days of the Crowds and the Plague – every silly word of it loaded to sparking-point with the Planet's inherited memories of horror, panic, fear and cruelty. And Chicago – innocent, contented little Chicago – was singing it aloud to the infernal tune that carried riot, pestilence and lunacy round our Planet a few generations ago!

> 'Once there was The People – Terror gave it birth;
> Once there was The People, and it made a hell of earth!'

(Then the stamp and pause):

> 'Earth arose and crushed it. Listen, oh, ye slain!
> Once there was The People – it shall never be again!'

The levellers thrust in savagely against the ruins as the song renewed itself again, again and again, louder than the crash of the melting walls.

De Forest frowned.

'I don't like that,' he said. 'They've broken back to the Old Days! They'll be killing somebody soon. I think we'd better divert 'em, Arnott.'

'Ay, ay, sir,' Arnott's hand went to his cap, and we heard the hull of the *Victor Pirolo* ring to the command: 'Lamps! Both watches stand by! Lamps! Lamps! Lamps!'

'Keep still!' Takahira whispered to me. 'Blinkers, please, quartermaster.'

'It's all right – all right!' said Pirolo from behind, and to my horror slipped over my head some sort of rubber helmet that locked with a snap. I could feel thick colloid bosses before my eyes, but I stood in absolute darkness.

'To save the sight,' he explained, and pushed me on to the chart-room divan. 'You will see in a minute.'

As he spoke I became aware of a thin thread of almost intolerable light, let down from heaven at an immense distance – one vertical hairsbreadth of frozen lightning.

'Those are our flanking ships,' said Arnott at my elbow. 'That one is over Galena. Look south – that other one's over Keithburg. Vincennes is behind us, and north yonder is Winthrop Woods. The Fleet's in position, sir' – this to De Forest. 'As soon as you give the word.'

'Ah no! No!' cried Dragomiroff at my side. I could feel the old man tremble. 'I do not know all that you can do, but be kind! I ask you to be a little kind to them below! This is horrible – horrible!'

'When a Woman kills a Chicken,
Dynasties and Empires sicken,'

Takahira quoted. 'It is too late to be gentle now.'

'Then take off my helmet! Take off my helmet!' Dragomiroff began hysterically.

Pirolo must have put his arm round him.

'Hush,' he said, 'I am here. It is all right, Ivan, my dear fellow.'

'I'll just send our little girl in Bureau County a warning,' said Arnott. 'She don't deserve it, but we'll allow her a minute or two to take mamma to the cellar.'

In the utter hush that followed the growling spark after Arnott had linked up his Service Communicator with the invisible Fleet, we heard MacDonough's Song from the city beneath us grow fainter as we rose to position. Then I clapped my hand before my mask lenses, for it was as though the floor of Heaven had been riddled and all the inconceivable blaze of suns in the making was poured through the manholes.

'You needn't count,' said Arnott. I had had no thought of such a thing. 'There are two hundred and fifty keels up there, five miles apart. Full power, please, for another twelve seconds.'

The firmament, as far as eye could reach, stood on pillars of white fire. One fell on the glowing square at Chicago, and turned it black.

'Oh! Oh! Oh! Can men be allowed to do such things?' Dragomiroff cried, and fell across our knees.

'Glass of water, please,' said Takahira to a helmeted shape that leaped forward. 'He is a little faint.'

The lights switched off, and the darkness stunned like an avalanche. We could hear Dragomiroff's teeth on the glass edge.

Pirolo was comforting him.

'All right, all ra-ight,' he repeated. 'Come and lie down. Come below and take off your mask. I give you my word, old friend, it is all right. They are my siege-lights. Little Victor Pirolo's leetle lights. You know *me*! I do not hurt people.'

'Pardon!' Dragomiroff moaned. 'I have never seen Death. I have never seen the Board take action. Shall we go down and burn them alive, or is that already done?'

'Oh, hush,' said Pirolo, and I think he rocked him in his arms.

'Do we repeat, sir?' Arnott asked De Forest.

'Give 'em a minute's break,' De Forest replied, 'They may need it.'

We waited a minute, and then MacDonough's Song, broken but defiant, rose from undefeated Chicago.

'They seem fond of that tune,' said De Forest. 'I should let 'em have it, Arnott.'

'Very good, sir,' said Arnott, and felt his way to the Communicator keys.

No lights broke forth, but the hollow of the skies made

herself the mouth for one note that touched the raw fibre of the brain. Men hear such sounds in delirium, advancing like tides from horizons beyond the ruled foreshores of space.

'That's our pitch-pipe,' said Arnott. 'We may be a bit ragged. I've never conducted two hundred and fifty performers before.' He pulled out the couplers, and struck a full chord on the Service Communicators.

The beams of light leaped down again, and danced, solemnly and awfully, a stilt-dance, sweeping thirty or forty miles left and right at each stiff-legged kick, while the darkness delivered itself – there is no scale to measure against that utterance – of the tune to which they kept time. Certain notes – one learnt to expect them with terror – cut through one's marrow, but, after three minutes, thought and emotion passed in indescribable agony.

We saw, we heard, but I think we were in some sort swooning. The two hundred and fifty beams shifted, re-formed, straddled and split, narrowed, widened, rippled in ribbons, broke into a thousand white-hot parallel lines, melted and revolved in interwoven rings like old-fashioned engine-turning, flung up to the zenith, made as if to descend and renew the torment, halted at the last instant, twizzled insanely round the horizon, and vanished, to bring back for the hundredth time darkness more shattering than their instantly renewed light over all Illinois. Then the tune and lights ceased together, and we heard one single devastating wail that shook all the horizon as a rubbed wet finger shakes the rim of a bowl.

'Ah, that is my new siren,' said Pirolo. 'You can break an iceberg in half, if you find the proper pitch. They will whistle by squadrons now. It is the wind through pierced shutters in the bows.'

I had collapsed beside Dragomiroff, broken and snivelling feebly, because I had been delivered before my time to all the terrors of Judgement Day, and the Archangels of the Resurrection were hailing me naked across the Universe to the sound of the music of the spheres.

Then I saw De Forest smacking Arnott's helmet with his open hand. The wailing died down in a long shriek as a black shadow swooped past us, and returned to her place above the lower clouds.

'I hate to interrupt a specialist when he's enjoying himself,' said De Forest. 'But, as a matter of fact, all Illinois has been asking us to stop for these last fifteen seconds.'

'What a pity.' Arnott slipped off his mask. 'I wanted you to hear us really hum. Our lower C can lift street-paving.'

'It is Hell – Hell!' cried Dragomiroff, and sobbed aloud.

Arnott looked away as he answered:

'It's a few thousand volts ahead of the old shoot-'em-and-sink-'em game, but I should scarcely call it *that*. What shall I tell the Fleet, sir?'

'Tell 'em we're very pleased and impressed. I don't think they need wait on any longer. There isn't a spark left down there.' De Forest pointed. 'They'll be deaf and blind.'

'Oh, I think not, sir. The demonstration lasted less than ten minutes.'

'Marvellous!' Takahira sighed. 'I should have said it was half a night. Now, shall we go down and pick up the pieces?'

'But first a small drink,' said Pirolo. 'The Board must not arrive weeping at its own works.'

'I am an old fool – an old fool!' Dragomiroff began piteously. 'I did not know what would happen. It is all new to me. We reason with them in Little Russia.'

Chicago North landing-tower was unlighted, and Arnott worked his ship into the clips by her own lights. As soon as these broke out we heard groanings of horror and appeal from many people below.

'All right,' shouted Arnott into the darkness. 'We aren't beginning again!' We descended by the stairs, to find ourselves knee-deep in a grovelling crowd, some crying that they were blind, others beseeching us not to make any more noises, but the greater part writhing face downwards, their hands or their caps before their eyes.

It was Pirolo who came to our rescue. He climbed the side

of a surfacing-machine, and there, gesticulating as though they could see, made oration to those afflicted people of Illinois.

'You stchewpids!' he began. 'There is nothing to fuss for. Of course, your eyes will smart and be red tomorrow. You will look as if you and your wives had drunk too much, but in a little while you will see again as well as before. I tell you this, and I – *I* am Pirolo. Victor Pirolo!'

The crowd with one accord shuddered, for many legends attach to Victor Pirolo of Foggia, deep in the secrets of God.

'Pirolo?' An unsteady voice lifted itself. 'Then tell us was there anything except light in those lights of yours just now?'

The question was repeated from every corner of the darkness.

Pirolo laughed.

'No!' he thundered. (Why have small men such large voices?) 'I give you my word and the Board's word that there was nothing except light – just light! You stchewpids! Your birthrate is too low already as it is. Some day I must invent something to send it up, but send it down – never!'

'Is that true? – We thought – somebody said –'

One could feel the tension relax all round.

'You *too* big fools,' Pirolo cried. 'You could have sent us a call and we would have told you.'

'Send you a call!' a deep voice shouted. 'I wish you had been at our end of the wire.'

'I'm glad I wasn't,' said De Forest. 'It was bad enough from behind the lamps. Never mind! It's over now. Is there any one here I can talk business with? I'm De Forest – for the Board.'

'You might begin with me, for one – I'm Mayor,' the bass voice replied.

A big man rose unsteadily from the street, and staggered towards us where we sat on the broad turf-edging, in front of the garden fences.

'I ought to be the first on my feet. Am I?' said he.

'Yes,' said De Forest and steadied him as he dropped down beside us.

'Hello, Andy. Is that you?' a voice called.

'Excuse me,' said the Mayor; 'that sounds like my Chief of Police, Bluthner!'

'Bluthner it is; and here's Mulligan and Keefe – on their feet.'

'Bring 'em up please, Blut. We're supposed to be the Four in charge of this hamlet. What we say, goes. And, De Forest, what do you say?'

'Nothing – yet,' De Forest answered, as we made room for the panting, reeling men. '*You*'ve cut out of system. Well?'

'Tell the steward to send down drinks, please,' Arnott whispered to an orderly at his side.

'Good!' said the Mayor, smacking his dry lips. 'Now I suppose we can take it, De Forest, that henceforward the Board will administer us direct?'

'Not if the Board can avoid it,' De Forest laughed. 'The A.B.C. is responsible for the planetary traffic only.'

'*And all that that implies.*' The big Four who ran Chicago chanted their Magna Charta like children at school.

'Well, get on,' said De Forest wearily. 'What is your silly trouble anyway?'

'Too much dam' Democracy,' said the Mayor, laying his hand on De Forest's knee.

'So? I thought Illinois had had her dose of that.'

'She has. That's why. Blut, what did you do with our prisoners last night?'

'Locked 'em in the water-tower to prevent the women killing 'em,' the Chief of Police replied. 'I'm too blind to move just yet, but –'

'Arnott, send some of your people, please, and fetch 'em along,' said De Forest.

'They're triple-circuited,' the Mayor called. 'You'll have to blow out three fuses.' He turned to De Forest, his large outline just visible in the paling darkness. 'I hate to throw any more work on the Board. I'm an administrator myself but we've had a little fuss with our Serviles. What? In a big city there's bound to be a few men and women who can't live without listening to themselves, and who prefer drinking out of pipes they don't own both ends of. They inhabit flats and hotels all the year round. They say it saves 'em trouble. Anyway, it gives 'em more time to make trouble for their neighbours. We call 'em Serviles locally. And they are apt to be tuberculous.'

'Just so!' said the man called Mulligan. 'Transportation is Civilization. Democracy is Disease. I've proved it by the blood test, every time.'

'Mulligan's our Health Officer, and a one-idea man,' said the Mayor, laughing. 'But it's true that most Serviles haven't much control. They *will* talk; and when people take to talking as a business, anything may arrive – mayn't it, De Forest?'

'Anything – except the facts of the case,' said De Forest, laughing.

'I'll give you those in a minute,' said the Mayor. 'Our Serviles got to talking – first in their houses and then on the streets, telling men and women how to manage their own affairs. (You can't teach a Servile not to finger his neighbour's soul.) That's invasion of privacy, of course, but in Chicago we'll suffer anything sooner than make crowds. Nobody took much notice, and so I let 'em alone. My fault! I was warned there would be trouble, but there hasn't been a crowd or murder in Illinois for nineteen years.'

'Twenty-two,' said his Chief of Police.

'Likely. Anyway, we'd forgot such things. So, from talking in the houses and on the streets, our Serviles go to calling a meeting at the Old Market yonder.' He nodded across the square where the wrecked buildings heaved up grey in the dawn-glimmer behind the square-cased statue of The Negro in Flames. 'There's nothing to prevent any one calling meetings except that it's against human nature to stand in a crowd, besides being bad for the health. I ought to have known by the way our men and women attended that first meeting that trouble was brewing. There were as many as a thousand in the market-place, touching each other. Touching! Then the Serviles turned in all tongue-switches and talked, and we –'

'What did they talk about?' said Takahira.

'First, how badly things were managed in the city. That pleased us Four – we were on the platform – because we hoped to catch one or two good men for City work. You know how rare executive capacity is. Even if we didn't it's – it's refreshing to find any one interested enough in our job to damn our eyes. You don't know what it means to work, year in, year out, without a spark of difference with a living soul.'

'Oh, don't we!' said De Forest. 'There are times on the Board when we'd give our positions if any one would kick us out and take hold of things themselves.'

'But they won't,' said the Mayor ruefully. 'I assure you, sir, we Four have done things in Chicago, in the hope of rousing people, that would have discredited Nero. But what do they say? "Very good, Andy. Have it your own way. Anything's better than a crowd. I'll go back to my land." You *can't* do anything with folk who can go where they please, and don't want anything on God's earth except their own way. There isn't a kick or a kicker left on the Planet.'

'Then I suppose that little shed yonder fell down by itself?' said De Forest. We could see the bare and still smoking ruins, and hear the slagpools crackle as they hardened and set.

'Oh, that's only amusement. 'Tell you later. As I was saying, our Serviles held the meeting, and pretty soon we had to ground-circuit the platform to save 'em from being killed. And that didn't make our people any more pacific.'

'How d'you mean?' I ventured to ask.

'If you've ever been ground-circuited,' said the Mayor, 'you'll know it don't improve any man's temper to be held up straining against nothing. No, sir! Eight or nine hundred folk kept pawing and buzzing like flies in treacle for two hours, while a pack of perfectly safe Serviles invades their mental and spiritual privacy, may be amusing to watch, but they are not pleasant to handle afterwards.'

Pirolo chuckled.

'Our fold own themselves. They were of opinion things were going too far and too fiery. I warned the Serviles; but they're born house-dwellers. Unless a fact hits 'em on the head, they cannot see it. Would you believe me, they went on to talk of what they called "popular government"? They did! They wanted us to go back to the old Voodoo-business of voting with papers and wooden boxes, and word-drunk people and printed formulas, and news-sheets! They said they practised it among themselves about what they'd have to eat in their flats and hotels. Yes, sir! They stood up behind Bluthner's doubled ground-circuits, and they said that, in this present year of grace, *to* self-owning men and women, *on* that very spot! Then they finished' – he lowered his voice cautiously – 'by talking about "The People". And then Bluthner he had to sit up all night in charge of the circuits because he couldn't trust his men to keep 'em shut.'

'It was trying 'em too high,' the Chief of Police broke in. 'But we couldn't hold the crowd ground-circuited for ever. I gathered in all the Serviles on charge of crowd-making, and put 'em in the water-tower, and then I let things cut loose. I had to! The District lit like a sparked gas-tank!'

'The news was out over seven degrees of country,' the Mayor continued; 'and when once it's a question of invasion of privacy, good-bye to right and reason in Illinois! They began turning out traffic-lights and locking up landing-towers on Thursday night. Friday, they stopped all traffic and asked for the Board to take over. Then they wanted to clean Chicago off the side of the Lake and rebuild elsewhere – just for a souvenir of "The People" that the Serviles talked about. I suggested that they should slag the Old Market where the meeting was held, while I turned in a call to you all on the Board. That kept 'em quiet till you came along. And – and now *you* can take hold of the situation.'

'Any chance of their quieting down?' De Forest asked.

'You can try,' said the Mayor.

De Forest raised his voice in the face of the reviving crowd that had edged in towards us. Day was come.

'Don't you think this business can be arranged?' he began. But there was a roar of angry voices:

'We've finished with Crowds! We aren't going back to the Old Days! Take us over! Take the Serviles away! Administer direct or we'll kill 'em! Down with The People!'

An attempt was made to begin MacDonough's Song. It got no further than the first line, for the *Victor Pirolo* sent down a warning drone on one stopped horn. A wrecked side-wall of the Old Market tottered and fell inwards on the slag-pools. None spoke or moved till the last of the dust had settled down again, turning the steel case of Salati's Statue ashy grey.

'You see you'll just *have* to take us over,' the Mayor whispered.

De Forest shrugged his shoulders.

'You talk as if executive capacity could be snatched out of the air like so much horse-power. Can't you manage yourselves on any terms?' he said.

'We can, if you say so. It will only cost those few lives to begin with.'

The Mayor pointed across the square, where Arnott's men guided a stumbling group of ten or twelve men and women to the lake front and halted them under the Statue.

'Now I think,' said Takahira under his breath, 'there will be trouble.'

The mass in front of us growled like beasts.

At that moment the sun rose clear, and revealed the blinking assembly to itself. As soon as it realized that it was a crowd we saw the shiver of horror and mutual repulsion shoot across it precisely as the steely flaws shot across the lake ouside. Nothing was said, and, being half blind, of course it moved slowly. Yet in less than fifteen minutes most of that vast multitude – three thousand at the lowest count –

melted away like frost on south eaves. The remnant stretched themselves on the grass, where a crowd feels and looks less like a crowd.

'These mean business,' the Mayor whispered to Takahira. 'There are a goodish few women there who've borne children. I don't like it.'

The morning draught off the lake stirred the trees round us with promise of a hot day; the sun reflected itself dazzlingly on the canister-shaped covering of Salati's Statue; cocks crew in the gardens, and we could hear gate-latches clicking in the distance as people stumblingly resought their homes.

'I'm afraid there won't be any morning deliveries,' said De Forest. 'We rather upset things in the country last night.'

'That makes no odds,' the Mayor returned. 'We're all provisioned for six months. *We* take no chances.'

Nor, when you come to think of it, does any one else. It must be three-quarters of a generation since any house or city faced a food shortage. Yet is there house or city on the Planet today that has not half a year's provisions laid in? We are like the shipwrecked seamen in the old books, who, having once nearly starved to death, ever afterwards hide away bits of food and biscuit. Truly we trust no Crowds, nor system based on Crowds!

De Forest waited till the last footstep had died away. Meantime the prisoners at the base of the Statue shuffled, posed and fidgeted, with the shamelessness of quite little children. None of them were more than six feet high, and many of them were as grey-haired as the ravaged, harassed heads of old pictures. They huddled together in actual touch, while the crowd, spaced at large intervals, looked at them with congested eyes.

Suddenly a man among them began to talk. The Mayor had not in the least exaggerated. It appeared that our Planet lay sunk in slavery beneath the heel of the Aerial Board of Control. The orator urged us to arise in our might, burst our prison doors and break our fetters (all his metaphors, by the way, were of the most medieval). Next he demanded that every matter of daily life, including most of the physical functions, should be submitted for decision at any time of the week, month, or year to, I gathered, anybody who happened to be passing by or residing within a certain radius, and that everybody should forthwith abandon his concerns to settle the matter, first by crowd-making, next by talking to the crowds made, and lastly by describing crosses on pieces of paper, which rubbish should later be counted with certain mystic ceremonies and oaths. Out of this amazing play, he assured us, would automatically arise a higher, nobler, and kinder world, based – he demonstrated this with the awful lucidity of the insane – based on the sanctity of the Crowd and the villainy of the single person. In conclusion, he called loudly upon God to testify to his personal merits and integrity. When the flow ceased, I turned bewildered to Takahira, who was nodding solemnly.

'Quite correct,' said he. 'It is all in the old books. He has left nothing out, not even the war-talk.'

'But I don't see how this stuff can upset a child, much less a district,' I replied.

'Ah, you are too young,' said Dragomiroff. 'For another thing, you are not a mamma. Please look at the mammas.'

Ten or fifteen women who remained had separated themselves from the silent men, and were drawing in towards the prisoners. It reminded one of the stealthy encircling, before the rush in at the quarry, of wolves round musk-oxen in the North. The prisoners saw, and drew together more closely. The Mayor covered his face with his hands for an instant. De Forest, bareheaded, stepped forward between the prisoners and the slowly, stiffly moving line.

'That's all very interesting,' he said to the dry-lipped orator. 'But the point seems that you've been making crowds and invading privacy.'

A woman stepped forward, and would have spoken, but there was a quick assenting murmur from the men, who realized that De Forest was trying to pull the situation down to ground-line.

'Yes! Yes!' they cried. 'We cut out because they made crowds and invaded privacy! Stick to that! Keep on that switch! Lift the Serviles out of this! The Board's in charge! Hsh!'

'Yes, the Board's in charge,' said De Forest. 'I'll take formal evidence of crowd-making if you like, but the Members of the Board can testify to it. Will that do?'

The women had closed in another pace, with hands that clenched and unclenched at their sides.

'Good! Good enough!' the men cried. 'We're content. Only take them away quickly.'

'Come along up!' said De Forest to the captives. 'Breakfast is quite ready.'

It appeared, however, that they did not wish to go. They intended to remain in Chicago and make crowds. They pointed out that De Forest's proposal was gross invasion of privacy.

'My dear fellow,' said Pirolo to the most voluble of the leaders, 'you hurry, or your crowd that can't be wrong will kill you!'

'But that would be murder,' answered the believer in crowds; and there was a roar of laughter from all sides that seemed to show the crisis had broken.

A woman stepped forward from the line of women, laughing, I protest, as merrily as any of the company. One hand, of course, shaded her eyes, the other was at her throat.

'Oh, they needn't be afraid of being killed!' she called.

'Not in the least,' said De Forest. 'But don't you think that, now the Board's in charge, you might go home while we get these people away?'

'I shall be home long before that. It – it has been rather a trying day.'

She stood up to her full height, dwarfing even De Forest's six-foot-eight, and smiled, with eyes closed against the fierce light.

'Yes, rather,' said De Forest. 'I'm afraid you feel the glare a little. We'll have the ship down.'

He motioned to the *Pirolo* to drop between us and the sun, and at the same time to loop-circuit the prisoners, who were a trifle unsteady. We saw them stiffen to the current where they stood. The woman's voice went on, sweet and deep and unshaken:

'I don't suppose you men realize how much this – this sort of thing means to a woman. I've borne three. We women don't want our children given to Crowds. It must be an inherited instinct. Crowds make trouble. They bring back the Old Days. Hate, fear, blackmail, publicity, "The People" – *That! That! That!*' She pointed to the Statue, and the crowd growled once more.

'Yes, if they are allowed to go on,' said De Forest. 'But this little affair – '

'It means so much to us women that this – this little affair should never happen again. Of course, never's a big word, but one feels so strongly that it is important to stop crowds at the very beginning. Those creatures' – she pointed with her left hand at the prisoners swaying like seaweed in a tideway as the circuit pulled them – 'these people have friends and wives and children in the city and elsewhere. One doesn't want anything done to *them*, you know. It's terrible to force a human being out of fifty or sixty years of good life. I'm only forty myself. *I* know. But, at the same time, one feels that an example should be made, because no price is too heavy to pay if – if these people and *all that they imply* can be put an end to. Do you quite understand, or would you be kind enough to tell your men to take the casing off the Statue? It's worth looking at.'

'I understand perfectly. But I don't think anybody here wants to see the Statue on an empty stomach. Excuse me one moment.' De Forest called up to the ship, 'A flying loop ready on the port side, if you please.' Then to the woman he said with some crispness, 'You might leave us a little discretion in the matter.'

'Oh of course. Thank you for being so patient. I know my arguments are silly, but – ' She half turned away and went on in a changed voice, 'Perhaps this will help you to decide.'

She threw out her right arm with a knife in it. Before the blade could be returned to her throat or her bosom it was twitched from her grip, sparked as it flew out of the shadow of the ship above, and fell flashing in the sunshine at the foot of the Statue fifty yards away. The outflung arm was arrested, rigid as a bar for an instant, till the releasing circuit permitted her to bring it slowly to her side. The other women shrank back silent among the men.

Pirolo rubbed his hands, and Takahira nodded.

'That was clever of you, De Forest,' said he.

'What a glorious pose!' Dragomiroff murmured, for the frightened woman was on the edge of tears.

'Why did you stop me? I would have done it!' she cried.

'I have no doubt you would,' said De Forest. 'But we can't waste a life like yours on these people. I hope the arrest didn't sprain your wrist; it's so hard to regulate a flying loop. But I think you are quite right about those persons' women and children. We'll take them all away with us if you promise not to do anything stupid to yourself.'

'I promise – I promise.' She controlled herself with an effort. 'But it is so important to us women. We know what it means; and I thought if you saw I was in earnest – '

'I saw you were, and you've gained your point. I shall take all your Serviles away with me at once. The Mayor will make lists of their friends and families in the city and the district, and he'll ship them after us this afternoon.'

'Sure,' said the Mayor, rising to his feet. 'Keefe, if you can see, hadn't you better finish levelling off the Old Market? It don't look sightly the way it is now, and we shan't use it for crowds any more.'

'I think you had better wipe out that Statue as well, Mr Mayor,' said De Forest. 'I don't question its merits as a work of art, but I believe it's a shade morbid.'

'Certainly, sir. Oh, Keefe! Slag the Nigger before you go

on to fuse the Market. I'll get to the Communicators and tell the District that the Board is in charge. Are you making any special appointments, sir?'

'None. We haven't men to waste on these backwoods. Carry on as before, but under the Board. Arnott, run your Serviles aboard, please. Ground ship and pass them through the bilge-doors. We'll wait till we've finished with this work of art.'

The prisoners trailed past him, talking fluently, but unable to gesticulate in the drag of the current. Then the surfacers rolled up, two on each side of the Statue. With one accord the spectators looked elsewhere, but there was no need. Keefe turned on full power, and the thing simply melted within its case. All I saw was a surge of white-hot metal pouring over the plinth, a glimpse of Salati's inscription, 'To the Eternal Memory of the Justice of the People', ere the stone base itself cracked and powdered into finest lime. The crowd cheered.

'Thank you,' said De Forest; 'but we want our breakfasts, and I expect you do too. Good-bye, Mr Mayor! Delighted to see you at any time, but I hope I shan't have to, officially, for the next thirty years. Good-bye, madam. Yes. We're all given to nerves nowadays. I suffer from them myself. Good-bye, gentlemen all! You're under the tyrannous heel of the Board from this moment, but if ever you feel like breaking your fetters you've only to let us know. This is no treat to us. Good luck!'

We embarked amid shouts, and did not check our lift till they had dwindled into whispers. Then De Forest flung himself on the chartroom divan and mopped his forehead.

'I don't mind men,' he panted, 'but women are the devil!'

'Still the devil,' said Pirolo cheerfully. 'That one would have suicided.'

'I know it. That was why I signalled for the flying loop to be clapped on her. I owe you an apology for that, Arnott. I hadn't time to catch your eye, and you were busy with our caitiffs. By the way, who actually answered my signal? It was a smart piece of work.'

'Ilroy,' said Arnott; 'but he overloaded the wave. It may be pretty gallery-work to knock a knife out of a lady's hand, but didn't you noticed how she rubbed 'em? He scorched her fingers. Slovenly, I call it.'

'Far be it from me to interfere with Fleet discipline, but don't be too hard on the boy. If that woman had killed herself they would have killed every Servile and everything related to a Servile throughout the district by nightfall.'

'That was what she was playing for,' Takahira said. 'And with our Fleet gone we could have done nothing to hold them.'

'I may be ass enough to walk into a ground-circuit,' said Arnott, 'but I don't dismiss my Fleet till I'm reasonably sure that trouble is over. They're in position still, and I intend to keep 'em there till the Serviles are shipped out of the district. That last little crowd meant murder, my friends.'

'Nerves! All nerves!' said Pirolo. 'You cannot argue with agoraphobia.'

'And it is not as if they had seen much dead – or *is* it?' said Takahira.

'In all my ninety years I have never seen death.' Dragomiroff spoke as one who would excuse himself. 'Perhaps that was why – last night – '

Then it came out as we sat over breakfast, that, with the exception of Arnott and Pirolo, none of us had ever seen a corpse, or knew in what manner the spirit passes.

'We're a nice lot to flap about governing the Planet,' De Forest laughed. 'I confess, now it's all over, that my main fear was I mightn't be able to pull it off without losing a life.'

'I thought of that too,' said Arnott; 'but there's no death reported, and I've inquired everywhere. What are we supposed to do with our passengers? I've fed 'em.'

'We're between two switches,' De Forest drawled. 'If we drop them in any place that isn't under the Board, the natives will make their presence an excuse for cutting out, same as Illinois did, and forcing the Board to take over. If we drop them in any place under the Board's control they'll be killed as soon as our backs are turned.'

'If you say so,' said Pirolo thoughtfully, 'I can guarantee that they will become extinct in process of time, quite happily. What is their birth-rate now?'

'Go down and ask 'em,' said De Forest.

'I think they might become nervous and tear me to bits,' the philosopher of Foggia replied.

'Not really? Well?'

'Open the bilge-doors,' said Takahira with a downward jerk of the thumb.

'Scarcely – after all the trouble we've taken to save 'em,' said De Forest.

'Try London,' Arnott suggested. 'You could turn Satan himself loose there, and they'd only ask him to dinner.'

'Good man! You've given me an idea. Vincent! Oh, Vincent!' He threw the General Communicator open so that we could all hear, and in a few minutes the chartroom filled with the rich, fruity voice of Leopold Vincent, who has purveyed all London her choicest amusements for the last thirty years. We answered with expectant grins, as though we were actually in the stalls of, say, the Combination on a first night.

'We've picked up something in your line,' De Forest began.

'That's good, dear man. If it's old enough. There's nothing to beat the old things for business purposes. Have you seen *London, Chatham, and Dover* at Earl's Court? No? I thought I missed you there. Im-mense! I've had the real steam locomotive engines built from the old designs and the iron rails cast specially by hand. Cloth cushions in the carriages, too! Im-mense! And paper railway tickets. And Polly Milton.'

'Polly Milton back again!' said Arnott rapturously. 'Book me two stalls for tomorrow night. What's she singing now, bless her?'

'The old songs. Nothing comes up to the old touch. Listen to this, dear men.' Vincent carolled with flourishes:

> 'Oh, cruel lamps of London,
> If tears your light could drown,
> Your victim's eyes would weep them,
> Oh, lights of London Town!'

'Then they weep.'

'You see?' Pirolo waved his hands at us. 'The old world always weeped when it saw crowds together. It did not know why, but it weeped. We know why, but we do not weep, except when we pay to be made to by fat, wicked old Vincent.'

'Old, yourself!' Vincent laughed. 'I'm a public benefactor, I keep the world soft and united.'

'And I'm De Forest of the Board,' said De Forest acidly, 'trying to get a little business done. As I was saying, I've picked up a few people in Chicago.'

'I cut out. Chicago is – '

'Do listen! They're perfectly unique.'

'Do they build houses of baked mudblocks while you wait – eh? That's an old contact.'

'They're an untouched primitive community, with all the old ideas.'

'Sewing-machines and maypole-dances? Cooking on coal-gas stoves, lighting pipes with matches. and driving horses? Gerolstein tried that last year. An absolute blow-out!'

De Forest plugged him wrathfully, and poured out the story of our doings for the last twenty-four hours on the top-note.

'And they do it *all* in public,' he concluded. 'You can't stop 'em. The more public, the better they are pleased. They'll talk for hours – like you! Now you can come in again!'

'Do you really mean they know how to vote?' said Vincent. 'Can they act it?'

'Act? It's their life to 'em! And you never saw such faces!

Scarred like volcanoes. Envy, hatred, and malice in plain sight. Wonderfully flexible voices. They weep, too.'

'Aloud? In public?'

'I guarantee. Not a spark of shame or reticence in the entire installation. It's the chance of your career.'

'D'you say you've brought their voting props along – those papers and ballot-box things?'

'No, confound you! I'm not a luggage-lifter. Apply direct to the Mayor of Chicago. He'll forward you everything. Well?'

'Wait a minute. Did Chicago want to kill 'em? That 'ud look well on the Communicators.'

'Yes! They were only rescued with difficulty from a howling mob – if you know what that is.'

'But I don't,' answered the Great Vincent simply.

'Well then, they'll tell you themselves. They can make speeches hours long.'

'How many are there?'

'By the time we ship 'em all over they'll be perhaps a hundred, counting children. An old world in miniature. Can't you see it?'

'M-yes; but I've got to pay for it if it's a blow-out, dear man.'

'They can sing the old war songs in the streets. They can get word-drunk, and make crowds, and invade privacy in the genuine old-fashioned way, and they'll do the voting trick as often as you ask 'em a question.'

'Too good!' said Vincent.

'You unbelieving Jew! I've got a dozen head aboard here. I'll put you through direct. Sample 'em yourself.'

He lifted the switch and we listened. Our passengers on the lower deck at once, but not less than five at a time, explained themselves to Vincent. They had been taken from the bosom of their families, stripped of their possessions, given food without finger-bowls, and cast into captivity in a noisome dungeon.

'But look here,' said Arnott aghast; 'they're saying what

isn't true. My lower deck isn't noisome, and I saw to the finger-bowls myself.'

'My people talk like that sometimes in Little Russia,' said Dragomiroff. 'We reason with them. We never kill. No!'

'But it's not true,' Arnott insisted. 'What can you do with people who don't tell facts? They're mad!'

'Hsh!' said Pirolo, his hand to his ear. 'It is such a little time since all the Planet told lies.'

We heard Vincent silkily sympathetic. Would they, he asked, repeat their assertions in public – before a vast public? Only let Vincent give them a chance, and the Planet, they vowed, should ring with their wrongs. Their aim in life – two women and a man explained it together – was to reform the world. Oddly enough, this also had been Vincent's life-dream. He offered them an arena in which to explain, and by their living example to raise the Planet to loftier levels. He was eloquent on the moral uplift of a simple, old-world life presented in its entirety to a deboshed civilization.

Could they – would they – for three months certain, devote themselves under his auspices, as missionaries, to the elevation of mankind at a place called Earl's Court, which he said, with some truth, was one of the intellectual centres of the Planet? They thanked him, and demanded (we could hear his chuckle of delight) time to discuss and to vote on the matter. The vote, solemnly managed by counting heads – one head, one vote – was favourable. His offer, therefore, was accepted, and they moved a vote of thanks to him in two speeches – one by what they called the 'proposer' and the other by the 'seconder'.

Vincent threw over to us, his voice shaking with gratitude:

'I've got 'em! Did you hear those speeches? That's Nature, dear men. Art can't teach *that.* And they voted as easily as lying. I've never had a troupe of natural liars before. Bless you, dear men! Remember, you're on my free lists for ever, anywhere – all of you. Oh, Gerolstein will be sick – sick!'

'Then you think they'll do?' said De Forest.

'Do? The Little Village'll go crazy! I'll knock up a series of old-world plays for 'em. Their voices will make you laugh and cry. My God, dear men, where *do* you suppose they picked up all their misery from, on this sweet earth? I'll have a pageant of the world's beginnings, and Mosenthal shall do the music. I'll – '

'Go and knock up a village for 'em by tonight. We'll meet you at No. 15 West Landing Tower,' said De Forest. 'Remember the rest will be coming along tomorrow.'

'Let 'em all come!' said Vincent. 'You don't know how hard it is nowadays even for me, to find something that really gets under the public's damned iridium-plated hide. But I've got it at last. Good-bye!'

'Well,' said De Forest when we had finished laughing, 'if any one understood corruption in London I might have played off Vincent against Gerolstein, and sold my captives at enormous prices. As it is, I shall have to be their legal adviser tonight when the contracts are signed. And they won't exactly press any commission on me, either.'

'Meantime,' said Takahira, 'we cannot, of course, confine members of Leopold Vincent's last-engaged company. Chairs for the ladies, please, Arnott.'

'Then I go to bed,' said De Forest. 'I can't face any more women!' And he vanished.

When our passengers were released and given another meal (finger-bowls came first this time) they told us what they thought of us and the Board; and, like Vincent, we all marvelled how they had contrived to extract and secrete so much bitter poison and unrest out of the good life God gives us. They raged, they stormed, they palpitated, flushed and exhausted their poor, torn nerves, panted themselves into silence, and renewed the senseless, shameless attacks.

'But can't you understand,' said Pirolo pathetically to a shrieking woman, 'that if we'd left you in Chicago you'd have been killed?'

'No, we shouldn't. You were bound to save us from being murdered.'

'Then we should have had to kill a lot of other people.'

'That doesn't matter. We were preaching the Truth. You can't stop us. We shall go on preaching in London; and *then* you'll see!'

'You can see now,' said Pirolo, and opened a lower shutter.

We were closing on the Little Village, with her three million people spread out at ease inside her ring of girdling Main-Traffic lights – those eight fixed beams at Chatham, Tonbridge, Redhill, Dorking, Woking, St Albans, Chipping Ongar, and Southend.

Leopold Vincent's new company looked, with small pale faces, at the silence, the size, and the separated houses.

Then some began to weep aloud, shamelessly – always without shame.

MACDONOUGH'S SONG

Whether the State can loose and bind
  In Heaven as well as on Earth:
If it be wiser to kill mankind
  Before or after the birth –
These are matters of high concern
  Where State-kept schoolmen are;
But Holy State (we have lived to learn)
  Endeth in Holy War.

Whether The People be led by the Lord,
  Or lured by the loudest throat:
If it be quicker to die by the sword
  Or cheaper to die by vote –
These are the things we have dealt with once,
  (And they will not rise from their grave)
For Holy People, however it runs,
  Endeth in wholly Slave.

Whatsoever, for any cause,
  Seeketh to take or give,
Power above or beyond the Laws,
  Suffer it not to live!
Holy State or Holy King –
  Or Holy People's Will –
Have no truck with the senseless thing.
  Order the guns and kill!
    Saying – after – me:

Once there was The People – Terror gave it birth;
Once there was The People and it made a Hell of Earth.
Earth arose and crushed it. Listen, O ye slain!
Once there was The People– it shall never be again!

READ MORE IN PENGUIN

In every corner of the world, on every subject under the sun, Penguin represents quality and variety – the very best in publishing today.

For complete information about books available from Penguin – including Puffins, Penguin Classics and Arkana – and how to order them, write to us at the appropriate address below. Please note that for copyright reasons the selection of books varies from country to country.

In the United Kingdom: Please write to *Dept. JC, Penguin Books Ltd, FREEPOST, West Drayton, Middlesex UB7 OBR*

If you have any difficulty in obtaining a title, please send your order with the correct money, plus ten per cent for postage and packaging, to *PO Box No. 11, West Drayton, Middlesex UB7 OBR*

In the United States: Please write to *Penguin USA Inc., 375 Hudson Street, New York, NY 10014*

In Canada: Please write to *Penguin Books Canada Ltd, 10 Alcorn Avenue, Suite 300, Toronto, Ontario M4V 3B2*

In Australia: Please write to *Penguin Books Australia Ltd, 487 Maroondah Highway, Ringwood, Victoria 3134*

In New Zealand: Please write to *Penguin Books (NZ) Ltd,182–190 Wairau Road, Private Bag, Takapuna, Auckland 9*

In India: Please write to *Penguin Books India Pvt Ltd, 706 Eros Apartments, 56 Nehru Place, New Delhi 110 019*

In the Netherlands: Please write to *Penguin Books Netherlands B.V., Keizersgracht 231 NL–1016 DV Amsterdam*

In Germany: Please write to *Penguin Books Deutschland GmbH, Friedrichstrasse 10–12, W–6000 Frankfurt/Main 1*

In Spain: Please write to *Penguin Books S. A., C. San Bernardo 117–6° E–28015 Madrid*

In Italy: Please write to *Penguin Italia s.r.l., Via Felice Casati 20, I–20124 Milano*

In France: Please write to *Penguin France S. A., 17 rue Lejeune, F–31000 Toulouse*

In Japan: Please write to *Penguin Books Japan, Ishikiribashi Building, 2–5–4, Suido, Tokyo 112*

In Greece: Please write to *Penguin Hellas Ltd, Dimocritou 3, GR–106 71 Athens*

In South Africa: Please write to *Longman Penguin Southern Africa (Pty) Ltd, Private Bag X08, Bertsham 2013*

READ MORE IN PENGUIN

RUDYARD KIPLING IN PENGUIN CLASSICS

'The most complete man of genius I have ever known' – *Henry James*

THE LIGHT THAT FAILED
A DIVERSITY OF CREATURES
THE DAY'S WORK
DEBITS AND CREDITS
WEE WILLIE WINKIE
JUST SO STORIES
TRAFFICS AND DISCOVERIES
KIM
THE JUNGLE BOOKS
LIFE'S HANDICAP
STALKY AND CO
LIMITS AND RENEWALS
SOMETHING OF MYSELF
PLAIN TALES FROM THE HILLS
SOLDIERS THREE
PUCK OF POOK'S HILL
REWARDS AND FAIRIES
SELECTED POEMS
SELECTED VERSE

'For my own part I worshipped Kipling at thirteen, loathed him at seventeen, enjoyed him at twenty, despised him at twenty-five, and now again rather admire him. The one thing that was never possible, if one had read him at all, was to forget him' – *George Orwell*

HENRY JAMES

The Aspern Papers and Other Stories

These three short stories are distinguished from Henry James's longer novels by a significant change in style. As always, they are deeply concerned with the subtleties and vagaries of character, but restricted as they are by the forms and conventions of short-story writing, they are necessarily more direct in tone and precise in their territory. *The Aspern Papers* (1888) is set in a crumbling Venetian palazzo where a determined scholar attempts to charm its inhabitants – the Misses Bordereau – out of a collection of letters by the important American poet Jeffrey Aspern. The plot is uncomplicated, yet the narrative develops with increasing irony towards an unusual and unexpected ending. *The Real Thing* (1893) and *The Papers* (1903) are set in London, and both stories, though utterly different in content, contrive a telling comment on social and artistic mores in the metropolis at the turn of the century. The stories, written during the author's flirtation with drama, are entertaining examples of the subtle range of James's writing, in which he unites pathos and humour with an immense knowledge of the European scene to brilliant effect.

Also published

THE AMBASSADORS

THE AWKWARD AGE

THE BOSTONIANS

THE EUROPEANS

THE GOLDEN BOWL

THE PORTRAIT OF A LADY

SELECTED SHORT STORIES

THE TURN OF THE SCREW AND OTHER STORIES

WASHINGTON SQUARE

WHAT MAISIE KNEW

THE WINGS OF THE DOVE